Ancient Matriarchs
Book Four

Moving into Light: Zehira, Wife of Enoch

Angelique Conger

SOUTHWEST OF ZION PUBLISHING / LAS VEGAS

Angelique Conger/Southwest of Zion Publishing
7401 W. Washington
Las Vegas, Nevada 89128
www.AngeliqueCongerAuthor.com

Book Layout © 2014 BookDesignTemplates.com

Moving into Light: Zehira, Wife of Enoch / Angelique Conger. -- 1st ed.
ISBN 978-1-946550-07-1

For strangers in a strange land--
May you find light,
And may all who meet a stranger—
May you find a new friend.

CONTENTS

CHAPTER ONE

Mama

I moved along the path, eyes down, watching for roots or rocks that would cause me to stumble. Aware of others on the trail, I moved to the side and stood leaning on my crutch, waiting for them to pass.

"Get out of my way, you lazy, good-for-nothing cripple!" Hadar shouted, pushing close to me, sending my crutch flying out of reach.

"Yeah, move. How could you be married to someone like Enoch?" one of the bullies surrounding me taunted as I struggled to maintain my balance and stay on my feet without the support of my crutch. I refused to crawl for it in the presence of these vulgar men.

"He was a cripple, too—c-c-c-could not g-g-g-get the w-w-w-words out." Another mocked.

Swallowing my tears, I stood silent. I refused to allow these rude ruffians the pleasure of seeing me cry. Long ago, I had learned that tears only encouraged the torments. I took a deep breath and waited for them to tire of persecuting me and to move along and give someone else grief.

Since things had become more difficult in the world, Enoch decided to leave me behind to protect me and the children. Men followed him regularly, determined to take his life. We trusted Jehovah to protect him, and me. However, for our safety, he often left the younger children and me with our parents in Aenon.

He had left me in there in Aenon on his latest journey months before this day. I wished he would return. I wished I could travel with him. But Hadar's digs hurt.

I am a cripple. My leg is twisted and will not support me.

But, our children waited for me to return to them at my parent's home. I sighed, relieved they did not witness this humiliation at the hands of the men I grew up with. I knew they were not my friends. I wanted them to be, but, once again, they proved they could not be friends with me.

Enoch's brother, Hadar, took immense pleasure in tormenting me. He had enjoyed it since long before Enoch indicated an interest in me. However, after Enoch openly befriended me, spending time with me, and especially after received his calling to be a prophet of Jehovah, Hadar had made a point to taunt me whenever possible.

I crouched in the dirt near my crutch, drawing abstractedly in the dirt with my finger while the men kicked dirt toward me. Eventually, they grew tired of my disregard for them and moved on down the path, with jeers and taunts pouring from their mouths. At least, they did not use the foul language I heard men use who lived in other villages and cities.

What did I draw this time? I stared at my picture. *Not flowers and vines. Faces. Ugly faces, like my tormentors. Ugh.*

I brushed the faces away and scooted over to grab my crutch and used its assistance in pulling me to my feet. *I do not deserve anything better than what these men give me. Teasing and tormenting have always been a part of my life.*

"A club-footed woman deserves no better. I am ugly." I settled the crutch under my arm and continued along the path toward Mama's home. "I do not know why Papa allowed me to live. Me, a cripple and ugly."

"You are not ugly." A voice startled me. "How many times must I remind you? You are not an ugly cripple. You are not even a cripple."

I turned into the arms encircling my waist. "Enoch! I thought you were still traveling."

"Not now. I am here with you. And just in time, I see."

"No, late as usual. Your brother and his cronies saw me as a perfect target, as usual, and kicked away my crutch."

A dark shadow crossed Enoch's face.

"It is all right, though, I am not hurt," I spoke in a rush, not wanting more problems. Especially not now Enoch had returned home.

"Not hurt, Zehira? That is why I hear those horrible words come from your mouth?" Enoch gazed into my eyes.

3

"Just a reminder of my place in the world. I am a "good-for-nothing cripple." I dashed away the rebellious tear that declined to stay inside.

Enoch wrapped me in his arms, enveloping me with his love.

He supported me on the side without my crutch while we walked toward the community of Aenon. As we walked, he drew me close to him, protecting and balancing me. As always, I appreciated his helpfulness and attention. His loving support drove away the focus from my foot and my difficulty walking.

"I built a home for us in Zion," Enoch said. "I am here to take you and our children back there with me."

"Is it safe there for us?" I gazed into his piercing blue eyes. He nodded.

"Really? I have heard stories. Men follow you during the day and turn on you at night, trying to take your life."

"Do you not believe me? I would not take you there if it were not safe." Enoch's eyebrows lifted as he squinted at me, a little frown on his face.

"I suppose you are right. You would not lie to me. Stop that!" I could not help but smile at the picture he presented. "When do we leave?"

"Tomorrow? We need to visit with your parents and mine tonight and gather up the children's and your things. A small cart sits beside my parent's home, waiting for you to assist me in loading it."

"And your mama does not yet know I am leaving, with a cart at her door?" I waggled my eyebrows at him.

"It is in the back. Shall we stop there first or last?"

I considered this a long moment. Would my parents be more offended if I waited to tell them last or if I told them first? It would not matter when I shared my good news, they would not be happy with me and would find a reason for offense. I shook my head as I thought about it.

"Why the long face, Zehira, my dear?" Enoch asked.

"My parents. They seek reasons to be offended. It has been difficult to live here in Aenon again." I allowed my voice to drop into nothingness. He knew my problem with my parents. He suffered their sharp tongues and easy anger beside me over the years. I shrugged.

"Umm hmm. It has been difficult for you. Where are the children?"

"With them. I needed to go for a walk to clear my thoughts. Mama and Papa continue to berate me. I needed a break from it. The children were there when I left."

Enoch pulled me tighter into his side. He had felt the sharpness of Mama' tongue, Papa's gruff unkindness, and knew my pain only too well.

"Let us gather the children and tell your parents first. They will believe what they will, regardless of anything we say." He said with a sigh, as he squeezed me a little tighter.

We fell silent, thinking as we walked to Mama's and Papa's home. When we arrived, children ran around the house and into the street.

Mama Lilah called to them in her usual whining shout. "Where are you running off to? Come back here and help your poor grandmama."

The usual uproar of shouting and whining greeted us as we approached the house.

Noam ran toward us, whooping in welcome. "Mama is back. Mama and Papa!"

Enoch stood firm, prepared for his onslaught as Noam threw his young body into us, nearly knocking both of us down in his exuberance.

"Hello to you, too, Noam. What is going on here?"

"Grandmama Lilah wants us to carry piles of clay so she can make jars. We have carried plenty of it, but she wants more." His lower lip poked out in a pout.

"Too much? Are you not big and strong enough to help your Grandmama Lilah?" Enoch brushed a finger across the boy's face.

I understood Noam's frustration. Mama often required more of children than they were capable of doing. I nodded over the boy's head with a frown.

I should not have been surprised by Enoch's cheerful response. "Let's go see. Shall we?" He glanced at me with a quick frown, then replaced it with a smile.

Grace and Tobiah saw us and hurried over to join us.

"Mama! Papa! Grandmama Lilah wants us to carry more clay. We carried a large pile, but it is never enough for her." Grace panted. She dropped her hands to her knees.

"We know, Grace. Come with us. You, too, Tobiah." Enoch calmed the children and took them by the hand to march back toward my screaming Mama. "We will see."

The children dropped his hands and trooped ahead of us, though only Noam, at nine, could be considered a child. Tobiah had grown tall over the past year and at fifteen had grown nearly as tall as Enoch. Grace, older than Tobiah by just over a year walked in a lithe motion.

I looked at Enoch and shook my head, attempting to prevent the venom I felt from leaking out in words. As we turned the corner and came closer to Mama, Enoch set me firmly on my feet so I could meet with her better. I tucked the crutch solidly under my arm and walked the last few feet in Mama's direction. Enoch stood quietly beside me, giving me support, knowing Mama's vile temper could not be cut short.

"Mama. What is the problem?" I stared at the huge pile of the sticky material.

"So, you decided to return, did you?" Mama snarled, not looking up from the container she formed. "Jars must be made to hold the grains your papa is harvesting this week. Your 'children,'" she said all but spitting out the word, "refuse to bring me an adequate amount of clay."

I stared at the pile, swallowed my retort and smiled. "What is all this here? Did they not bring it? Is it not sufficient for many jars and huge pots? And yet you are not using it." I struggled to be kind in the face of her anger. Mama's behavior toward my children threatened to push me into uncontrollable anger.

Enoch set a warm, calming hand on my shoulder.

"Where have you been?" Mama continued to growl. "These would be finished if you were here to push your children to carry the material I need."

"You have all you can use. My children are not your slaves, Mama. We are not here only to give you the assistance you demand." I began to shout and I stopped speaking trying to control myself.

"You are here to support me in the way I choose," Mama yelled. At last, she stood and turned toward us.

"And that choice is to make slaves of us all? To demand that we carry much too much and work harder than you?"

Enoch squeezed my shoulder in a gentle warning.

Mama's voice became impossibly shriller. "And you ran away, as usual, unable to meet my demands."

Anger overcame me and I shouted, "Because I could no longer cave in to your demands another moment. My only fault was to leave my children here to bear your cruelty!" I stopped speaking to take a deep breath and glanced at Enoch. I dropped the hand I had raised.

Enoch gazed at me with a creased forehead and sadness in his eyes.

I have disappointed him, again. I try so hard and still I rise to her bait. I swallowed the ugly things I wanted to say and instead said, "I am sorry, Mama. I should not have left the children with you." I glanced at Enoch, seeing him lift an eyebrow. "Nor should I have left at all today."

"You should be sorry!" Mama ranted. "You left me with all your children and all this work to do. You are a disgrace. You, and that foot of yours. Why did Jehovah curse us with such a weak daughter?"

"Enough, Lilah," Enoch spoke with unexpected force. "This is my wife and you will not say those things to her. You have had the use of Zehira and our children long enough. We are leaving for Zion tomorrow. Until then, we will be at the home of my parents, Jared and Helsa."

He stopped our children's little cheer with a wave. "Gather anything you have in this house. We leave in the time of one finger span's movement of the sun."

The children and I rushed into the house to gather our possessions. I could hear Enoch speaking gently.

"Gavi is harvesting grain today? And the jars from last year?"

Mama's voice slowly softened from the strident shouting. "Not sufficient numbers are left. Some broke, others are full of last year's crops. We have need of many more than we have."

"How many have you made today? There is plenty here for many large jars."

"I made three, already. I need more clay to have sufficient for all the grains Gavi will harvest." Her response changed from anger to surprise. "Where did all this come from? It was not here earlier."

I could not believe Mama did not see. She had always been an angry, unhappy, and spiteful woman. This was no different. Her next words supported my belief.

"It was here when Zehira and I arrived. Did you not see the children lugging it here to refill your pile?"

"It is right they did." Mama refused to back down, even for my Enoch. "They should help their grandmama."

"Yes, they should. And they should be loved by their grandmama. Do you love my children?" Enoch's voice hardened a bit. I wanted to stare out the window, but my hands were full of folded clothing.

"Love? Grandchildren? They are here to assist me, not to be loved."

I heard him sigh. "It is as I suspected. They will not be here for you to use any longer. We will leave you to your work."

The children and I filed out the door, our clothes and other possessions filling small bags. Enoch took my bag and pulled me close. The children danced ahead of us, out the gate and down the road away from Mama's home and her griping and complaining.

We had been taught to honor and obey our parents, so when they demanded that the children and I move in with them, I did, reluctantly. Enoch's mama, Mama Helsa tried to convince me to stay with her and Papa Jared, but after listening to Mama rant and threaten them and me, she tearfully relented and allowed me to go. They were my parents and I did owe them honor and obedience.

CHAPTER TWO

Surprise

The streets we walked through overflowed with people hurrying to and fro. Some men and women called out greetings to Enoch. A few hurried over to seek a blessing at his hand. Most ignored him.

"Why do they not care that you are here?" I whispered.

Enoch shrugged. "A prophet is without honor in his own city. Most of my neighbors recognize me as the stuttering, weak son of Helsa and Jared. I do not worry. My God knows me. Papa preaches to these people, making them his responsibility, not mine."

We continued to stroll toward Enoch's childhood home. I leaned on his strength and support. Though the people in the crowds were my neighbors as well as his, they left me tinged with fear. Too often they purposely bumped into me or brushed my crutch from beneath my arm. But with Enoch's support, my fears stilled.

Papa Jared and Mama Helsa greeted us with a warm hug. "So good to see you. We have missed you. You have been so close, yet so far away," Mama Helsa murmured into my ear.

"I am sorry, Mama Helsa," I responded. "My Mama did not give us leave to visit you."

"I know, Zehira. I have known Lilah for many years. You need not say anything." A hardness crossed her face before quickly fading. "We are happy you are here with us now."

I am certain she remembered the day Mama and Papa drug the children and I from her home.

Papa Jared put his arm around me and walked with us. "We have prepared a meal, waiting for your return, and we set up a table under the trees in back. Come, let us eat. I am hungry."

The children cheered and trooped around the house toward the table. We adults followed more slowly.

"Thank you, Mama." Enoch waved his hands. "We appreciate your hospitality, especially ..." His voice drifted off, not wanting to continue.

I knew what he wanted to say, but as a man of God, he refused to share anything that even appeared like gossip. *Why are my parents not as accepting?* I knew the answer, but could not bring myself to name it.

We ate together in noisy, happy love, a feeling I yearned to feel from my parents. Papa Jared and Mama Helsa showed no surprise when Enoch shared the news we would leave for home on the following morning.

"We feared your stay would be short when we saw your cart," Mama Helsa leaned forward in her chair.

I glanced at Enoch and mouthed the words, "Told you." He just smiled.

Papa Jared nodded. "We knew you came to gather your family and take them to Zion. We hoped you could stay longer."

"I know, Papa. I have a house ready for us and need my family closer. Jehovah needs us to return." Enoch shrugged with a smile.

"Will it be safe?" Helsa reached to refill her glass and offered the pitcher to me.

I took the pitcher and refilled my glass and each of my children's glasses, listening for Enoch's reply.

"The walls are thick. The gate closes tight at night. Yes, it will be safe." Enoch smiled for me. "And you know, Jehovah protects us as we obey."

Papa Jared nodded in understanding. He had recently been ordained a High Priest as a son of Adam. He, too, knew well the ways of Jehovah.

Mama Helsa leaned forward in her seat. "I saw no oxen or horses to pull your cart. Surely, you do not plan to pull it yourself?"

"I do. I have nothing more to trade for an animal. We can pull it." Enoch shrugged.

Mama Helsa glanced at Papa Jared and lifted an eyebrow.

"We will be fine. We are strong. We can stop to rest. It will be well." I closed my eyes a moment, hoping I spoke the truth.

"It will be fine," Papa Jared said. "How many days do you think it will take you to return to Zion, Enoch?"

"Pulling the full cart, probably three weeks. I came in a week, but I walked alone, with no cart. Liam brought it ahead for us."

While the conversation turned to Enoch's teaching the Gospel of Jehovah, I listened with only a part of an ear. I worried for the safety of our family and that we would have sufficient food to eat on our journey, especially hearing that Enoch had nothing else to trade. I realized he knew what he was doing, or at least, Jehovah did, and focused on the conversation.

Much later that night, as we lay together, I allowed the fears to bubble up and voiced my concerns. "How will we travel? My foot is twisted and I walk slow. The cart will help support me, but ..."

"Do not fear, my love. All will be well. Jehovah told me to bring you to Zion. It is time we were together once more. All will be well."

I breathed out a deep sigh and snuggled closer to him. "I wish my faith were as strong as yours. I fear ..."

Enoch covered my complaint with a kiss, deep and long. I sighed, enjoying his touch, his sweet kisses.

"Fear not. My faith will suffice, for now. Trust the Lord. Trust me." He kissed me again, longer this time. My longing for him took over, joining his.

I woke during the night and studied Enoch's sleeping face. No fears marred it. He snored softly. I sighed and closed my eyes, ready to sleep once more. I trusted this good man.

Later, the first rays of sunlight streamed into my eyes. I opened them and glanced to where Enoch slept. He had left our bed, already. I stretched, amazed no one had come yet to arouse me, demanding me to join in the morning chores. Then a thought came to me. *Today we leave for Zion.* I tossed the quilt off and rose from the bed, as well.

I washed, dressed, and braided my hair, and then prepared to help with the morning chores. After slipping my feet into my shoes and grabbing my crutch from the wall near the bed, I hurried into the kitchen where I found Mama Helsa pushing the coals around and breathing on them to bring them back to life.

"Good morning, Zehira," she said. "Did you sleep well?"

Her cheerfulness amazed me, so different from my mama. "Good morning, Mama Helsa. I did sleep well. How can I help?"

We worked together to make bread and a grain mush, chuckling and talking happily together. Grace joined us, setting the table with plates and spoons. I absorbed the love and joy of women working together. It would be so nice to experience this with my own Mama. I shook my head at the impossible thought.

Enoch and the other men and boys paraded in, damp from washing in the outside water trough. Papa Jared brought in milk freshly milked from the cow while Enoch, Tobiah and Noam each carried a small basket of freshly picked strawberries, raspberries, and gooseberries to mix into our mush. Chairs scraped on the wooden floor and laughter filled the room as we all sat down to eat.

Much too soon, we gathered together, preparing to leave the love and acceptance of Enoch's family home. I carried my bag of belongings to the cart, wondering how we would be fed on the journey.

I glanced up from my feet to a surprise. "Papa Jared!" I cried. "Where did this ox come from? Enoch said we would walk."

"Helsa and I could not allow you to walk for three weeks." He reached out to pat the oxen. "This ox is extra. You need it more than us. We could not sleep well if we kept it, knowing you were walking that far."

I reached over the side to place my bag inside. Tears suddenly blurred my vision. Huge earthen jars of grains, dried fruits, and meats filled the bottom. Fresh fruits and vegetables rested in baskets on top of the jars. Stacks of warm quilts rested beneath the seat, enough to keep all of us warm at night. Cooking pots and water bags hung from the tall poles outside. Everything we needed for our journey waited for us inside.

I wiped my eyes and stepped away from the cart to see Mama Helsa and Papa Jared beaming at my surprise. Enoch stood nearby with a silly grin dancing on his face. I fell into Mama Helsa's arms, allowing the tears to flow.

"How can you manage so much for us?" I bit back the rest of my unvoiced thought. *My parents would never do this for me.*

"Our crops are bountiful, providing enough and more to share." Mama Helsa's smile broadened, somehow.

Tobiah placed his bag in it with a surprised "Oh!" Grace lifted Noam so he could set his bag inside, then bent for her own. When she turned back toward us, her eyes were wide.

"What?" Noam asked.

Grace lifted him to see.

"Food." Noam nodded as if he expected it.

"Thank you, Grandmama, Grandpapa." Grace hugged them.

Enoch embraced his parents. "You were right. It is a good surprise."

CHAPTER THREE

Travel

Hours later, our family halted to rest in a shady grove of trees. By this time, the children realized this trek was no game. It would take time to reach our new home. Little Noam slumped to the ground, too tired to eat. Tobiah sat munching on an apple and a piece of cheese while Grace sliced cheese and bread.

I reached for apples for Enoch, Grace, and myself, then sat by Noam. There, I gratefully accepted the bread and cheese Grace offered. I watched my daughter offer her papa his share and sit gracefully near her brothers and me. Grace would never be taunted for her awkwardness.

Enoch set his food aside and stooped to pick Noam from the ground, placing him in the cart, nestled among the jars and baskets of food. Enoch tousled Noam's little blond head and smiled. I felt his love for us, and returned the gesture. He sat beside me while we ate and rested.

Suddenly, Enoch stood, looking all around. I drew Grace and Tobiah close, holding onto Tobiah to prevent him from jumping up to stand beside his papa. My heart beat rapidly, pulsing loudly in my head.

I heard voices of men coming closer. Enoch stayed standing, alert and gazing in all directions all around us. Men tromped into view, swirling dust about their feet. Enoch stiffened. We were alone and had no way to protect ourselves.

Liam pushed forward, embracing Enoch. "You got the cart. Good."

Enoch relaxed a bit, but I saw his eyes flick to the right. I followed where he looked, seeing many other men crowding in toward us. My heartbeat somehow increased and my stomach tightened. I gripped my crutch tighter, prepared to swing it at the men, to protect my children.

Twenty men surrounded us. Once again, I wished Enoch would carry a sword. However, even if he did, he could not protect the children and me against this many men. He said we would be safe. How could we be safe, now?

"Enoch, we need your assistance." Liam turned toward me and shrugged. "News came this morning after you left Aenon. Efran is besieged near Ziklag. He and a hundred men stand for Jehovah, surrounded by a thousand Shemites."

Liam raised his arms as if he had no choice. "They call for Efran to bow to their gods, or else they will take his life, and the lives of all who stand with him. Efran managed to send a message, begging you to help."

Liam glanced at me again. "I am sorry, Zehira. We need your husband to support us. Those men will die without his aid."

I bowed my head. What could I say? Those men would die without Enoch. If he left me behind, I would be stranded. I needed his assistance to get us to Zion safely, but I refused to beg. He would do the right thing.

"Excuse me, men. I must discuss this with Zehira."

At least Enoch wants to discuss this with me. Our long separations left me unsure.

I remembered all the times we traveled together in the early days of our marriage. We rode our horses throughout the land, meeting and speaking with men and women who sought to know and understand Jehovah's words. Those were special days. I loved listening to my good husband share. Then, the babies started to come to our family. That ended my travels with Enoch. I hoped to travel with him to Zion. Now, even that had become questionable.

I felt his warmth near me, his hand on my elbow, lifting me. I gazed into his eyes, afraid to say anything, knowing anything I said would be wrong. As a cripple, I held Enoch back. I swallowed back my tears so he could not see them.

"Zehira, come with me."

Enoch guided me out of the circle of men, out of the little grove where we had stopped. When he stopped, he gently turned me to face him.

"Can you find your way to Zion alone?"

Find my way to Zion alone. I had been there twice before. Probably I could, but would I want to?

"I can, I remember the way." I did not want to show my fear, of the men among us, or of the dangerous journey alone to Zion, although I felt certain Enoch felt me quiver.

Enoch embraced me. "I do not want to leave you. I promised to protect you."

I tried to contain my shudder and buried my head in his shoulder.

"Efran and his men will die without me. I thought to get you safely to Zion before this happened. Zehira, you are strong and brave. You can do this."

My shudder escaped. Grace and Tobiah joined us, crowding close.

"We will help you, Mama. Papa, I can be sure the ox moves onward." Tobiah stood tall and pushed his chest out.

"I know you will, son." Enoch placed his hand on Tobiah's shoulder. "You are strong and the ox listens to you. Grace, can you help your mama?"

"You know I will, Papa," Grace said.

I lifted my face and whispered, "My children are braver than me. I will not hold you back. My fears for us are small compared to my fears for you."

Enoch touched my face. "You need not fear for me. Jehovah carries me in the palm of his hand. I will be safe. I will give you a blessing. Jehovah will protect you and the children. All will be well with you as you travel."

A tear spilled past my defenses. "You just came for us, and now you must leave us." *In the wilderness, alone.*

"I must. Jehovah will be with you. He will protect you. Sit on this log. I will give you a blessing."

The blessing served to settle my fears. I saw Noam peek over the edge of the cart as we returned. My fears had lessened, but I still feared the men would want the food we had with us in the cart.

"Mama. Where were you?" Noam cried. "I woke up and you were gone."

"Papa and I needed to talk. We are here, now." I patted his back, calming the little boy's tears.

Enoch lifted Noam from the cart. "I must leave you and Mama. These men need my guidance. Will you help Mama, Tobiah, and Grace? You are such a big boy. Can you be sure they pray every night?

Noam soberly nodded his head.

Enoch ruffled his hair. "That's a big boy. Papa will be there soon after you get to Zion. Here, eat something. You fell asleep before you could eat."

Enoch handed Noam an apple and a chunk of bread while Grace sliced him some cheese and handed it to him. He solemnly chewed his food, bravely watching his papa prepare to leave. Even little Noam showed greater bravery than me.

Enoch reached beneath the bench and retrieved a pack. For a moment, it surprised me, until I remembered he had walked from Zion to Aenon. Of course, he would have one. I looked closer at the other men. Each of them also carried a pack on his back.

Enoch reached into the cart to choose dried meats, vegetables, and fruits to place in his pack. I found small bags and scooped some of each grain into them. I gave him most of the bread and a bag of water. He chose a few apples and closed his pack.

I breathed out the breath I held, not happy for him to leave us, but I had no choice.

Enoch embraced me for a long moment. I clung to him, silently willing him to stay, all the time knowing he had to leave us. He bent down and kissed me.

"I will return soon," he whispered. "You will be safe. Trust in Jehovah."

He pulled away, slung his pack on his back, waved, and disappeared. The other men followed. Within less than a finger span of the sun's movement, the children and I were alone. I refused to show my fear to the children, so I smiled and moved to the ox. Tobiah joined me, helping to hitch him to the cart and get us all moving along the trail.

The sunlight dimmed as the sun dropped toward the tops of the mountain. I had been watching for a safe place for us to sleep. I wanted someplace that would hide the ox and cart from prying eyes. I did not trust the men who wandered the trails between the villages and larger communities.

At last, I found a grove of trees with a gigantic fallen tree along one side and a stream flowing nearby. Greenery grew within the grove, providing food for the ox to eat, water for all of us to drink, and trees to screen us from others. What more could I hope for?

I moved the cart into the grove, near to the fallen tree. Tobiah staked and hobbled the ox so it could wander far enough to eat, though not wander far away from us. I lay my hand on Tobiah's shoulder and realized he had grown taller than I thought. He would soon be as tall as me, or taller.

Dinner was cold bread, cheese, and dried fruit and meat. After eating, the four of us crawled into quilts tucked into the cavity between the tree and the grass, with the cart in front of us.

After praying with the children, I poured out my fears and worry in a heartfelt silent prayer. I wanted to pray aloud as I had been taught, but I did not want my children to know the depths of my fears. I lay awake in the dark for a long time, working to slow my heartbeat.

CHAPTER FOUR

Assault

I startled awake and looked for Enoch, until I remembered with a shiver that he was traveling with men in another direction. Pink light heralded the rising sun. I glanced to my left to see my children still sleeping.

What woke me? I lay silently listening, trying to discern the difference. Then, I heard it. The ox bellowed and a voice hushed her. I reached out and touched Grace. Her eyes opened, she had been listening.

"Keep your brothers quiet—and here," I whispered into her ear.

She nodded.

I moved carefully and slowly from between our quilts. In the light of the early morning sun, the shadows of two men lay long on the grass. One man attempted to move the ox toward the wagon while the other dug into our cart. Our troubles would multiply if they took the ox and cart with all our food and water.

Water bags hung from the side of the cart near me. I quietly moved to the cart removed two water bags and carried them to the cavity in the tree, setting them next to Grace and the boys. Tobiah sat beside her, his eyes wide. He moved to join me, but Grace held his leg, keeping him on the quilts.

I returned to the cart and picked up a rock tossed it out a way from the cart. When the man rummaging through our cart turned toward the sound, I reached into the cart and grabbed the bag of dried meats, then ducked low before he turned back toward me.

Another stone sailed over my head, hitting a branch of the tree in to the left of the cart. When the man cursed and moved quickly toward the sound, I reached into the cart again and grabbed another bag of food, ducking out of sight as he called to the other man.

A third rock landed in another direction and I turned to see Grace drop her hand. I shook my head at her and grabbed another bag of food from the cart. I ducked low and carried the bags of food to where the children sat and dropped it beside the water.

I moved back to the cart, planning to claim a jar of grain, and leaned my crutch against the cart. As I reached inside, concentrating on the jar of grain, a foot kicked me.

Anger from all the tripping I received through my life rose up black with in me. I grabbed his foot as he swung it toward my face and pulled him down. I scrambled up and grabbed my crutch and beat him on his back. He found his feet and yelled and kicked at me.

I swung the crutch at his head, hoping to knock him over, maybe even knock him out. I heard Tobiah wrestling with Grace. If he escaped her grasp, he would be by my side in an attempt to protect me. A fist hit me in the chest, another on the chin. I stepped backward and looked into his face.

"You?"

"Yes. You thought I would stay with your weak husband. We slipped away and circled back. We saw your food. You do not need it all. You can share it with us." Liam's snarl twisted his face.

"Share means we agree! We do not agree that you may take our food, our cart, and our ox. You will not take our food!" I shouted.

Liam stepped toward me, snickering. "What will you do about it? You are a cripple."

I screamed, swinging my crutch from the ground toward his back with all my strength. Liam ducked, but my swinging crutch caught him on the back of the head. He dropped to the ground, twitched once, and did not move again.

Liam's partner ran toward me, shouting and cursing. He tried to hit and kick me. In my rage, I swung my crutch around wildly, trying to hit him, as well, or at least, keep him away from me. He ducked beneath my swinging crutch and slammed his head and shoulders into my body. I fell backward, hitting my head on the top edge of the cart as I fell. Bright lights filled my vision before everything went black.

When I opened my eyes, the brightness of the sun forced them immediately closed. I tried to move, but movement caused my head to pound and my stomach to heave. My chest and sides felt battered and bruised. After lying still for the space of a hand span, I tried to lift my head once more, but bright lights exploded behind my eyes and I let it fall back with a groan.

"Lay back, Mama," Grace said. "He kicked you in your sides after you fell."

"Unh. Water?"

"We have a little, the two bags you brought back to us. Tobiah will refill them when we need. Lie still."

"The cart? The ox?" I mumbled, fearing her answer.

"They took them. Tobiah and Noam chased them a distance, but with the ox, they were faster." I heard the resignation in Grace's voice.

"Where are Tobiah and Noam now?"

She set a cool cloth across my eyes. "I sent them to find some dry moss and vines. Your ribs feel like they are broken. I will wrap them so you can walk."

I pulled my arms close and tried to sit up.

"Do not move yet, Mama. You are badly hurt. Let the darkness ease before you try. She touched my face with a soft touch. "The cool cloth should help."

"Thank you," I mumbled, "but is there enough water?"

"There is. Do not fear. Remember, there is a stream running past our little glen." She lifted my head gently and helped me sip from a cup.

I lay back, fighting the blackness and waiting for the nausea to settle. In the distance, the gurgle of running water reached me. I heard the boys return. Grace thanked them and sent them searching for an aloe plant, with instructions to cut two big spears. Two? I must have more than a few cuts and scrapes.

Grace lifted the cloth. I heard her dip it into water and wring it out. I worried about water as she replaced the cloth on my head. Soon, the nausea stilled and the blackness began to recede.

"Will this do, Grace?" Tobiah asked. "This is the only one we could find and it was small. We know better than to take the whole plant."

This will have to do. You did well." Grace sighed softly. "Is the water clean? Would you check above the stream a distance to be certain no dead animals have fallen into it? Be extra careful, though. The men seem to be gone, but ... well, stay quiet and alert."

"We will, right Noam?" Tobiah said.

"Yeah. Those bad men will not come close with us on guard," Noam agreed.

"Be sure you do not let them know you are here," Grace called softly as they moved away.

Stream? I do not remember a stream? Where?

"Mama, I am going to put some of this aloe on your cuts. I will need to lift your robe."

"Unh huh."

29

I lay with my eyes closed while Grace lifted my robe and daubed aloe on the cuts on my legs and sides. She gently moved me to my side and daubed more aloe on cuts on my back. Fighting back groans and tears, I submitted to my daughter's gentle ministrations. Eventually, she helped me roll back onto my back and tugged my robe down around my legs, then gave me another sip or two of water.

Liam, that evil man, really hurt me.

The boys returned with news. "No dead animals. The water is pure and sweet," Tobiah said.

"We followed the cart tracks," Noam announced, "but Tobiah would not let me get close."

"Which direction are they traveling?" Grace asked.

I listened for the answer.

"East, toward Nod," Tobiah said. "Probably running to those idol worshipers for safety."

"Perhaps, or trying to disguise their true direction. We must stay on guard," I mumbled.

I tried to push myself up to sit. The nausea returned and the world spun, but the blackness receded into gray. I gave up and let my head rest on the ground, no, too soft to be the ground. Someone must have folded something under my head.

"How late is it?" My voice sounded stronger than I felt.

"The sun is nearing the apex, Mama. You were asleep a long time. We were worried about you." Fear tinged her calm voice.

I lay with my eyes closed for a while, listening to the children whisper to each other, I worried about the man I had hit with my crutch, Liam. He fell hard. I had to ask Grace. I waited until she lifted the cloth from my forehead. I cracked an eye open and watched her dip the cloth into a container of water and twist the water out.

"What about the man I hit?"

"He moaned when the other man dumped him into the cart. The ox did not like to be hitched to the cart so early, but she went with them." Disgust filled Tobiah's voice.

"Poor ox," I murmured.

Good. I did not kill Liam. I have enough to repent of already. I do not want to repent of killing a man, even in defense of my children.

"We need to leave this place," I struggled to sit.

"No, Mama. We need to stay here tonight." Grace touched my shoulder and pushed me back down. "You cannot travel yet. Your head is hurt too badly. We have food and water. We can stay tonight, if we are careful."

"No. We need to go." The pounding in my head increased as I tried to stand. I slumped back to sit. "I guess we stay the night."

Grace lifted my head and gave me another drink. She gave me a small piece of dried meat. She handed the boys small pieces of dried meat and a cup of water. With pure water nearby, we could drink all we wanted while we stayed here.

"Rest, Mama. You need to heal. We need you well enough to leave in the morning. Sleep."

When did Grace get old enough to tell me what to do? When I got beat up by that creep, Liam. Though she was right, I still worried about her and the boys.

"You will watch for others who may want to hurt us?"

"We will." I watched Noam thrust out his chest.

"I will sleep then." I closed my eyes against the brightness of the sun and slept.

CHAPTER FIVE

Struggle

Twice more before dark, I opened my eyes. Grace offered me a drink and a bit of dry fruit each time, before encouraging me to rest some more. The third time I woke, I listened to the night sounds. Little nocturnal animals rustled in the grass and trees. The sounds comforted me. I knew the animals would not move so if dangers were present.

This time when I opened my eyes, no nausea or blackness affected me, to my joy. I carefully pushed myself off the quilt and sat up. My head still hurt, but did not pound as it had earlier. I probed the cuts and scrapes Grace had doctored earlier with aloe. Though still tender to the touch, they hurt less. I sighed and lay back down, falling into dreamless sleep.

Sunlight pierced my eyelids, waking me. Though still early, Grace, Tobiah, and Noam spoke quietly together. I smiled at their resilience as I managed to sit. No nausea. No blackness. Even the spinning and pounding in my head had reduced to a manageable throb.

Grace glanced my way. "Mama is awake. We should be able to leave soon, if she is feeling better."

I stood slowly, wary of a relapse of my symptoms. I wobbled a bit with dizziness, but it lessened as I walked to where the children squatted.

"We can leave after we eat. Be sure the water bags are filled and ready."

"Are you sure, Mama? We can stay here another day. This is a nice place to camp." Grace stared at me, watching for weakness.

"No, we cannot stay another day. It is too dangerous to stay here. I can leave."

We ate breakfast and rolled the quilts to sling them across our backs, along with the food and water containers I managed to retrieve before my beating. Tobiah refilled the water containers and Noam found my crutch in the trees, dented, but usable. Soon, I led my little family from the quiet of the glen onto the path leading to Zion at as quick a pace as my head and twisted foot would allow.

Every hand span or so of the sun's movement, Grace called a halt, insisting I needed a rest. I argued with her, though secretly grateful for her thoughtfulness. My head pounded, bringing with it a thread of dismay. This much could be dangerous.

Tobiah saw a little cave in the hill as the sun set behind the mountains. No gurgling brook sang nearby to refill the empty water skin. I allowed us each a small sip from the second skin before the little ones lay down to sleep.

I slept fitfully that night, waking often to listen to the small sounds of the night. Little animals skittered through the grass away from night birds hunting them. When I finally slept, I dreamed of men attacking my family and stealing our cart and ox.

I roused the children as purples and pinks painted the eastern sky. We trudged on toward Zion, thirsty from the dry food. We rationed the last of our water, hoping to find another clear stream. Late in the afternoon, we crossed one. I waited to drink of its coolness, watching in all directions while the children quenched their thirst and refilled the water skins. Only then did I allow Tobiah and Grace to stand guard while I knelt and dipped water up with my hands until my thirst was quenched.

Our little family marched on until nearly dark before we found a dip in the grass a distance off the path, near a pool of water. Tall grass concealed our presence and I managed to sleep through the night, waking only twice to listen to the sounds of the night, comforted by the movements of small animals.

Once again, we marched toward Zion before purple and pink streaks of sunrise disappeared. We moved slower, as my leg buckled under me, forcing us to rest.

Near mid-day, Noam stopped and turned toward us with his finger to his lips. "Men," he whispered.

We slipped into the cover of the nearby trees and listened as boisterous men passed, laughing at crude jokes. I knelt behind a tree and quivered, reminded of the ugliness of men and my encounters with them. Grace reached out and set her warm hand on my arm. I looked into the girl's face and saw my own reflected.

This would never do. I straightened my back and smiled. I could be brave for my children, even while I worked to ensure their safety.

At last, the voices faded along the path and I dared to continue our journey.

Enoch walked from Zion to Aenon in a week's time. I counted the days we had trudged along the path. One-half day with Enoch and the cart, the rest of the day with the cart. One day lost to my beating and now, this third day of walking, or limping in my case. Between my limp and my crutch, we walked much slower than Enoch, but we had his help and the help of the ox that first day, taking us farther in that one day than he could walk. I decided we were half way to Zion.

That meant three more days of trudging along the path, hiding when others passed along the path, nibbling on dried meat and fruits, and sipping at the limited water. Each time we came to a stream or river, we filled our water skins. Without water, we could never arrive at our destination.

On the next day, we hid more often for the path became busier.

"Will we hear the great Enoch speak when we arrive in Zion?" we heard a young man ask his companion.

"They say he helped Efran against the Shemites. He called upon a great river to leave its banks and rush between his men and the enemy. Some Shemites drew to close to the raging flood and were drowned. The others turned and ran. Enoch should return to Zion soon."

Their voices passed us and were lost in the distance. Grace and Tobiah stared at me.

"Papa called on the river to protect them?" Awe filled Noam's voice.

"Jehovah protects him," I said.

No others came along the path, so we stood and moved on. Late in the morning of the tenth day, Grace tugged on my robe. "Mama, what is that? It looks like a garden wall, but it is as tall as a mountain."

I gazed in the direction she pointed.

"Zion. That is Zion. Your papa told me it has high walls to protect it and tight gates that close at night. We will be safe there."

"Hurry, Mama. Let's hurry to Zion!" Noam cried.

We moved a little quicker along the path that had broadened into a road, beaten down by the many traveling feet. The wall grew larger as the sun crossed the zenith and moved toward setting, but it seemed not to be any closer. Even Noam slowed his pace.

"When will we see Papa?" he moaned.

"I do not know if he is here. You heard those men earlier. We are almost there, though. Look. See the gates."

I glanced up at the western sky where gold and orange streaked among the purple and pink.

"We must hurry, or we will find ourselves locked out. Hurry."

The children picked up on my fear and excitement and rushed the last distance to the gate, slipping past as the last rays of sunlight gleamed golden on the brass gate hinges.

"You barely made it," a large man said. "We are closing the gate for the night."

"Thank you," I gasped and bent with one hand on my knee, fighting to regain my breath. When I finally could breathe well enough to talk again, I asked, "Is there a place for travelers to rest? A place we can sleep and be safe?"

"You will be safe here. Those who live here love Jehovah. We will protect you. An inn for visitors sits down this road. Wait, while I finish locking the gate, and I will take you there."

The man lifted a heavy log into place across the gate before turning to my family and me. "Come with me. I will show you the way to the Visitor's Inn."

He turned and walked away at a brisk pace. I tried to keep up, but my twisted foot and aching bruises, combined with exhaustion from the extra effort to get inside, slowed me. Tobiah and Grace paced on either side of me, helping me move forward. Noam followed, as tired and slow as me. The man turned to say something to me and noticed we were far behind.

"I am sorry. My long legs move faster than your shorter ones. I am James. Enoch entrusted me to close this gate, and help travelers."

"Thank you, James. We have traveled many days to get here."

"Alone, without a man? You are brave."

"No, not brave. Just needing to find our way here." I held my free hand up to ward off the complement.

CHAPTER SIX

Traveler's Inn

Grace, Tobiah, Noam, and I followed James through the crowds of people hurrying home along the clean city streets. As night fell, men walked through the streets with torches, lighting those along the streets, illuminating little gardens of flowers fronting the neat homes. Although it was a larger city than I ever visited before, Zion was beautiful with smiling people who nodded as they hurried past.

A larger building came into view ahead of us on the side of the road. James led us to the door of this building and showed us in. A large room filled with tables and the fragrances of cooking food greeted us. James seated us at a table near the edge of the room and disappeared through a door, while I leaned my crutch against the wall near the table.

"Welcome! Welcome! Traveler's Inn welcomes all who are new to our city." A small man bounced the door open and wiped his hands on a bright yellow kitchen towel. "We welcome all seekers of truth."

"Thank you. We are very tired," I said.

"I am Bain, your innkeeper. And you are?"

"Zehira. These are my children, Grace, Tobiah, and Noam. We have walked far and are tired and dirty."

"And hungry," Noam added.

"Now that you are in Bain's capable hands, I will return to my gate," James said with a smile.

"You have clean clothes?" Bain asked.

"We ran into bandits along the way. They took everything except a little food and two skins of water," Grace said with a frown.

The boys nodded.

"I will bring you something to eat. Food is most important, first. Then we will get you into rooms and find you baths and clean clothing."

"We have nothing to trade for this. How can we repay you for your kindness?" I frowned, fearing we would be forced out in the morning.

"Tonight, it is not a problem. Tomorrow, you may help in the kitchen and laundry, if you desire," Bain said.

"That would be wonderful. I would not want to abuse your kindness."

Bain nodded and smiled. "I will return soon with food. Sit and rest."

We sat at the table, leaning our elbows on the table and resting our chins on our hands until Bain re-entered the room, followed by two young women. He carried a bowl of delicious smelling stew, which he set in the center of the table. The tall girl placed a basket of bread, bowls, spoons, and napkins in front of us. The shorter girl set a pitcher of clear water and four cups on the table. They smiled and nodded at us and withdrew, allowing us to eat in privacy.

The children and I bowed our heads in thanks to Jehovah, then I dished a bowl of stew for each of us. Grace sliced the bread, handing a slice to each of us. We dipped our spoons into the delicious smelling stew and ate.

"Mama?" Grace set her spoon down. "I have been thinking about something."

"What would that be?" I set my elbows on the table.

"Why did you not tell James we are the family of Enoch? Would they not be watching for us?"

"Probably. That would make sense. Your papa did not manage to travel with us. As it is, I suppose this is easier."

"How can it be easier, Mama?" Tobiah asked between bites.

"You boys may not understand. Maybe Grace will. It has always been a challenge for me to make friends, with my twisted foot." I glanced at my crutch.

Grace nodded.

"I would rather the women of Zion get to know me before they know I am married to Enoch."

"I can understand that, Mama. I feel the same." Grace picked up her spoon and returned to spooning the delicious stew into her mouth.

We said little more as we ate.

As I sopped up the last of my stew with the bread, Bain entered the room.

"Wonderful food," Tobiah said.

"Yes, delicious," Grace added.

"Yum," Noam said.

I nodded my thanks with a smile.

"You are our only guest this evening. We are glad you enjoyed the food. Would you like that bath and bed?"

I sighed deeply. "Please."

The children stood. Tobiah helped me stand while Noam reached for my crutch, giving it to me when I stood. When I settled the crutch beneath my arm, Bain led the way up sturdy stairs and down a hall. Two rooms stood open, one for Grace and me, the other for the boys.

"A warm bath awaits you in this room." Bain indicated a door on the right near the rooms. "Who would like to be first?

"Mama will go first," Grace announced. The boys nodded their agreement.

"We guessed at sizes, but we think the clothes we have provided will fit. Please leave your dirty clothing in the basket in the bathing room. We will ensure they are cleaned and ready for you tomorrow."

"Thank you, Bain. We appreciate your help." I nodded, too tired for any more.

"We welcome seekers of truth. You are a seeker, or you would not have come to Zion. We are happy you have come." Bain nodded and left us alone.

In the room Grace and I shared, I found a soft, blue robe that matched my eyes, while a light green robe matched Grace's. I lifted the blue the robe and found small clothes folded neatly beneath it.

"Mama, take the clothes and enjoy your bath. You deserve it," Grace urged.

I nodded and crossed the hall to the bath. There, a large tub filled with hot water waited for me. I stripped off my dirty clothing and unceremoniously dumped them into the waiting basket. Then, I climbed into the hot bath and leaned back. The hot water relaxed and soothed away all my aches and pains from my beating and the long hike to Zion. Leaning back, I thought about Enoch, remembering the first time he stood up for me.

I had watched the sons of Jared from the safety of my older sister's skirts. I watched Enoch with his little brother, Hadar, tagging behind as he went to the community log pile for wood for his Mama's fire. Hadar kept a running conversation going, often ending with, "Right, Enoch?" I could tell he adored his brother.

One day, when Hadar was nearing his teen years, my sister and I were drawing water from the well when Hadar led Enoch toward the well. Hadar had grown taller and bigger than his older brother.

"I am too important to carry water for Mama. That is *girls* work, not something a future prophet should do. You can carry the water to Mama," Hadar growled.

Enoch bent to reach the rope attached to the bucket we women used to draw water and started pulling.

"Remember, I got the water, not you. Mama asked me to get the water."

Enoch nodded and pulled on the rope, bringing the bucket full of water out of the well.

"H-h-hand m-m-me the j-j-j-jar, H-H-H-Hadar."

The younger boy handed the water jar to his brother. As he turned, he saw us and thrust his chest out.

"Getting water is girls work, not for someone like me. I will be a prophet someday. You there." He pointed at me. "Give me one of your dates."

I glanced into my basket. Only one date remained. Mama had allowed me only three that day.

"I do not have enough for you to share my dates with you."

"Yes, you do. I see a date in your basket. Give it to me," Hadar demanded.

"No."

Hadar reached his hand into my basket and took the last date.

"That is mine," I shouted and stomped my foot.

"You do not need it. You are a cripple," he shouted back and kicked my crutch out from under my arm.

I fell, landing hard on my hands.

"H-H-H-Hadar!" Enoch yelled. "That w-w-w-was n-n-not n-n-n-nice. G-g-g-give it b-b-b-back."

"N--n-no." Hadar said, dancing away from his brother. "Do not forget Mama's water." He pushed the bucket into the well. "Mama is waiting for me to bring her water. You had better hurry."

Enoch retrieved my crutch and helped me up. He silently turned back to the well, reaching for the rope. When the bucket again appeared above the well, full of water, Enoch carefully poured the cool water into our water jug. Then, he dropped the bucket back into the well, dragging up the full bucket and poured water into their mama's water jug. He smiled shyly at me and followed his brother toward their home.

I smiled at the memory, thinking about how wrong Hadar had been. I stood and reached for a soft towel that waited for me on a stool and stepped from the tub. Grace and the boys deserved some of this lovely hot water. I wrapped the towel around myself and limped back to my room. After Grace left to bathe, I flopped across the bed and slept.

CHAPTER SEVEN

Zion

Early the next morning, I woke to find someone had turned me around, so my head lay on my pillow, and had covered me. I stretched, climbed out of bed, and slipped on the beautiful blue robe lying there, waiting for me. I glanced at Grace, who still slept and opened the door, tucked my crutch under my arm and hobbled out, concentrating on finding the latrine. I nearly tripped over Tobiah, who jumped to his feet.

"What are you doing on the floor?" I asked. "Did not Bain provide you with a comfortable bed?"

Tobiah glanced down the hall. "There are no locks on the doors. After our journey, I fear strangers and feel safer protecting your door."

I smiled at my son, understanding his concerns. "Thank you."

Grace sat in her bed, rubbing her eyes. "Where is Noam, then?"

"He tried to stay with me, but when he fell asleep, I carried him to his bed." Tobiah stretched.

I walked to the door to their room when the door opened.

"Why did you bring me here?" Noam demanded. "I could help."

"I know, brother, but you were snoring. Everyone would know we were in the hall."

"I do not snore."

"No more than the old ox," Grace teased.

Soon, even Noam joined in the laughter.

"We are all awake. Get dressed and we can go down to the dining room and see if there is any breakfast." I said. "But move quietly. We do not want to wake any other visitors."

"We are the only ones. Bain told us last night," Noam reminded me.

"If Bain or the girls still sleep, we do not want to disturb them."

The children were soon dressed and quietly walked down the stairs behind me. As we neared the dining room, lovely odors of breakfast filled the air. The tall girl opened the kitchen door as we entered.

"Good. You are awake," she said with a smile. "I will bring you your breakfast."

Before we could say anything to her, the door closed on her back. We chose a table close to the kitchen door, to make it easier for them to bring us the food. We did not wait for we had just settled into our chairs when the girl was back setting plates of food in front of each of us. The other girl followed with spoons, cups, and a pitcher of cold milk.

"Enjoy," they chorused.

"Where is the latrine?" I asked before the girls could leave the room.

"The latrine? Oh, did Bain forget to show you?" the tall girl laughed as her face colored. "Follow me, I will show you."

She led us down a passageway and outside to a little house.

When we returned to the dining room, we tucked in to the food. We did enjoy it. It tasted excellent. I had not realized how much I missed simple things, like warm cooked food and cold milk. We did not say much; we were too busy focusing on the food.

When all the plates were empty, we stacked them in a pile and Grace stood to pick them up. Noam took the cups and Tobiah carried the pitcher. I tucked my crutch beneath my arm and carried the spoons. We marched into the kitchen with our burdens.

"We came to help," Grace announced. "Our only means of repayment is to help you in the kitchen."

The girls smiled and stepped away from the pan full of dish water.

"Mama, you and Tobiah go straighten our rooms," Grace suggested. "Noam and I will wash the dishes."

I nodded. Grace probably wanted to be alone to learn more about these girls. Tobiah and I returned to our rooms upstairs. Together, we pulled quilts up and straightened each bed. We found our old clothes on a stool, cleaned and ready to wear.

"Should we change?" Tobiah asked, fingering the fine robe he wore. "This is so much nicer than our traveling clothing."

"They are much softer." I shrugged in the softness of my robe. "When Grace and Noam return, we should change."

Tobiah frowned and then nodded.

We found brooms and swept the floors of each room, the halls, and down the stairs. As Tobiah held the door open for me to sweep the little pile of dust into the street, one of the girls from the kitchen rushed in.

"We do not sweep our dirt into these streets," she cried. "We brush it into a dustpan and take it to the garden. We work to keep the streets of Zion clean."

I dropped my eyes. "I did not know. How do you sweep it into a dustpan?"

The girl showed me how to sweep the dust into a flat sided container. She carried the dirt from the floor to a round basket and dumped it there.

"You do not know about Zion, yet. We keep it clean and beautiful. You will learn. I am Susanna."

"Thank you for teaching me. I suppose Grace did not throw the dishwater from the window?"

"No. Hanna showed her the flower garden that needed watering. We share the water with our flowers and vegetables."

"Makes sense," Tobiah said.

"Should we change back into our own clothing?" I winked at Tobiah.

"Not unless you prefer it. What you are wearing is now yours. We keep clothing to share with our visitors. Do you want to see our city?"

"We would, if we have repaid you for our rooms and meals."

Susanna nodded. "You have more than repaid us for your meals."

"Tobiah, would you fetch my crutch?"

He nodded and bounded up the stairs. Grace and Noam joined me as Tobiah returned with the crutch.

"Do you have a map?" he asked. "This city is large and unfamiliar to us. How will we find our way back here?"

Hanna shook her head. "No, no maps, but ask anyone. We are near the South Gate. If you travel south, you will find us again."

We walked into the bright sunshine, so bright I noticed others shielding their eyes with their hands or broad-brimmed hats. I blinked a few times, then squinted before I could take in the brightness and drop my hand to observe the flowers growing in front of each building.

My twisted foot kept our pace to a stroll. We walked down roads, turning without thought toward the center of the city.

I did not want to be a country bumpkin, pointing out all the wonders of the city, but I could not help saying, "Look at the well. They have built it with neat stones that glisten in the sunlight."

We sat on its walls and dipped our hands in the cool water for a drink.

"Mama?" a voice from within the crowds spoke. "Mama? Is that really you?"

A big man stepped through the throng of cheerful people until he reached us.

"Methuselah!" I cried, throwing my arms around him. "I did not know you were in Zion."

Methuselah greeted his brothers with a bear hug and a gentle kiss on the cheek for Grace.

"Papa sent me. When he arrived in Ziklag to help, he realized Liam and Evron were no longer in the group. He feared for your safety. You were safe, after all?"

"We are safe now, but no, Methuselah, we were not safe. They came back and took our cart and ox. Liam fought with me. The other man, Evron, did you say?"

Methuselah nodded.

"He attacked me, knocking me against the edge of the of the cart, then he viciously kicked me. We were delayed while the blackness faded. We walked here with only the little food I managed to retrieve before they saw me and the water bags I managed to grab. We hid from anyone who passed, fearful they would return for our lives. We managed to pass through the gate before James closed it last night."

"James did not say you came through his gate. I asked him this morning. He was watching for the family of Enoch," Methuselah growled.

"Do not fault James, son. He took us to the Traveler's Inn. I told him only my name. I did not think to say Enoch was my husband." Then under my breath, I added, "Who would believe Enoch would marry a cripple like me?"

"Cripple? Not you, Mama!"

I shrugged. "I do not want to only be known as Enoch's wife. I want friends who like me because of me, not as status as Enoch's wife. It happens, when you are a cripple."

"I suppose that makes sense. I am glad you arrived safely. Let me show you to your house."

"House?" I said through the noise of the children's excitement. "Yes, I remember, Enoch did say there was a house for us. The bump on my head must have caused me to forget."

"We must retrieve our belongings and thank Bain, Susanna, and Hanna," Grace said.

"I will take you there later," Methuselah said. "Mama needs to see her new home, first."

Methuselah took my arm and drew me close, much like Enoch, to help me walk more firmly down the road. I tried to memorize the turns to take to get back to the well. I would need to return for water for cooking and cleaning.

Methuselah turned along a path to a house no bigger or smaller than the other homes we observed as we walked down the many streets. In front of the house bloomed purple iris, pink rock roses, colorful spikes of lupine, with gold and blue pansies and tiny purple violets lining the path. I paused to inhale the fragrances wafting on the gentle breeze. Bees buzzed in the flowers. Birds chirped in the trees. I smiled appreciating the pleasant experience.

"Who lives here? Who will we visit?" I asked.

"Such a lovely home. Someone nice must live here," Grace added.

Both Tobiah and Noam chimed in, wondering who lived there.

"Do you not know, Mama?" Methuselah asked. "You live here. This is your home."

CHAPTER EIGHT

Our House

Methuselah stepped forward, opening the front door. "Welcome to your home, Mama."

I struggled to find the words to say as I gazed around. *This beautiful home is mine?* I walked through the sitting room, filled with warm wooden furniture and colorful pillows and rugs. I ran my hands across the wood, appreciating the smoothness. Noam sat in a rocker, leaning back and grinning as it rocked back and forth with him.

"I like this chair," he said.

I smiled at my youngest son and nodded. I understood his joy.

We moved down a hall, opening doors to rooms with beds and wardrobes. Grace stepped into one and opened the door to the wardrobe. Inside were soft robes of many colors.

"My room?" she asked.

Methuselah nodded. Grace stayed, dropped her pack on the bed and fingered the colorful robes, moving about her room.

Robes that fit the boys were in the next room. Tobiah and Noam chose a bed and dumped their traveling packs on them. They upended the packs on the bed and sorted through them, preparing to sort through their belongings and find new homes for them.

The last room in the hall held two wardrobes filled with clothing for a man and a woman. Questions filled me as I turned to Methuselah.

"Yes, Mama, this room is yours and Papa's."

I resisted the temptation to stay and sort through my belongings as the boys did. Instead, I set my traveling pack on a chair and followed Methuselah on a tour of the rest of the house.

A small study was located next to our bedroom. Enoch had already placed his books, ink, pens, and vellum on the desk, ready for work. A smile played on my face as I fingered his books. Yes, they were his. Now, I knew I was in my own home.

Methuselah led me to the kitchen, stocked with all the dishes I would need to feed a large family, along with the necessary pots and pans. I saw a tall door in a corner and pulled it open. Jars of grains sat on the floor, containers of dried fruits and vegetables sat on the shelves above them. Another door opened to a cool area filled with jars of milk and cream, fresh fruits, vegetables, and slabs of mutton and beef.

A large basin for washing dishes sat on a counter. I searched, unsuccessfully for a water jar.

"No water jar?" I asked.

"No, Mama, you will not need a large jar for water. That smaller one is big enough. See?" Methuselah opened a door leading to the back yard. By then, Grace and the boys trooped in to join us in the kitchen. We followed Methuselah into the bright sunshine. There, near the house, stood a well with a handle to turn. When Noam turned it, a bucket full of cold water lifted from its depths.

I slumped next to the well. "But how will I get to know the other women here, if we do not meet at the well each evening?"

The grin on Methuselah's face fell.

"Meet the women? I thought you would like your private well. All the houses have private wells. The women find other ways to meet.

Grace moved closer. "All the houses? No evening trips to the well? No excuse to meet and share the news?"

"I do not know how they do it, Grace, but trust me, they still get together. They still share the news. I will find out for you how they do it."

Grace waved a hand at him. "No, I will find out on my own. For this, I do not need your help."

We returned to the kitchen and Grace sat in a chair by the table, her chin resting in her hand, a glumness surrounded her. I knew exactly how she felt.

At least, she is tall and beautiful. She will make friends easily. Not like me. I stared down at my twisted and bent foot and the crutch under my arm. I, too, plopped into a chair and sat with my chin in both hands. I had a difficult time finding friends in Aenon, the town I grew up in. How would I ever get to know all these strangers, even a few of them? All these people loved and honored Enoch. What would I do? I did not want them to like me only because I married their leader.

"I thought you would like to have water close. I am sorry, Mama, Grace. You will find a way to meet other women."

We glanced up at him, almost in unison.

"I can do that," I murmured.

Methuselah and the boys went out to gather wood from the nearest community woodpile. Grace wandered back to her room. I sat in my chair thinking and remembering.

My sister, Deni. was tall, lithe, and perfect. Her feet were straight, her hair dark, long, and straight. None of that described me. Untamed curls filled my light-brown hair. I could only be described as short and dumpy. Worst of all, my right foot twisted under so far I could only walk on the toes. Walking, even with the crutch Papa carved for me, filled my whole body from my toes to my shoulders with pain.

Deni treated me well, most of the time, except when friends visited. I knew, then, to stay hidden from them.

None of the girls my age spoke with me. Instead, they taunted and teased me. No other person in Aenon had a foot twisted like mine. My childhood was lonely until Mele moved in. Mele did not notice my crutch and twisted foot. She stood not much taller than me, with long blond hair tied up in braids around her small head. We met each morning and evening at the well, sharing gossip and friendship. We laughed together and shared secrets. It was a lovely time.

We girls loved days when our mamas sent us to dig clay for pots. This allowed us time to play a few minutes, out of the stern gaze of our mamas, especially mine. For, Mama Lilah acted angry that I lived.

We were happy in our friendship, until Mele met Hadar. His tall, dark, handsome looks drew her attention. I could not stand to be around the bragging bully. He walked through our village with an entourage, demanding drinks from the well from all the girls, expecting to be first in everything. I could not understand how my friend could be drawn to him.

Hadar was interested in Mele, as well. Her blond beauty stood out from the other girls in Aenon. Once more, I lived in a lonely place. Mele not only became aware of my twisted foot, she joined in Hadar's taunts.

I dug clay alone after that, missing my friend.

"You got away from your mama?" Mele dropped her basket and digging shovel near where I worked one afternoon.

I looked up at her in surprise. *Why was she talking to me?*

"Yeah. Mama is making more jars and needs lots of clay. Said I cannot dawdle like I usually do. Not that it matters. I have no one to talk with."

"I am here."

"Until Hadar whistles." In my loneliness, I allowed the sarcasm to leak into my voice.

59

"Hadar does not whistle for me." Her hand went to her hips. "He is good to me."

"I am glad for you." I continued to fill my clay basket.

"You should be. I am going to be Hadar's wife. We will be betrothed tonight."

I stopped digging and stared at my one-time friend. "You are going to marry him?"

"Yes. He will be the next High Priest. His Papa is a priest, and he will be. I will be important."

"You are important to me, Mele. You are my friend. You do not need to marry that bully." I watched her shoulders droop a moment until she rolled them back and stood tall and confident once more.

"But, I do. He will be wealthy. Do you not see how people give to him, give him precedence? He is always first."

"Because he demands it. People do not really like Hadar. He is a bully." I ground out the words, struggling not to raise my voice.

"And, am I a bully, too, because I love him?" Mele stood with her hands on her hips.

"Because you follow him, sometimes. He is …"

"He is my betrothed." She stamped her foot.

"I am sorry about that." I dug into the clay and finished filling my basket. I stood and limped away.

Mele stood with her hand on her hips, jaw slack in surprise. At last, as I moved down the path she shouted, "I am sorry you were my friend."

I moved on, so angry I could not think of anything to say until a lump of clay hit me in the back. I spun around on my good foot to see Mele bending over for another lump of clay. Before she could fling another glob of clay at me, I grabbed a hunk from my basket and threw it. In my rage, it did not surprise me that I hit her on the back. She threw another handful of clay toward me, hitting me in the face. We were soon covered in the brown clay.

I caught a glimpse of myself in the stream and started tittering.

"Why are you giggling?" Mele stood with a glob in her upheld hand.

"You look funny."

"Funny?" Mele pointed at me. "No funnier than you."

"We are a mess."

"We are."

We stood with our hands on our knees, giggling. At last, we stopped laughing and stepped into the creek to wash. Dripping wet, we fell into each other's arms.

"I am sorry, Zehira. You are my friend and you always be."

"And you will always be my friend, Mele. Even married to Hadar, you will be my friend."

We had been better friends—for a while.

"Mama." Methuselah touched my shoulder. "Are you well? You have been sitting there, staring, for a long time."

"Yes, son. I am well, and happy. I was just remembering."

CHAPTER NINE

Wells

Enoch returned that night. I fell into his arms in tears.
"You were gone so long. Are you well? Were you
hurt?" I babbled.

"I am well. And you? Tobiah told me about your run in
with Liam and his friend. You were brave to fight them alone.
A bit silly, perhaps, but brave."

"I will not let some thieves hurt my children. If I had not
retrieved food and water, we would have starved on the road
here." I dropped my fists to my hips.

"But you were hurt. You could have been killed by them.
It was dangerous to fight them with your crutch."

"It was dangerous, but I had no choice. I was attacked. We
required water and food. I got it." I tapped my foot.

Enoch shook his head and pulled me close. "I know. I am
sorry I left you. Efran could have handled the Shemites." He

raised his eyebrows. "Not as easily, but he could have handled them. I am sorry those wicked men attacked you."

I buried my head in Enoch's shoulder, allowing him to pull me close.

Sometime later, I pulled away and looked at Enoch. "I forgot to gather our things from the Traveler's Inn. I should go thank them for their kindnesses."

Enoch pulled me back and murmured into my hair, "Grace told me she did that earlier today. She wanted to spare you the effort."

I wanted to thank them personally. I appreciated Grace's concern, but it prevented my contact with those women. I sighed. "I will send them a note of thanks."

"They will appreciate that." Enoch bent to kiss me on the forehead.

I pushed myself back and away from him, putting space between us. "How will I get to know the women of Zion if every home has a well? We meet at the well to share. What can I do to get to know these women? They do not know me. They will see me only as the wife of Enoch," I kissed him on the forehead, "whom I love, or that crippled woman—or both. I want to be known for myself."

Enoch brushed his hand along my face. "You will figure this out. You are a smart woman," he reassured me. "I believe the women will forget your twisted foot and your crutch as they get to know you."

"But where will I meet them? How will they get to know me?" The question came out almost in a wail.

"You are an intelligent woman. You will find a way." He pulled me close again and kissed me like were newlyweds again.

Enoch had kissed me deeply many years before. He returned after a visit with Adam and a long journey through the land. His visit with Adam resulted in his ordination as a High Priest at a younger age than any of his grandfathers, except Adam. His Papa, Jared, still had not received that honor. Few in Aenon could believe the change in him. Fewer believed the honor. Enoch no longer stuttered, even a little bit. In those early experiences teaching the word of Jehovah, he developed an unprecedented confidence.

Enoch had found me in Mama's house, weaving and dreaming of him. I liked his kindness when he helped me carry clay and water for Mama. Love for him grew when he stopped his brother's constant bullying.

Hadar decided I was a good target for his torments. It made him look tough among his friends who frequently surrounded me.

"What do you think you are doing, cripple?" Hadar taunted one day when we were younger.

"You do not belong on this road," his buddy added.

"I do belong here. I was born in Aenon before you were," I had replied.

Hadar stood with a fist on a hip staring at me. "That does not give you the right to be on my road, where I will see you," he snarled. "I should not have to see a cripple like you."

"Then go the other way or close your eyes," I retorted.

"No. You need to go the other way. You do not need that crutch." Hadar swept my crutch from beneath my arm.

I fought to maintain my balance.

"Give me my crutch!" I yelled.

"No. I think not. You need to learn to turn the other way when you see me. Maybe this will teach you."

"Give my crutch back. I have every right to be on this road. I have as much right as you do."

Hadar just snickered and held the crutch out of my reach.

I tried to reach it while trying to maintain my balance. The last thing I wanted to do among these bullies was to fall.

"G-G-G-Give her the cr-cr-crutch b-b-b-back!" Enoch had come up behind them, unseen by any of them.

"Oh?" Hadar had said. "My st-st-st-stuttering brother thinks I should give the cripple b-b-b-back her crutch." He giggled at his own sick joke.

"Yes. Give it b-b-b-back. N-N-Now." Authority filled his voice, in spite of his stutter.

"No. I will not. What will you do?" Hadar said. His bully friends stepped back, making way for the two brothers, expecting a fist fight. Enoch had grown and now stood taller than Hadar. His blond hair and blue eyes set him apart from Hadar, who stood just as tall. His swarthy skin and dark straight hair intrigued the young women of Aenon and captivated the young bullies.

Hadar thought Enoch would fight him, too, and dropped my crutch to raise his fists.

Enoch surprised Hadar and the others. He reached down and picked up my crutch.

"Thank you, brother," he said. Then he turned to me. "Here is your crutch. May I escort you?"

I tucked my crutch beneath my arm and nodded. Enoch turned his back on Hadar and his ring of bullies and took me by the arm and pulled me close. I felt my cheeks heat in embarrassment, but I clutched tightly to his arm and walked away.

Then, when he returned that day from his first journey, he came to mama's house and took me away to the trees near the stream. He bent down from his height, lightly running his finger along my arm.

"Jehovah has called me to an important mission," he said. "I am to warn the people to repent."

"Has not Adam and the other prophets called people to repentance?"

"They have, with small success, lately. I am to travel among the people and teach them of the love of God. I am to tell them to repent, or be destroyed. It will be difficult. Many will taunt me, many have ridiculed me. Even so, Jehovah gave me the charge to call them to repent in a way even Adam has not been able to do. It is fearful for me." His voice trailed off.

"Surely, it is. Did the Lord take—" I reddened. "I am sorry. I do not want to embarrass you." I looked at my feet.

"You cannot embarrass me. The Lord strengthened me and I trusted him. My stutter disappeared."

"How wonderful for you." Then, I added in a whisper, "I wish He would straighten my foot."

"Someday, He may." Enoch drew me close again and kissed me. Though surprised, I leaned in, enjoying the kiss, enjoying being with this good man.

Enoch pulled back and gazed into my eyes. "Zehira, I have loved you for many years. I am still young. I have a mission from Jehovah that will not end. Will you join me on my mission? Will you marry me?"

I returned his gaze, loving him, wanting him, and unsure of what I heard. "You could have any woman in the land."

Enoch reached for my hand and stroked it. "I do not want any woman in the land. I want a woman who will stand beside me with Jehovah."

I needed to be certain. "Many of those women would want to be with you. Why would you want me? A short, dumpy woman? A cripple?"

Enoch held my hand and stared into my eyes. "Zehira, you are beautiful. Your foot is twisted, not your heart. I have watched you for years. You are gentle, yet you stand for yourself. You did not turn from Hadar's taunting. I knew that day when I got your crutch from him, I wanted you to be my wife. I did not think you would want me, and my stuttering."

I snorted. "I have loved you since you drew water for Hadar that day when you were young. You have always been humble. I love that."

"Will you marry me?" He stared into my eyes.

"When?" I countered. Secretly, I hoped he would suggest that day, or the next. I wanted out of mama's house.

"Next month."

I sighed.

"That will give us time to travel to Home Valley. I want Grandpapa Adam to marry us. It must be Jehovah's way.

Joy fell from me as quickly as the tears I hid from Hadar. "Yes. I will marry you. Next month will be wonderful."

He kissed me.

"My papa. You must ask my papa. He will want you to reimburse him for me. He and Mama depend on my help." I allowed my frustration to expel with a sigh.

Enoch's joy, too, had dampened. "What will he demand?"

I looked at my feet. "I do not know, but I know my papa. He will demand something."

Papa Gavi demanded a team of oxen and a wagon. Enoch did not have an ox or a cart for himself and nothing to give to papa. He went to his papa, Jared, asking for his recommendation. Papa Jared tried to convince Papa to allow me to marry Enoch without recompense. He refused.

We met often, until Jehovah required him to continue his mission. Before he left, we clung together many long moments until Enoch gently stepped away and walked down the road.

He returned three months later, filled with power and might. It did not impress Papa. He continued to demand a bride price. Jared counseled us to join him on a journey to visit Grandpapa Adam. He would have an answer for us.

Grandpapa Adam agreed with Jared. My Papa had no right to demand a bride price for me to marry Enoch. He married us one quiet morning at the altar on the hill, repeating the words spoken when Father married him to Grandmama Eve.

Afterward, Enoch and I held each other close and kissed deeply then, and often later.

Now, in our new home, I remembered his love for me. "I will not let you down. I will find a way to meet these women," I whispered.

CHAPTER TEN

A Friend?

Getting to know the women of Zion did not come easy. Enoch took me with him to the tabernacle the next Sabbath. As he walked to the front of the room to preach, I found a seat with the children near the back. From there, I heard the whispers, wondering which woman in the crowd had married Enoch. They all knew I had arrived, but none had found a way or a reason to see or meet me.

"She must be beautiful," one woman in front of me whispered to another. "Enoch is such a magnificent leader. His wife must be strong and beautiful."

The other woman nodded in agreement. *They will be surprised. I am neither beautiful nor strong.*

The buzz of interest filled the room as people craned their heads searching for the wife of their leader until the meeting began and they became absorbed in his teaching of the love of Jehovah. At the end, Enoch spoke of being accepting of those who were not perfect. I knew he spoke for me. The congregation murmured in agreement. Still, as the meeting ended, no one spoke to me. They stood and moved toward the exit, chattering together about Enoch's preaching.

"Mama," Grace asked, "why do you not stand by Papa and let them know?"

"Not today. I want to get to know these women on my own terms. I do not want them to befriend me because I am married to your papa."

"That is silly," Tobiah said.

"For you, maybe," Grace put her hands on her hips. "Mama is right. She needs to make friends for herself, not just because she is married to Papa."

"How do you plan to meet the women?" Noam asked.

"I have no idea. I am still thinking. If you have any ideas, I will be happy to hear them," I sighed and moved my crutch under my arm to hobble out.

"You are new to Zion, are you not?" a woman said as I reached the outer door.

I glanced up. A hand reached out in welcome, taking mine.

"Welcome! I am Talia. I hope you have enjoyed your time with us, so far."

"Thank you, Talia. I have. My name is Zehira. This is my daughter, Grace. My younger sons are here," I glanced around and realized they were gone, "somewhere. Zion is a beautiful city. All the lovely flowers add to its charm."

"The flowers do add to the beauty. What do you think about the wells in every back yard?"

I thought a moment, not wanting to offend a possible new friend. "They are convenient. It is nice to have water readily available in the morning when I need it—" My voice trailed off.

"But, you miss the central wells."

"I do. How do you meet the other women in this city?" I flopped my free arm and shrugged the one holding my crutch.

"I miss them, too, for that very reason." Talia frowned.

"How did you meet your neighbors? What can I do?"

Talia shrugged with a little sigh. "I knocked on their doors with apricot cakes. Who can ignore you with a gift of food?"

"That is one way, I suppose. Where is everything grown? I found my garden, planted and growing, but where do we get our grains? We have a tree or two, but where are the orchards?"

"Have you looked all the way back to the back of your back yard?"

"No, not far. I wandered into the garden and found some luscious raspberries. I could make raspberry tortes for my neighbors."

"Tortes? One for each? That is a lot of work." Her eyes opened wide.

"No, not really." I shrugged and reddened. "I make big tortes and smaller ones. I can bake smaller tortes to give to my neighbors."

"Mama makes good tortes," Grace said.

Talia touched my arm. "You will want to explore all the way to the back of your garden. We have community fields and orchards in the center of each section."

"Community fields and orchards?" Grace asked.

"Who has rights to the crops?" I asked.

"We harvest and share. No one goes hungry here. One section grows grapes, another grows peaches. One section grows wheat, while another section grows oats or amaranth. We share our efforts." Talia waved her hands around as she spoke.

I stood in silence a long moment. "Share? Where is the sharing done?"

"We take from the things we grow what we need and store the rest in the warehouses. Everyone is welcome to visit the warehouses and take what they need." Talia spoke, certain in her knowledge.

"Who does the work of harvesting and caring for the community plots of food? Men or women?" Grace stood with her arms folded, contemplation filling her face.

"It depends on the family. Some families prefer to help with the animals or build homes and carts for others. Each person gives and shares in the bounty." Talia dropped her hands to her side.

"Everyone helps? What if someone refuses to work?" I lifted my eyebrows in question.

"No work, no eat. People are given time and a chance to learn, to become comfortable with this life. If they choose not to help others, or to only take without giving, they find themselves locked out of the warehouses. People who cannot share

are not happy in Zion and eventually leave. Do you plan to
not work?" Talia frowned at me.

I shook my head. "No. I will do my share. I just wondered."

"It is good to meet you, Zehira, Grace. My Joam will be
wondering where his dinner is. Maybe we will meet in the
fields, orchards, or in the warehouses. If not, I will see you in
the tabernacle."

With that, Talia turned and walked away with a wave.

CHAPTER ELEVEN

Harvest

Pink and purple streaks joined the gold of the rising sun as I pushed a cart stacked high with large baskets through an ivy-covered wall the next day. I stopped a moment to gaze into the light and allow it to fill my soul. I took a deep breath and pushed the cart on through the wall and into the orchard.

Enoch and I had wandered through the peach orchard the night before, the fragrance of ripe peaches wafting on the air. He warned me that people rose early to get the peaches picked. I intended to be one of the first there.

Others were pushing their way through walls similar to ours. I raised a hand in greeting and moved to the tree I inspected the evening before. I inhaled the sweet fragrance a long moment before unloading the baskets from my cart. I lifted one, set it on the ground near me, and began to pick the ripe, sweet fruit. Now was not the time to worry about befriending my neighbors, there were peaches to pick, lots of huge, juicy, itchy bulbs of sweetness.

Noam, Tobiah, and Grace joined me, pushing carts filled with the baskets we found in the garden shed. After a time picking, Tobiah lifted the six filled baskets into his cart and pushed it back through another gate. Work would begin soon to preserve all this fruit, but, first we needed to clear the fruit from all the many trees.

I picked up another empty basket and reached up to strip off the last of the fruit. Grace and Noam each took an empty basket and trudged to the next tree. I stared up into the branches of the tree and determined all the fruit had been picked. I filled a large basket with the fruit and left it on the ground under the tree. Tobiah would gather it up when he returned. I retrieved an empty basket and joined the children in carefully removing peaches from the other side of the tree.

"Mama, are we responsible for preserving all the peaches we pick, or will others help us?" Grace asked.

"I did not think to ask your papa last night." I frowned in thought and stretched as high as I could for another peach. "It would be a lot of work for us to do all these alone. I hope we work together."

"You will." Tobiah pushed his cart close to our tree and bent to gather the filled baskets. "Joam gave me instructions to take the peaches to the warehouse in the next street. I emptied the peaches into great vats there and brought back the empty baskets. You will need them with all these peaches."

He groaned as he lifted another heavy basket into his cart and trundled away with them.

I nodded and kept picking, happy to hear I would not be required to preserve all the peaches on my own. Even with the children's help, I would be stretched to care for this many peaches before they spoiled.

When I reached the fifth tree, the sun stood high over our heads. I felt the effects of so much stretching and bending in my arms and back, not to mention my legs. My crutch got in my way, but without it, I toppled over. It amazed me that I still stood on my feet. I took a moment to stretch and glance down the row of trees. Many people spread out among the scattered trees, plucking the sweet fruit.

"You found our orchard," a friendly voice called.

I looked around before seeing the owner of the voice on the other of the tree I was picking.

"Talia!" I cried. "I heard you lived around the corner from us. And here you are."

Talia set a handful of peaches in her basket. "I wondered if you would live on our block and get to share in the care of our trees."

Together, we removed all the fruit from the tree, all the while talking and enjoying each other. Noam had joined Tobi-ah in pushing carts through the orchard to retrieve the full baskets of fruit and then to bring all the workers empty ones. Grace worked beneath a nearby tree, visiting with other young women who had joined her.

When every peach on our tree had been picked, Talia and I moved on to the next tree, joining other women already picking fruit from it.

"This is my new friend, Zehira," Talia gaily called to the women. "Zehira, this is Rani, Ana, Chiba, and Deborah."

The women waived in my direction, calling their "hellos" as they stretched to pluck the globes of fruit from the highest branches. I joined them, though my back and arm had progressed from hurt and ache to spasms and agony. I glanced at the sun which neared its zenith and realized I had forgotten to bring any food for the mid-day meal. Other women glanced at the sun and rubbed their backs. At least, my sore muscles were shared by those who did not share my lack of experience.

"Time to stop for the mid-day meal," Ana declared. "This first day of picking is hard."

The other women agreed and set the peaches they held into the baskets and plopped to the ground. Each of them pulled food from the packs on their backs. I steadied my crutch under my arm and stepped away from the tree, thinking I needed to return to my kitchen for something to eat.

"Where are you going?" Chiba asked.

"I did not think to bring food." I felt my neck and cheeks flush red.

"You do not have to leave," Deborah said. "We always bring more than we can eat. We will share with you today."

The other women chimed in, encouraging me to stay.

"My children will not have any food either, I should …" I said, wishing I could stay with these friendly women.

"The others will have enough for your children," Ana said. "No one is allowed to be hungry during peach harvest."

"But my sons are pushing those heavy carts." I felt compelled to resist, hoping they would convince me to stay.

"They will be fed. Sit. Enjoy." Rani patted the ground.

Glancing toward the tree where I had last seen Grace, I saw her chuckling with other young women, enjoying their meal. I slowly lowered myself to the ground, laying my crutch next to me.

"Try my sesame bread." Ana offered sliced bread to each of us.

"Take some of my pickled fish," Rani offered. "It will taste good on Ana's bread."

Each woman opened her pack and shared with the others, tasting some from each woman. Laughing and visiting with them, I relaxed and enjoyed their freely-given friendship. No one seemed to notice my crutch or twisted foot. Though I stretched out my legs and massaged the muscles to relax them, I felt more comfortable with these women than I had in many years. Never before had I sat with so many women who accepted me.

"I am new here and have no idea what we do after all these peaches are picked. What is next?" I waved a hand at all the trees and the filled baskets.

"I thought you were new here," Chiba said with a smile. "With so many hands, all these trees will be stripped bare of fruit by the time we leave tonight. Tomorrow we meet at the peach warehouse. There we preserve them."

Deborah must have seen the confusion on my face. "We dry some, make some jam, and put some in a sweetened syrup in small jars and seal them with wax. Fresh tasting preserved peaches taste wonderful in the winter."

I raised my eyebrows in amazement. "I have never heard of keeping peaches fresh tasting for so long."

"It is a new process. We have been preserving fruit like this for only three or four years," Ana said. "It takes time and lots of jars, but it is so worth it in the middle of the winter when we are hungry for fruit."

"Here." Talia handed each of the women a peach. "Desert. Zehira's addition to our meal."

The women gladly took a peach and bit into it. I giggled with them as sweet juice dripped down my chin.

"Great addition to our mid-day meal," Rani said between bites. "Thanks."

I took another bite and then said with a nervous laugh, "You are very welcome. Thank you for sharing your food with me. With all the wonderful food and a rest, I think I can help pick the rest of these peaches."

The women agreed and dragged themselves up. I stuck my crutch in the dirt and used it to push myself up, then slipped it under my arm once more. Grabbing a basket, I reached out and picked the nearest peach. I spent the rest of the day picking, visiting, and giggling with my new friends, thanking

Jehovah for the gift of neighborhood orchards to take the place of a central well.

Grace, too, enjoyed the friendship of the other young women. A handsome young man returned often to speak with her as he gathered their baskets of fruit. Noam and Tobiah stopped by occasionally to gather our filled baskets, as did the other young men. I asked the boys if they had eaten. They had, so I relaxed and stretched up to pick more peaches.

As gold, pink, and purple streaked the evening sky and the sun fell behind the far mountains, the last of the peaches were set into baskets and carted to the warehouse. I dropped my hands and shrugged my shoulders in circles, trying to relax the knots in them. I bent to pick up a small basket of peaches for our family dinner and turned to go home. I stopped suddenly, staring at all the ivy-covered walls. *Which one led to my home?*

Talia must have seen my bewilderment. "You do not know where home is?" she gently asked.

"No. They all look the same. Can you help me?"

"I see your children heading toward Enoch's house. Are they traveling the right direction?" She pointed toward them.

"Yes." I followed her pointing finger. "Oh, I see them. Thank you." I started to limp toward them.

"Enoch is your husband?" Chiba asked.

"Yes," I answered, too tired to be defensive.

"Welcome, double welcome. We wondered when we would get to know you," Ana said.

"We are glad to have made your acquaintance before we knew you were Enoch's wife," Deborah added. I must have had a questioning look on my face for Deborah quickly added, "Now we know you for yourself, not just as Enoch's wife."

"I look forward to seeing you early in the morning, at the warehouse." Talia gave me a little hug as Tobiah joined us to help me home.

"Tomorrow, early," I cheerfully called as I waved at my new friends. As Tobiah and I pushed our way through our own gate, I groaned, "Tomorrow early. Oh."

We stopped by our garden to pick tomatoes and spinach for dinner and moved slowly through the back door. I dropped into the nearest chair by the table, unable to go any farther. Though exhausted herself, Grace took the vegetables and prepared a meal for the family. I sat, head in my hands, watching.

CHAPTER TWELVE

Injury

Carrying a basket filled with fresh raspberries, tomatoes, carrots, and my sharpest knife, I pushed my way into the peach warehouse that Tobiah and Noam showed me to early the next morning. Grace and the boys followed me, each carrying a similar basket, though the boys' baskets included flat bread and dried meat to share with others for our mid-day meal.

We spent the day peeling and slicing peaches. Some of these we dropped into small jars into which other women added sweetened water and capped the jars with beeswax. Others we sliced into thin slices and set onto huge trays and then placed them into an oven with low heat to be dried. Still other peaches, too ripe for any other purpose, we cut into small chunks and cooked with honey and made into peach jam and placed into smaller jars and, once more, sealed with beeswax. My time was spent, sitting on a tall stool, my crutch leaned against the wall behind me, peeling and slicing peaches, talking, and tittering with my new friends.

At mid-day, I opened my basket to share the vegetables and raspberries. My new friends happily shared the food they brought. We ate together, enjoying the same camaraderie as the day before. By the end of the day, a third of the peaches had been sliced and preserved.

Grace stood with other young women over a hot stove, stirring and cooking the jam. Noam filled baskets with peaches from the huge vats where they waited in cool water, carrying them to the other women and me who were peeling and cutting the peaches. Tobiah carried jars, both full and empty, for the women, setting the full jars of peaches and jam onto shelves to await the winter. Other men carried baskets of dried peaches, fresh from the drying ovens and placed them on the shelves. With surprise, I heard it was evening and time to leave.

We were all tired by the time our day ended. But because I sat on my stool through the day, my legs were not as tired. Together, I walked home with my children, all of us exhausted. Noam and Tobiah flopped onto chairs near the front door and Grace dropped onto the wide sofa.

I limped to the kitchen to finish cooking the pot of beans I had started early that morning. I ground wheat and mixed together a flat bread that always tasted good with those beans. While the bread baked, I moved out the back door to my garden, where I picked lettuce, tomatoes, spinach, onions, peppers, and carrots for a salad. Enoch walked into the kitchen and slipped his arms around my waist from behind.

"Good day, huh?" He kissed the back of my neck.

"Yes, very." I turned in his arms and returned his kiss. "I met some good women. They took me into their group and loved me. I do not have to go to the well to meet and share with them, at least not yhis week. We worked to preserve peaches together. And, do you know what?"

Enoch shook his head, gazing into my eyes.

"No one seems to notice my crutch. I am just another woman. Zion is a good place."

I threw my arms around him, holding him tight in my joy. We stood together with my eyes dripping onto his shoulder, until he sniffed the air. "Is something burning?"

"My bread!" I flew to the oven and pulled my bread from within its depths. The top was a darker brown than I liked, but it would be edible.

Grace and her brothers trooped into the kitchen just then.

"Do we smell fresh bread? And at night?" Tobiah asked.

"And beans?" Noam asked. "I like beans."

"I know you do, and yes, it is ready to eat. Wash up and sit at the table."

I watched them push each other aside in a friendly tussle, trying to be first to the table. I had hoped for this for many years: happiness at home and friends nearby.

The next morning, I took a small pot of the beans with me to share with my new friends. Once more, we sat at the tall table on stools, peeling and slicing, talking and giggling.

When we opened our baskets, the other women exclaimed in amazement that I had time to prepare beans, and that I would share them.

After our mid-day meal, we returned to our stools and picked up our sharp knives and returned to peeling and paring. I picked up a peach and ran the blade around it to split it in half. It felt wrong, somehow, with nothing in the center to stop the sharpness, no pit to prevent its slipping. I had no time to pull it back. The blade bit into my hand, cutting across my palm.

"Ouch!" I cried and clutched at the injury with my good hand as my knife rattled to the table top.

"What?" Rani asked looking at me. "Blood! She cut herself. Grab a cloth, quick!"

Talia grabbed a towel lying on the table and rushed to my side. Gently, she pulled my hand away from the injured one.

"Oh, dear. You cut it bad. Your knife is sharp. Here, let me wrap it in this clean cloth."

Talia wrapped the cloth around my hand, pulling it tight. Blood seeped through in moments. Ana handed Talia another cloth, which she added to the top of the first.

"Push on it here," she instructed.

My stomach flipped and my head spun with dizziness. In a distance, I heard Deborah call to Tobiah, telling him to come help them get his mama home to his papa.

What can Enoch do for me? I need a healer.

The pain increased my dizziness. Tobiah arrived and put his arm around me. Ana supported me from the other side, while Talia led the way. Noam ran ahead, searching for Enoch, who usually spent time away from home during the day, teaching and helping the people of Zion while he was in the city. I wondered if they would find him for me.

Noam opened our door and called. "Papa? Papa! Mama is hurt! Papa, Mama needs you!"

For some reason, Enoch stayed home, working in his study that morning. He ran toward me and swept me into his strong arms.

"What happened?"

"She sliced her hand. The bleeding is bad," I heard Talia say, as though from a distance. "It has soaked through a second cloth."

"I see," he said. His voice receded into the distance.

I wondered about a healer and mumbled, "When is someone going to call for healer, someone to sew up my hand?"

"Do not worry," Talia whispered, her voice suddenly close. "Enoch is here."

"Enoch does not need a healer to sew you up, He will heal you," Ana added.

I had been away from him for too many years. I did not know when he learned to heal.

Enoch lay me on the lounge chair in the sitting room.

"Rest here, love," he said. "Hold that cloth across your hand."

I clutched the cloth with my good hand and listened to him go to our bedroom and rummage among his things. He must have found the thing he looked for, because he went into the kitchen to wash his hands. I could not understand his actions. Healers needed a needle and thread and a salve. But, my weakness and dizziness increased. I closed my eyes, waiting to see what he planned.

Enoch returned to the sitting room and smiled into my eyes. "Zehira, do you love Jehovah?"

I had no idea what this had to do with my injured hand as my ability to feel in it increased. Still, I nodded. "Yes. You know I do."

"Do you know that he created this world? Created you and me?"

Though nothing he said solved my confusion, I nodded once more. "Yes."

His quiet, gentle voice continued. "Do you believe Jehovah can heal your hand?"

My eyes flew open wide and I stared into his eyes. He nodded. "Yes, of course, He can. Will He?"

"Yes, He will."

Enoch lay his hands on my head and prayed to Jehovah, ending with, "In the name of Jehovah, I command your body to heal, the muscles and skin to knit together in their proper way, allowing you to continue working with your friends and family."

I felt a tingling along the length of the injury. An itch indicated something occurred to the skin. I felt the skin join. I stared into his eyes, feeling his love and the love of Jehovah.

The tingle reduced. The pain was gone. Enoch gently unwrapped the cloths wrapped around my hand. Tobiah started to ask about it, but I saw Talia nudge him quiet. When the wrapping had been removed and air touched it once more, I heard Tobiah gasp and thought to join him. Some blood stained my hand, but the slice across the palm had healed. A thin line marked the path of my knife.

"Flex your hand slowly," Enoch suggested.

I tentatively opened and closed my hand a few times. No pain crashed through me. The injury did not reopen.

I gazed up into Enoch's eyes. Wonder and awe filled me. "I am healed. You healed me."

"No, my love, Jehovah healed you. Because of your faith, you are healed."

CHAPTER THIRTEEN

Acceptance

Though I felt fine, and the damage to my hand had disappeared completely, my new friends insisted that I stay home "to rest" for the afternoon. My hand no longer hurt, there was no blood, no open wounds, or other damage, I believed I could return to my stool, but they encouraged me to stay home.

After the women left, Enoch helped me to bed. I could not remember the last time I napped in the afternoon, except when ill or had just delivered another child.

"I do not need to sleep," I argued.

Enoch won, telling me he would stay close.

He sat in the chair near the window in our room to read as I fell asleep. He still sat there when I woke. I lay in bed, watching him, loving the curve of his head, the bump of his nose, the softness of his lips. He had a gentleness, and an unseen power. Many could not see both sides of his personality.

After watching him bend to his reading in the sunlight for many long moments, I asked, "Enoch? When you were healing my hand, why did you not heal my foot? Surely, Jehovah can heal my foot as easily as he healed my injured hand." I caught my lower lip in my teeth.

He turned toward me, a slight frown crossing his face. "You are awake. How do you feel?"

"Better. But, Enoch, why not my foot, as well?"

He let out a deep breath. "I wanted to heal your foot. The words were in my mouth, but Jehovah denied me," he whispered. "He tells me this is not the time. There is more for you to learn."

"Enoch sat still, his eyes focused on me. I could see his fear and I wondered at it.

"You wanted to heal my foot?" I swung my feet across the side of the bed.

Enoch pulled me into his lap. "Yes. I have wanted to heal your foot for many years. However, each time I beg for that privilege, Jehovah has forbidden it."

"Why? Is my faith not strong enough?" I ran my fingers along his strong chin.

"He has not shared with me the reason why, only that now is not the time. Your faith is strong, or your hand would continue to bleed and be folded and unusable. There is something more you must learn. What that something is, I do not know." A tear slipped from his eye and rolled across his cheek.

"You have asked again?" I caught his tear on my finger and stared at it.

"I have, as you slept, and the answer is the same. You must live with your twisted foot."

I dropped my eyes and brought my left hand up to look at the thin line across my palm. Enoch took my hand in his and traced the thin scar.

"I am sorry, my love. I did all I was allowed."

"I know." I leaned into his strong body. "I hoped."

We sat together for a long time.

The next day, when I returned to the peach warehouse, I found all the peaches peeled and sliced, waiting to be pre-served. Ana sent me to seal the bottles with beeswax. Deborah showed me how to lift a spoonful of the warm wax from the pot where it softened above the low fire. I drizzled the wax across the top of the fruit, making sure it covered all the top and edge of the jar, sealing in the sweet goodness. Together with Ana, we sealed many jars of fruit until time for our mid-day meal.

When the clatter of peach preserving settled and women's voices rose, we joined our other women friends, and some other men and women from other blocks, who assisted us in preserving peaches, to share our food at one of the paring ta-bles. My women friends welcomed me back, happy to see my hand had no lasting damage.

"We did not know Enoch is your husband," one new friend said, tasting some of the cake I brought to share.

"Does it matter? I asked as I took a bite of the cake.

"Not really. We have learned you are a hard worker, not one who will take advantage of your husband's status," she said.

"I have never done that." I stared at her. "Do women really do that?"

"Yes. We have had some who think their men are important and they are not required to work."

"I am required to work and I would even if I were not required. I wanted to meet the women of Zion."

"One of those women, the women who believe they are too good to join us in working, is expected to move back next week." Talia made a face and shuddered. "You may know her. Mele of Aenon. She is married to—"

"I know her. She is married to Hadar. Mele was my friend in Aenon before she married Hadar. She changed ..." I drifted off, remembering the last time I spoke with Mele.

Papa Gavi accepted my marriage to Enoch without a bride price many years after we first asked. Enoch had been required to leave me in Aenon with Jacob and Helsa sometime after our marriage, because I carried our second child. The first had not survived his birth and expelling him from my body had been difficult. I had been ill for a month after the child's loss, taken in by Grandmama Eve who helped me heal. Enoch journeyed to villages near Home Valley in those months while I healed.

Two years later, I found myself to be with child, again. Enoch feared for my health. Jehovah required him to continue his mission and we returned to his mama and papa's home where Helsa could help me during this difficult period. When my parents learned of my pregnancy, they demanded that I return to their home. As always, I bowed to their demands. Obedience to parents, as taught by our culture, ran deep in my soul, even when those parents are demanding and unkind.

For the first few days after I returned to Mama's home, they were kind and concerned for my health. However, they soon returned to their old ways, demanding that I cook and clean, carry water and clay, and help with other difficult tasks. Five months into my pregnancy, I again lost my child.

Mele had married Hadar and become mother to three sons already. They lived in Aenon. Hadar continued to demand the best of everything, as did Mele.

She came to visit her sick friend. "I am so sorry you lost a child," she said in a sing-song, sweet voice. "Do you want to hold my little Yehu?"

Mele thrust the little boy into my arms and chatted about her children, their wondrous abilities and growth. I struggled to swallow my tears as I had during our youth, but my time with Enoch allowed me to be open, and I forgot the skill.

"Do not allow your tears to fall on my baby!" Mele exclaimed, when at last she noticed. "Just because you cannot have children is no reason to cry on mine."

Mele gathered up her bag and baby and flounced out of the room, much to my relief.

Soon after that, Hadar and Mele moved with their children to another part of the country. We had not seen each other since then. Now, they were moving to Zion—again.

"Again?" I set my spoon on the table beside my slice of cake, suddenly, no longer hungry. "Mele and Hadar have lived here before? Many years ago, when Zion was a small village, they visited Aenon and did so again a few years ago. I have not seen her since. I never heard that Hadar and Mele lived here."

"They came here for a month or so, never left Traveler's Inn." Rani leaned her head on her hand. "Mele demanded that everything be done for her, rarely even climbing out of bed. She expected Susanna and Hanna to care for her child while she slept. Hadar behaved no better, swaggering around the city and expecting the men to listen to his crazy schemes because he was Enoch's brother. Neither of them lifted a finger to help. When Enoch returned and insisted they help or leave, they chose to leave."

"And now they are returning?" Ana asked, with a small frown.

"It seems they plan to stay this time." Talia gathered up the empty dishes and stacked them together. "Joam tells me there is an empty house across from ours. A message came to the city council from Hadar, requesting that they live here once more. He promises to live by the laws of the city."

"They say they will do their share. Do they know there is a bean field in their block? Harvesting beans requires a lot of lot of work. And their block is responsible for one of the wheat fields. Can you see Hadar working in a wheat field?" Deborah popped the last of her cake into her mouth and wiped away the crumbs.

"Or Mele harvesting beans?" Ana gathered her empty dish into her bag. "I hope they have really changed. This is the harvest season. Everyone must help. People from other blocks are here helping us. They will expect us to help them when the time comes to harvest their crops."

"I wondered about that." I stared at the many people sitting around the tables, eating and visiting noisily. "There are many more people working here than those who live in the homes around our block. There are, what, ten homes around a block?"

"Twelve." Chiba drew the shape of a square in the air above the table, pointing to the sides. "Three on each side. Twelve families can sometimes harvest and preserve all the food that grows within, if there are many children, but not when we are blessed with bountiful harvests, like this year."

"If you look on the shelves, you will find apricots and plums preserved here already. Our peaches will join them on the shelves. During the season for harvesting fruits of many varieties, they bring each fruit here to preserve them, in much the same way we preserve peaches." Talia waved her hand around the room. "We help with their fruits. They help with ours. Some of those whose responsibility is grains join us in preserving fruit. We all help each other. We all have free access to all the stored foods in all the warehouses."

The women around us were putting away their lunch baskets and returning to work, so my friends and I joined them. In another two or three hours, all the peaches were drying or put into jars as jam or near-fresh fruit. We would return each day to turn the fruit until it dried. Then we would put it in baskets to be used by the community. The women called out their goodbyes as they left the warehouse. I joined Talia and the other women from my block walking home. All the other women naturally slowed to my pace, whether from exhaustion or charity, I did not know. Either way, I appreciated it.

CHAPTER FOURTEEN

Criteria

Every time I thought I could talk with Enoch about Hadar and Mele moving to Zion, he was busy with the city council, running the business of the city, and I was busy working in the fruit warehouse. At night, we fell into bed, too exhausted to talk with each other, and I forgot to ask him. Before I had time or memory to ask him about them, he was called to preach in a nearby city.

"Will you be happy here now that you have new women friends?" he asked the morning before he left.

"I do have many new friends, and although I will be happier here, you returned from teaching only last week. I will miss you." I filled his travel bag with dried meats, vegetables, fruits, and bread.

"I will miss you, as well. It would be nice if you could travel with me, but …"

I knew he could not take me. I moved too slowly and it had become much too dangerous for a slow moving, crippled woman. I would put Enoch in danger. I missed our early days together. I sighed and shook away my frustration.

Enoch stuffed the food bag into his travel pack and slung it across his back. "My mission is to preach the gospel. You know I must go." He shrugged to adjust his pack more comfortably.

I reached for his large drinking skin and dragged it to the counter near the water and filled it. "It has always been your mission, and I do not resent it. This is your city. You will return sooner than you returned to Aenon. I have friends and a home that I do not have to share with my mama here. I will miss you, but not as much as I did in Aenon. I will be happy here, working among the women."

I handed his water skin to him and he slipped it over his head, settling it on his shoulder. He hugged me close as he gave me a long kiss.

"I will be home before the Sabbath. This is the Sabbath for sacrifice." He gave me a quick kiss and walked out the front door. I stood in the doorway watching him until he turned the corner and was out of sight.

Grace helped me clean the house and sweep the dust into a flat piece of metal, dumping it into the garden as Hanna had taught her. Tobiah and Noam left earlier, joining other boys at the local school.

Grace left to find her friends who were working on making the great jugs used to store the wheat nearly ready to harvest.

My loom held a piece of fabric I had started the day before and I thought to return to it when Talia knocked at my door.

"Some of us are setting up the house across the street for the newcomers. We thought you might like to help us," she said after we shared a kiss on the cheek.

"I would love to help. Someone helped set up my house for us. Was that you?" I gathered my cloak from the hook behind the door. The changing weather over the past few days reminded me of the need for extra warmth later in the day.

"I did help," Talia said. "Those of us who live near always try to be sure the house is ready before a new family arrives."

"How did you know we were coming?" I tucked my crutch under my arm, closed the door, and walked with Talia down the street.

"We knew you were coming because Enoch went to get you. There were two or three houses empty. He chose this one for you. Said he wanted one near the center so you would feel safe."

"I do feel safer here in the middle of the city. I did not know of his caring choice." A flash of sudden tears blurred my sight.

"Hadar and Mele sent a message. Some people arrive without notice. Those are taken to Traveler's Inn until we know them better. If they agree to abide by our laws, a house is provided for them. Turn here, we go to the meat warehouse first."

We turned right and continued down the street filled with other citizens of Zion, each busy with their own errands.

"What laws must we obey? I did not get the message." I followed behind as Talia pushed open the door to the warehouse on our right.

The building stored both fresh and dried meats. Talia struck her flint and lit a torch hanging near the wall.

"I should have brought a cart," I said as I stared at the slabs of mutton and beef.

"No. There is one here for us to use. We need to return it, but that is no problem." Talia retrieved the cart and maneuvered it close to the slabs of fresh meat. "This cart is easier to pull than it appears."

Together, we loaded slabs of fresh meat into the cart. "Dried meats are on the other side." She pointed then slid between the handles of the cart and pulled it behind her to the other side of the warehouse. "One law is to work—do your fair share. If you are sick, injured, or have a new baby, you are exempt for the time. However, each citizen of Zion is expected to participate in the work of the city."

"Like helping to harvest and preserve the foods?" I followed my friend across the building. "I can do that."

"You do." Talia slipped under the cart and picked up two bags of dried meats. "Or keeping the city streets clean and the front of your house neat. Choosing nice plants that harmonize with the others along the street. Things like that."

I took the bags from her, one at a time, and set them in the cart beside the fresh meat. Then I ducked between the handles, set my crutch in the cart, and took my place behind the cross handle. Talia joined me, and we pulled the cart to the door.

Talia ducked down to slide out from between the handles of the cart and opened the door, tipped the torch into the basket of sand sitting nearby to quench the fire. She tugged at the cart and helped me move it past the door, and then shut and latched it.

We pulled the cart toward Talia's home together. It moved easily, though filled with heavy meat.

"Hanna and Suzanna told me not to sweep dirt from the house into the streets and to pour house water into the garden. That is easy to do." I continued my discussion about the rules of Zion as we walked down the street among the other carts.

"You must be a believer, believe in Jehovah and obey his laws," Talia said. "As Enoch's wife, that is understood. You would not have been healed if you were not a believer."

I lapsed into thought, thinking of my belief in Jehovah and my love for him. Mama and Papa did not always obey, but they did allow me to listen to Jacob's teachings. I liked to hear the stories of Grandmama Eve and Grandpapa Adam, our first parents. I loved to listen to the promises of Jehovah, learning of their time before coming to this earth, and their leaving the Garden of Eden. Knowing I could return to Jehovah and Father when my time on earth ended comforted me.

It had not been easy for me. My twisted foot kept me from playing with the other children, so I sat at Helsa's feet, learning to read and write. Mama taught me to cook and clean, weave and form jars and jugs from clay. She forgot about the

Sabbath, frequently demanding that I work alongside her. But soon, I learned to slip away and attend Sabbath meetings and learn of Jehovah on my own. Yes. I was a believer.

I realized we had reached the home to be occupied by Mele and Hadar. Overwhelmed by my thoughts, I had not noticed.

I grabbed my crutch and tucked it buck under my arm before slipping out from between the handles of the cart. I grabbed a bag of dried meat and carried it through the house into the cool closet, followed by Talia, with her arms filled with bags of meat. When all the meat hung in the closet, I knew we would be required to return the cart and gather fruits, vegetables, and grains.

A table and chairs set up in the kitchen, along with pots and pans, surprised me. Chairs and loungers were set in neat arrangements in the sitting room, along with tables and lamps. Men entered with beds for the two rooms. Mele and Hadar must be bringing a child or two with them. Other women followed carrying bedding to make the beds.

Talia and I crouched down between the handles of the cart. She waited while I placed my crutch inside, and we pulled it behind us, bouncing and banging across the stone roads toward the warehouse. There, Talia pushed the doors open and we pushed it back to its place. Then, we walked down the street to another warehouse, where Talia again lit a torch. This warehouse seemed emptier.

"This is where we keep grains. They have not yet been harvested this year. The shelves have been emptied by the citizens of Zion over the past year," Talia told me as we chose jars of wheat, rye, oats, and amaranth, placing them in another cart I pushed to the shelves.

"These shelves are still more than half full. Did you use fewer grains than last year?" I asked.

"These are only the ones we keep available for easy access. Inside the north gate, two streets in, are granaries filled with grains. The men bring it here, when the jars are gone, and the women refill the empty jars."

"Grains do keep us busy. Poor Mele," I murmured, chuckling inside at the thought of all she would be required to do.

We took care of the torch and door before moving on to another warehouse. In this one, we added four small baskets of dried vegetables, quenching the fire and latching the door as we left. Next, we pulled our cart across the street to the fruit warehouse. Familiar with this building, I lit the torch and helped Talia pull the cart to where peaches, apricots, plums, and other dried fruits were stored. We filled smaller baskets with some of each fruit, quenching the fire and latching the door on our way out.

Talking about the methods of feeding the many people of Zion, we were soon back at what would be Mele's home, setting jars and baskets of food on the shelves.

"When will we bring milk?" I asked as we closed the door to the house.

"I believe Mele and Hadar arrive two days after the Sabbath. We will send girls to fetch fresh milk that morning. Our work is done."

Enoch returned in time to participate in the Sabbath worship and sacrifice, teaching us of Jehovah. The children and I sat with Talia and Joam, near the front of the tabernacle. My heart swelled within me, knowing I had friends who loved me before they knew I was Enoch's wife.

CHAPTER FIFTEEN

Welcome

Enoch and I were pulling the bedding back for bed the next day, when he finally shared the news of the city's newest residents. "I am certain you know by now, but my brother and his wife will arrive tomorrow. I did not know before today." His eyes were locked on mine, almost begging me to understand.

I allowed a half-frown to cross my face. "I have known since before you left. Joam is on the committee to provide housing."

Enoch sat heavily on the chair in the corner to remove his boots. "I should have known. Why did you not tell me sooner?"

I sat in the other chair and removed my foot coverings. "I waited for you to tell me. I thought you knew everything that happens in Zion."

He stood and removed his robe, folded it, and carefully lay it on the back of the chair. "No. I am not always here. There is a committee to accept or reject newcomers. Hadar and Mele were here two years ago, before we put up the walls. They could not live by our laws then. If you do not work, you do not eat. They would not work. When Bain refused to feed them, they left."

I lay down on the bed wearing a sleeping robe, my daytime robe folded neatly and draped on the back of the chair. I admired Enoch's broad, hairy chest as he reached for a sleep shirt. "Will they work this time?"

He joined me in bed, pulled the quilts around us and flung an arm around me, pulling me close and snuggling. "Who knows. This is my brother who thinks the world owes him a living. I was not part of the decision. I do not know what Hadar said to convince the men and women on the committee to change their minds."

I kissed his forehead, then his lips. That night's loving was one of the best in a long time.

The next morning as I ground wheat for the day's use, Grace brought a jug of fresh milk in and placed it in the cool closet. "Hadar and Mele are here already. They came into their house as I was leaving. I took them their milk."

"Did they speak to you?" I poured the ground grain into a bowl and reached for oil and water.

"They nodded, but did not seem to recognize me, their niece. I thought they had changed." Grace crossed her arms beneath her breasts.

"The committee is giving them another chance. Jehovah teaches us to forgive and believe others will repent." I spooned the starter and honey into the mixture and stirred it in.

"I know people can change and repent, Mama," Grace said, reaching into the cupboard to set the dishes on the table for the morning meal. "But Uncle Hadar does not seem to be one who thinks he needs to change."

I sprinkled a pinch of salt and fresh thyme into the mixture and began to knead it. "Who would think hard wheat kernels could change into something as tasty as bread for our family? Even someone like Hadar can change." I smiled at my daughter, knowing well the feelings raging within her. "Stranger things have happened."

I kneaded the dough and formed two loaves of bread and set them onto baking sheets to raise.

Grace raised her eyebrows. "Why two loaves, Mama?"

"Mele will not have the energy to bake bread this morning. I am taking a loaf to her. Would you like to go with me?"

"For you, Mama, I will go."

After the bread baked and after we cleaned the morning dishes, we walked along the early morning street, quiet at this time of day, to the home of my old friend.

Mele exclaimed as she opened her door," Zehira! How long have you been here in Zion? Come in! Come in!"

Grace and I entered and sat in the chairs others had placed in her sitting room. "We have been here nearly a month now. Where have you been?"

Mele sat on the edge of her seat, glancing back into the house frequently. "We spent the last year in Pisgah. Hadar helped Cainan in his fields and in preaching. Elsa and Cainan were kind to us, but Hadar was not happy there. He still thinks ...," she looked back into the house as though afraid of something. "He still thinks he deserves more, thinks he should be 'the one.'"

"Is he here now?" I glanced toward the bedrooms and kitchen.

"He is in the back, sleeping in the sun." She looked back once more. "But I am never sure if he is sleeping or waiting to catch me in something." Mele's voice caught and I felt her pain. Mele had chosen Hadar, but her choice had not made her happy.

"Come visit me, Mele, where we can visit more freely." I glanced at Grace and we stood to leave.

"Thank you, Zehira. You have always been my friend."

As we neared the door, Hadar walked into the sitting room from the back of the house and plopped onto a chair. "Hello Zehira, hello Grace. How is the little cripple today?" The sneer not quite gone from his voice.

"Just fine, Hadar. Zion is good to me. I hope it will be good to you." I did not know where the gentleness in my voice came from. Even the anger I had felt in Aenon refused to surface. I gave Mele a quick hug and took Grace by the hand and left. I heard Mele close the door quietly behind her. Hadar's voice raised in a roar behind the door, the words unintelligible and angry.

Grace shook her head as I turned back toward the door. She was right. I shook my head and walked away.

CHAPTER SIXTEEN

Experiences

Grace kissed me goodbye as we reached the street in front of Mele's house, telling me she planned to meet friends and help with the bean harvest. I continued down the street toward our home when I heard a friendly voice calling from the doorway of the house I passed. I looked over to see Talia waving and calling.

"Zehira! So good to see you. You will never believe what just happened," she said and then put her hand over her mouth. "Oh, I guess I was not supposed to say anything, but I am so excited, I had to tell someone."

I reached out and touched her arm. "You have already started to tell me. Now you must. What is your good news?"

Talia drew me into the comfort of her sitting room, filled with plants and soft pillows. She had lived here long enough to make it hers. "Joam just spoke with Jehovah!"

"Jehovah?" I stared at her with an open mouth. "Do people talk with Jehovah often?"

"He walks with us here in Zion. Sometimes, we see Him, and sometimes we do not. He allows us to see Him when it is to our benefit. Occasionally, He talks with us."

I sat in amazement, my hands limp in my lap. I finally found my voice. "What did Jehovah say to Joam?"

"He thanked Joam for his willingness to give Hadar another chance. He said he understands our hesitancy in accepting Hadar and family after the last time, but Hadar needs this opportunity to prove himself."

"Prove himself? To whom?"

"Joam didn't say. I doubt he asked."

I slowly shook my head, remembering my recent experience with Hadar and Mele. "Was that all?"

"Yes, or at least all Joam shared with me. His excitement about speaking with Jehovah overflowed. It has been a long time since he last visited with Him personally."

We sat in silence, each of us in our own thoughts. I did not know Jehovah walked and talked with the people of Zion. Something else new for me to learn.

I hesitantly broke the silence. "Talia, have you spoken with Jehovah?"

"Oh, yes. I spoke with him recently."

"Oh?"

"The evening after we picked the peaches. He joined me on the walk back to my home."

I lifted my eyebrows, waiting for more.

"He thanked me for befriending you, said you needed a good friend, and that he was happy I was your friend."

Somehow, my eyes opened wider. "Thanked you for befriending me?" I whispered. "Yes. I did need a good friend at the time. Thank you, Talia, for being my good friend."

Talia nodded and smiled.

"Have you told others of Jehovah's visit? I would be embarrassed—"

"Do not be embarrassed. I am happy to be your friend. You are a friend to me. I, too, needed a friend. I would never share something so special as this with others. I did not even tell Joam, though I was tempted to tell him this morning when he shared his most recent experience with me. I should not have shared his experience, it is sacred, not for sharing. But, I was compelled to call out to you."

"I needed to know Jehovah is aware of me," I murmured.

"And of me," Talia added.

Our conversation turned to other topics, until I remembered I needed to start dinner. We hugged at the door and kissed each other on the cheeks, promising to see each other soon.

I was lost in thought as I started preparing the evening meal, then moved to my loom. Why had no one told me of Jehovah's presence in Zion? What had Enoch told Jehovah of me? Of course, he communicated with Jehovah often. It would be nothing new for him. Would He even need to be told?

The question that really caught my attention was more personal. Would Jehovah speak with me? He knew me, knew my needs. Would I make Him happy and give Him cause to share His pleasure with me?

"Mama?" A voice startled me out of my thoughts. I jumped and turned.

"Oh, Methuselah." My heart pounded within my chest. "I did not hear you come in."

"You were busy. Were you thinking?"

"I was. What brings you here this afternoon?" I rose from my chair by the loom to embrace my older son.

He returned the embrace and stepped away. "It is time for me to return home. I have been away from Qitarah and Pisgah for two months. It is time to return. I leave early in the morning.'"

"Will you have enough traveling food?" As always, I worried about my children having enough food.

"I will. Suzanna and Hanna have prepared a traveling bag of dried food and some hard biscuits for the trip."

We walked from my workroom toward the sitting room. "How long will it take to travel to Pisgah?"

"About a month, more or less, with preaching along the way. I wanted to tell you goodbye before I leave."

"Will you stay for dinner? See your papa?"

"Yes, thank you."

I glanced out the window to see the sun near setting, its bright light streaming into the room. "Sit and rest while I finish the meal. Your brothers and sister should return home soon, along with your papa."

Methuselah chose a book from the shelf and sat in a comfortable chair to read while I hurried into the kitchen to complete the meal.

Joy filled our home that evening. All my children were on their best behavior, jesting and teasing each other without hurting anyone's feelings. I basked in the love of my family, though I missed the older children and my grandchildren. My family had never reached the size of Eve's. Others came before Methuselah. After losing the first two, two sons and a daughter joined our family before Methuselah, and another son and daughter before Grace. With my struggles carrying babies, I felt blessed to have my ten children. Our other older sons still lived in Aenon, farming. The daughters married good men, men who listened to Enoch's teachings of Jehovah, most of the time.

"Before you go, Methuselah," Enoch said at the end of the evening, "I have received a message from Home Valley. Grandpapa Adam and Grandmama Eve are aging, as you know, and have called a conference of their believing children."

Everyone responded with excitement. Our first parents had lived long and healthy lives, now into their nine-hundredth year.

"When is the conference to be held?" Methuselah took a sip of his pomegranate juice.

"In six months. That will give time for all to receive the message and travel to Home Valley. The conference will be held on the mount of Adam-ondi-Ahmen, near Home Valley." Enoch leaned forward setting his elbows on the table. "Will you have time to gather your family and join us?"

"I will meet you there. There is much for me to do before then. I leave in the morning."

"Will we all go to Home Valley?" Noam asked, jumping up and down in excitement.

"We will all go. We leave here in four months. I desire to arrive before the conference begins." Enoch pushed his chair back from the table.

"Will you send messages to the other children to join us?" I asked, looking forward to being with all my children and grandchildren again.

"I have already, though they may already know. I am certain Papa Jared received the same message from Adam."

"It will be good to gather all our children around us again." I reached out a hand to take Enoch's and the other hand toward Grace.

Grace smiled a small smile and pushed the hair from her face and shuffled her feet.

After Methuselah left and the boys were in bed, I tapped on Grace's door. "Can we talk?" I asked as I entered.

My sweet daughter nodded and I sat beside her on the bed. "You are not so happy about this trip to Home Valley?"

"No. Happy about the trip to see our first grandparents, but…" Her voice trailed off.

"But?"

"Lucas will ask Papa for his blessing for us to marry tomorrow. I love him. We want to be married in five months. How can Papa marry us if we are journeying to Home Valley? How can I plan a wedding if we are on the road?"

I slipped an arm around my daughter, embracing her. "There will be an answer, surely your papa will know how to solve this problem. I have seen Lucas working with you. He is a good worker. Has he been honorable with you?"

"Of course." Grace traced the pattern on her nightdress. "He loves me and he loves Jehovah."

"What are you not telling me, Grace?" I placed a finger under her chin to tilt her face toward me and gazed into her eyes.

"He wants to leave Zion, to seek a living elsewhere," she whispered.

"Doing what?" I struggled to keep my voice soft and loving.

"He thinks he can gather wild horses and train them. He plans to trade or sell them to others around this land and perhaps in others."

"Sell? For money?"

Grace nodded sadly.

"And you want to marry this man?"

"I did until he shared his most recent plans. Now, I am not so sure." Tears began to leak through her eyelashes.

"Is he testing you? Did you express your concern?" I asked as Grace lay her head on my shoulder.

"No, I was too surprised. Would he test me?" Hope filled her eyes and she glanced into my eyes.

"Perhaps. How could Lucas even think about leaving Zion, a place of so much love? Did you know Jehovah walks in our city? He even talks with some of the citizens."

"He talks with Papa. I know that. But He walks through Zion? Talks with its citizens? Who, Mama, has talked with Jehovah besides Papa?"

"Talia and her husband Joam both have. Apparently, it is not a rare thing here. How can Lucas leave this?"

"I do not know," Grace moaned. "I have lived elsewhere and no other city is as loving or busy helping others as Zion. I am not sure I even want to leave to go to the conference with the rest of our family. I do not want to leave Zion."

"I understand. I am happy here, too, but I know I will return after the conference." I stroked my daughter's hair, soothing and calming her, and myself. "Wait to hear what your papa says after Lucas visits with him."

She nodded tearfully. Eventually, she lay back on the bed, and relaxed. I tiptoed out of her room.

CHAPTER SEVENTEEN

Grace Decides

Enoch told me the following evening about Lucas's visit with him that morning. "He asked for permission to marry Grace. When the discussion turned to the future, he spoke of his dream to catch wild horses."

I turned the quilts and sheet back on the bed. "What does he plan to do with wild horses?"

He sat on his comfortable chair in our room. "He hopes to trade them or sell them for money. My shock was so great, I could not respond for a long moment. All I could do was listen in horror to his dreams."

"Did you give them permission to marry?" I sat on our bed near him and gazed into his eyes.

"It is up to Grace. I have to give her the right of choice, as you desired the right to choose me, so many years ago." He leaned forward and took my hands.

"I understand your concern." I could not understand how he managed to keep his voice calm. "Grace must be given the right of choice, as Father gives choice to all of us."

"Even when she could choose wrong, even if she does choose wrong?" My voice continued to be loud and strident.

Enoch leaned forward and kissed me gently. "Even when she is choosing wrong." Somehow his voice stayed quiet. "Each of us has the same responsibility to make correct choices, even Grace. She has the right to make wrong choices, as do all of Father's children. We taught her right. You taught her correct principles. Trust her."

I spluttered in an attempt to say what I wanted. I lost almost all control over my voice.

"I spoke with Grace about it this afternoon. At that time, she had not decided. She may go with Lucas, or she may stay here with us. Trust her, Zehira, she is a good young woman. Whatever decision she makes, it will be right for her."

I breathed deeply and walked around the room, muttering to myself until I regained control and could sit down calmly.

"Grace loves Jehovah and is a remarkable young woman. She will make the right decision," I whispered as I sat back on the bed and dropped my hands into my lap. "I hope her decision is the decision I prefer."

Enoch took my hands and gazed into my face. "Whether she does or whether she does not, it is her choice to make and she will have to live with the consequences, whether they are right or wrong. You have taught her well. You love the Lord and have taught her to do the same. Trust her."

I stared at our hands. "Of course, you are right. She must have a right to choose, as I did. Papa did not want to allow me to choose you."

Enoch shook his head. "No, he did not. I remember."

We sat together, remembering.

After my third pregnancy, producing our first living child, Chayim, I returned to Aenon. I decided to try to make amends with my family, taking my little son to meet my parents. Enoch and I spent the night with his parents, Jacob and Helsa. The next morning, we dressed our baby and ourselves early and walked to the home of my parents. We arrived as they were finishing their morning meal.

"Should we knock?" Enoch asked, knowing the animosity my parents felt toward us.

"This was my home all the time as I was growing up, but I have never felt comfortable here." I snuggled Chayim close in my arms. "Yes, knock."

Enoch rapped on the door and we waited. We were turning to leave when the door finally opened. Mama stood in the door, her perpetual scowl filled her face.

"Mama." I reached out tentatively to touch her arm. "This is Chayim, your grandson. We wanted you to meet him."

I lifted the babe, allowing his blanket to fall back from his little head. Mama reached out to brush her hand through his dark curls, a hint of a smile played at her lips.

"Would you like to hold him?" I lifted the babe toward her. "He is a sweet child."

Silently, Mama reached out, taking the small weight of the babe into her arms. She began to coo and make little sounds common to women holding little children. Her face softened into a gentle smile I did not remember ever seeing.

"Come in." She turned toward the interior of the house with the child.

Enoch and I followed her through the sitting room and into the kitchen in time to hear Papa's gruff voice ask, "Who was at the door?"

"Visitors."

"Oh? Who is that you have there? Where did he come from? Whose child is he?" His voice softened a tiny bit.

"Our grandson, Chayim," Mama said. "Zehira and Enoch brought him."

"They are not welcome here," Gavi growled. "You know that."

I stepped forward to take the baby. "If we are not welcome, our child is not welcome. Come to Mama, Chayim."

Papa stared at the babe in his wife's arms, and then at me.

"You have a child? We have a grandson?" he whispered.

"Yes, Papa Gavi. We wanted you to meet him," Enoch said.

I stood with my hands reaching for Chayim while Mama held tightly to him. I wanted my son. I wanted to leave that house. Why had I agreed to take him there?

Papa reached out to the babe and brushed back a tiny golden lock of hair from his face. As he did this, his frown softened.

"No. You do not have to leave," he said.

Papa spoke nonsense to the babe, tickling him. Mama handed my baby to him, saying, "Take him for a moment, but I want him back."

Papa raised Chayim high into the air over his head, gently squeezing and shaking the child's tummy. Chayim squealed and burped up a small amount of milk, just missing Papa's mouth. I held my breath, knowing how quickly Papa's mood transformed from cheerful to raging angry. Instead, he chuckled. I shook my head and stepped back into Enoch's comforting arms.

"Where are you three staying?" Mama's eyes never left Chayim.

"With Jared and Helsa, for now. They have more space," I said.

That was not the whole truth, but it softened the real reason. Enoch's Mama and Papa were more consistent in their welcome. Mama nodded her head.

"My turn." She reached to take the baby back. "You have had him for long enough."

"For now." Papa hesitated to return the child. "I get him later."

"Of course." Mama cuddled little Chayim close. "It has been a long while since we have had a little one in this house. He smells good."

The child whimpered. "His bottom is probably wet. He needs a dry cloth around him."

Mama checked, then lay him down to change him. When she finished, she picked up his little feet and kissed his little toes.

"One, two, three, four, five, on that foot, and one, two, three, four, five, on the other foot. Perfect." She continued to examine the babe, kissing and touching all over him. Papa leaned over her, joining in the silly noises.

I smiled to see Mama and Papa be so silly with my little boy. The usual harshness of their faces had smoothed, replaced by love and tenderness for my child.

I leaned over Enoch and kissed him on the forehead. "You are right. We cannot deny our Grace the same opportunity we claimed for happiness. She has the right and the responsibility to make her own choices, even if they are not what we would prefer."

Enoch nodded. "Your mama and papa finally softened, for a while. Grace does not deserve the pain and sorrow we were forced to overcome in the early years of our marriage. It is better to allow her to choose."

Grace knocked on our door, something she rarely did after we closed it for bed. I opened it and invited her in, especially when I saw her swollen eyes and her tear-stained, red face. I pulled her into an embrace and stood rocking her as she sobbed.

"Oh, Mama," Grace sobbed. Her sobs were all we could hear for many long moments. At last, she controlled her sobbing enough to speak and be understood. "Lucas has decided to leave Zion. His desire for wealth and things of the world are greater than his love for Jehovah, or me."

Enoch put his arms around us, helping to comfort his daughter. "He decided to hunt horses?"

We took a half step back to allow us to see each other's faces.

"Yes, even after I begged him to stay. I remembered your counsel, Papa. Lucas must choose for himself. I could not force him to be with me, but I cannot go with him. I love Jehovah. I love living here in Zion. I cannot leave in search of the world. We lived there with Grandmama Lilah and Grandpapa Gavi. I thought I could leave, but I cannot. I choose to stay in Zion."

My arms encircled her once more. Tears splashed from her face onto the shoulder of my robe and my tears fell on her back, while Enoch's dropped onto her shoulder as the three of us held each other close. Enoch stood aside, watching our tears. At last, our tears ended. We wiped our faces with our hands and the corners of our robes, even Enoch wiped his eyes. Grace gazed into my eyes and then Enoch's.

"Thank you, Mama, Papa. This is the hardest decision I have been required to make."

Enoch touched her face. "You will find other decisions difficult, but if you remember Jehovah, you will make the correct choice."

Tobiah and Noam walked past our room and glanced in to see our tear-streaked faces. They entered our room.

"You chose to let him go?" Tobiah asked.

Grace nodded. He gave her a quick hug.

Noam threw his arms about her waist. "I am sorry, Grace. I know you love him."

She patted his head and slipped out of our room. I heard her door click closed.

"Time for you boys to go to bed, as well," I said. Grace will survive this decision, as will all the rest of us. Sleep well."

The boys gave us a quick hug, kissed us on our cheeks, and bid us good night before leaving for bed.

Enoch stood with his arms embracing me, his head resting on the top of mine. "She made the right choice. She will need our support over the next days."

I nodded.

Lucas stopped by the next morning to say goodbye. I watched Grace kiss him sweetly on the lips and separate from him. She waved to him as he left, then silently closed the door.

"He will return," she whispered. "He will discover the world is not a friendly place. He will find Zion is more than he thought he wanted."

"Will you be here for him?"

"I do not know. Time will tell."

CHAPTER EIGHTEEN

Invention

The season of late harvest arrived. Some blocks harvested wheat, rye, oats, or other grains. Pears, pomegranates, dates, and grapes were being preserved in the fruit warehouse. Every person was needed to ensure the preservation of enough food for everyone for the raining season. Grace and I gathered our sharp knives and walked together to the fruit warehouse and joined in preparing pears.

Rather than join the other young women, Grace chose to work with my friends and me peeling and slicing pears. We spent the day peeling and slicing fruit, and sharing lunch with the others. We brought baskets of sliced, roasted beef to share with the others. By the time we left that evening, most of the pears were ready and in the process of being dried or preserved.

We peeled and sliced many fewer pears than peaches. We looked forward to pomegranates, persimmons, and all the other fruits next to preserve and store. Soon the nuts would be ready to process, breaking open the outer husk and shelling them. We could always find something needing to be done in Zion. For this, I was grateful, knowing I would always have something to do, and friends to do it with.

The work in the fruit and nut warehouses helped keep Grace's thoughts off Lucas. Sometimes, at night I heard quiet sobs from her bedroom. During the day, she smiled with a fierceness that made my heart hurt. Eventually, she rejoined the young women, though she kept her distance from the young men. I supposed it was for the best and wondered if she hoped Lucas would return sooner rather than later.

I tried to support my daughter without getting in the way, though it was difficult to allow her to feel the pain and work it out on her own. I understood Grace's challenge and let her work out her feelings on her own unless she asked for help.

Noam loved to read. Enoch allowed him to borrow books from his collection. Some were copies of the Books of Remembrance Adam had written. Others were histories of other men and women who had lived on our earth. Some of the books were books of scriptures, written words of God. I often found him sitting with his legs crossed on his bed, a book in his lap, reading.

Other days, Noam returned home full of talk and excitement about the animals. He had found the corner of the city that held sheep, oxen, camels, and horses. These he loved. Soon he convinced me that a small dog would be a good addition to our family. He brought home a small, tan puppy, that soon joined Noam on his bed and followed him everywhere he went.

Tobiah quietly went about his work. Many days he left before the morning meal, returning only in time to join our family for the evening meal.

"Where does he go?" I asked Grace one morning when Tobiah again missed our morning meal together.

"He helps with preserving many of the foods. I think there must be a girl he cares for. He often finds himself near Sari when we work together."

"He also ends up in the carpenter shops," Enoch added. "He is learning to work wood. The master carpenters keep him late."

"Will he make carts and wagons?" Noam asked. "Maybe he will make a cart for me. I will ask him tonight."

Noam finished eating and ran off to his morning classes with Ester, followed by his new pup. He sat at her feet three mornings a week. Ester had grown too old to work in the warehouses any more. Now, she taught the young to read and write, telling them stories and keeping the very young children safe when their mamas were busy. Babies stayed near their mamas.

One day, later in the harvest season, Grace and I helped clean the recently harvested cotton with other women in that warehouse. I noticed Tobiah enter with a new, interesting tool. He carried it to Sari, who sat across from me. He wrapped his arms around her, the new tool on the table in front of her.

"Tobiah!" she squealed. "What is this?"

"I listened to your concerns that cotton is hard to straighten and hard to pick out all the sticks and burrs. I thought this claw may help solve your problem." Though the room was full of women, he had eyes only for Sari.

"You listened to me? And you figured a way to solve my problem?" Sari turned in her stool to throw her arms around him.

"I want to make your work easier. This is a busy time, everything we do to make it better gives us more time to do other things." He winked and returned her embrace.

The women around me tittered. We could all see he wanted to use some of his extra time to be with Sari. She ducked her head so he could not see her smile. They were still too young for marriage, but that did not stop their growing love.

"Try it," he urged.

Sari took the wooden claw and admired its four claws, the smoothness, and the comfortable handle. At last, she stabbed a boll of cotton with the claw and dragged it through. Sticks, weeds, and other unwanted trash were brushed away while the fibers straightened. A few more passes through the boll and it looked almost smooth with clean fibers ready to twist together into long threads.

"Not quite right," Tobiah said. "It is taking you to long. Let me work on it."

He reached for the claw, but Sari refused to return it.

"This works better than nothing. You know how you made it," she laughed merrily. "Go back to your workshop and make another."

"If you insist," he said, blushing.

"I insist." She gave him a brief peck on the cheek and went back to cleaning the cotton with his claw. Tobiah glowed as he walked past me and out the door, totally unaware of my presence.

Sari shared her claw among the women who exclaimed at how much easier it made the work. I sat listening, not taking any of the pleasure from Sari. I liked the girl's enthusiasm for the tool, and my son.

Two days later, while she sat working, Tobiah brought in a second try. This tool had two parts, a flat part with spiky points of wood and another claw. Sari pushed the cotton boll onto the flat part and brushed the claw through it.

"Better," she said after running two bolls through it. "What do you think, Zehira?"

It surprised me to have Sari ask for my opinion. "It works better. But, what would happen if you use the claw to scrape away the trash?"

"And two of these flat things with spikes, brush them against each other?" Sari said. "What do you think, Tobiah?"

"Try it. I brought two of these, so more of you could use it."

He produced another set. Sari took the flat part with spikes and began to brush a piece of the cotton she had cleaned. The fibers straightened, all laying in the same direction.

"How do I get it off this?" she asked.

Tobiah had thought of this and handed her a flat stick that fit between the spikes. She slid it under the cotton fibers and lifted. Most of the fibers lifted.

"Tobiah," Deborah said, "your new tool will work for wool, too."

Tobiah reddened with embarrassment.

"I was trying to help Sari, and the rest of you, to solve this problem."

"You did, thank you," Talia said.

"Can you make more of these for us, please?" Chiba asked.

"Back to work for me." He gave Sari a quick hug and left the warehouse.

During this time, Enoch left to preach in the wilderness to seekers. Some wanted to know the truth. Others were seeking to hear a prophet. "Sometimes," he told me later when he had returned to Zion. "I thought the crowd had come to say they had seen me, rather than being seekers of truth."

"You are an important man, Enoch"

He shrugged, and continued his story.

"Often, enemies showed up trying to break up the gathering with angry words and actions. If that did not work, they returned with bullies in an attempt to hurt the individual members of the crowd. I called on Jehovah to protect the seekers."

Jehovah had given him great power over the elements of the earth.

"What did you do?"

"The Destroyer is determined to destroy Jehovah's work. Yesterday, many men left their herds with their servants and came to listen to my preaching." He reached for a freshly baked cookie.

"They left their servants home?" I stepped toward the cool closet for the jug of milk.

"No, they left them by wells or rivers, with servants who would ensure the animals would not run away or get hurt. Sometimes, lions attack the sheep in the wilderness."

"I have heard about the lions. What happened yesterday?" I reached into the cupboard for a glass.

"A nice crowd had gathered to listen, not as many as other times, but a nice size."

I nodded and poured the milk into the glass, then handed it to him.

Enoch took a long swallow of the milk. "As we neared the end of the discussion, a crowd of mockers joined us at the edge of the crowd. They shouted out, mocking and deriding my words. When the men in the crowd ignored their words, they began to push their way forward, trying to get close to me." He began to pace around the kitchen with his cookie in his hand.

"Were you frightened?" I asked.

"No. Father protects me. I never fear for my safety, but I worry about the safety of those who come to listen to me. The mockers began to throw their fists, attacking those who were there to listen to the word of the Lord." He stopped pacing and stood in front of me and pushed the last bite of cookie into his mouth.

"What did you do?" I stared into his eyes.

"I called on the Lord, asking for a whirlwind. A wind blew up, blowing dust amongst the crowd and into the eyes of the mockers. They lost their anger, rubbing the dust out of their eyes. The wind blew away, leaving only true seekers. Any of the mockers left were serious seekers. All the others were gone, blown away in the wind."

"The Lord does protect you. For that, I am grateful." I reached out and ran my fingers down his face.

We embraced for a long time until I lifted my head. "I have known for a long time that Jehovah protects you. Do you not remember the time we were protected, before Chayim?"

"I have been protected many times, over the years. Which time was that?" Enoch swallowed the last of his milk, sat in a nearby chair, and pulled me onto his lap.

"We were in the wilderness, on the plains of Pisgah."

"I have been on that plain many times." Enoch kissed my nose.

I smiled and continued. "Men and women gathered around to listen to you teach. Many were asking good questions, seriously interested in the truth."

Enoch nodded.

"A large mob appeared across the river shouting, cursing, and threatening the lives of everyone. You stopped teaching. I saw you bow your head, and then a flood roared down the river, trees bounced down it along with huge boulders. The water overflowed the river banks, washing away those nearest the river and stopping their shouting of the loudest vile comments. Some near the back were drenched. All who were not washed away left, allowing you to complete your teachings."

"I remember that day," Enoch brushed the hair from my face. "That was one of my earliest experiences with protection. I forgot you were with me that day."

"I will never forget that day. Since then, I have never feared for your safety when you left me to teach others. I knew you would be safe. Jehovah loves and protects you."

I leaned in close, kissing my husband with a passion, having missed him while he was gone. He picked me up and carried me to our room.

CHAPTER NINETEEN

Burned Bread

One day, when all the work in the warehouses had been completed, I sat at my loom, finishing a rug I had been working on for nearly a month. Enoch came in as I finished it and helped me to take it off the loom.

"I think I will give this rug to Mele. She has not had time to weave anything new since she arrived. The cotton has kept her busy much of the time."

Noam wandered in, munching on a fresh cookie.

"Such a pretty rug. All that work for Uncle Hadar?" he asked wrinkling his nose.

"All that work for Aunt Mele." I stared at him. "Is that a problem for you?"

"Hadar yelled at me yesterday, said I was in his way at the cotton warehouse. I just tried to catch some of the falling cotton. It was my job to sweep up the fallen cotton and the dirt brushed out of the bolls. I did not trip him, not even close," he said, then whispered, "I would not do that."

"I know, son," Enoch said. "Uncle Hadar forgets what it is like to be a boy. He did not have to help at home like you do. It makes it harder for him to be a man."

"Will you help me carry the rug to Aunt Mele?" I asked Noam. "You will be happier when you see her get this beautiful rug."

"Sure. I am strong. I can help." The boy brightened and ran into my workroom.

Enoch chuckled and followed him in to help him roll the rug. Then, the two of them carried the rolled rug down the street to Hadar and Mele's door. I limped behind, my crutch under my arm to support me. When we arrived, I knocked, hoping to find Mele home alone. We were about to leave the doorstep when I heard footsteps inside. The door opened slowly and Mele peeked around the edge of the door. Tears streaked her red face.

"Mele!" I cried. "Are you well?"

"Yes. No. Not really." Mele stayed behind the door.

"I brought you a new rug. When I took it off the loom today, I thought of you. Can we bring it in?"

Mele opened the door wider. Noam led the way as he and Enoch carried it into her sitting room. They busied themselves moving the furniture to the side and unrolling the rug. I stared at my friend as they worked.

"What happened to you?" I whispered.

Mele had a bright red hand print across her face. She clutched her robe to her chest, hiding the tear down the front. A red mark peeped above her neckline and bruises showed black and purple on her arms.

"I burned the bread for the morning meal today," she murmured. "Hadar got angry with me."

"There you go, Aunt Mele," Noam crowed. "Is not this new rug pretty?"

"Beautiful, Noam," Mele smiled. "Your mama does fine work. Thank you for helping her bring it to me."

"You are welcome," he said, suddenly shy. "Mama, may I go to Ester's now?"

"Run along, Noam. Enjoy learning."

Noam gave me a hug and rushed out the door. Enoch sat in a chair.

"What did Hadar do to you, Mele?" he asked. "You do not cry for no reason."

She moved to a chair and sat down. I sat next to her and reached out to take her hand.

"Tell him," I encouraged. "Enoch will do the right thing for you."

Mele swallowed a sob and nodded. "I burned the bread for the morning meal today. I deserved it."

I lifted my eyebrows. Enoch shook his head.

"He beat you because you burned the bread?" he asked.

"He has been extra angry this week. Noam tried to help yesterday when Hadar yelled at him. Noam did not see him kick at him. He shouts at me for everything. Nothing I do is right. This morning, he slapped me, grabbed my arm, knocked me down, and kicked me. My side hurts." She held her side. "He sent me to the well for water at the time I needed to remove the bread from the oven. I tried to tell him, but he insisted he needed water. When I came back in, it was too late. The bread had burned."

Mele's tears fell freely, soaking the front of her robe.

"What happened to your robe?" I patted Mele's hand.

"He grabbed my robe and tore it. He called me horrible names."

Mele dropped her head into her hands and sobbed quietly. I glanced at Enoch over her head. He nodded.

"Take her to bed. See what you can do for those bruises, please. I am going to find Hadar."

Mele looked up, fear filling her eyes. "Be careful. You have been the subject of Hadar's anger lately. He believes he should be the leader of this beautiful city."

"I will be careful, but it is time my brother understands." Enoch's jaw tightened.

I caught his eye. "Please, be careful," I mouthed. He nodded and stood to leave.

"I will send Joam and Talia to stay with you. Joam will keep Hadar out."

"He will be furious if he returns and cannot come in." Mele's chin trembled.

"I will ask Joam to bring Benjamin. They are both bigger and stronger than Hadar," Enoch said as he left.

I gently slipped my arms under Mele's and helped her stand. We limped together down the hall. Mele leaned heavily on my strength, while I leaned on her for stability. I started to take her into the room she shared with Hadar, but turned away when I saw clothing torn and scattered across the room.

"We will go to the guest room." I helped my friend across the hall.

This room appeared to have been unused since the couple moved in, until I pulled the bedding down. Dried blood spotted the rumpled sheets.

"Here, Mele, sit here in the chair while I change the bedding," I said.

Mele sat in the chair, staring unseeing and shaking in the warm room while I bent to open the bottom drawer of the chest where sheets were usually placed there when we set up homes for new families. Finding a clean set, I stripped the dirty ones from the bed and replaced them with clean, fresh linen. I dropped the soiled sheets into a basket to show Enoch later.

In the torn-up room, I found one nightdress and returned to my friend, whose shaking had increased. Knowing Mele was sick, I slipped off the torn robe and pulled the soft nightdress over her head, then helped Mele move to the bed. I tucked the covers around her to help warm her, then sat in a chair to watch and be with her.

I heard the front door open and held my breath for a moment, fearing Hadar had returned. Then, I heard Talia's voice coming down the hall.

"In here, Talia." I softly called. "I am glad you came."

"Why here? Why not their room?" Talia murmured.

I pointed across the hall with my head. Talia handed me the basket of medicinal herbs she brought and crossed the hall to investigate. While she was gone, I searched through the basket for comfrey and the blood clotting herb. Finding the blood clotting herb first, I rubbed it across Mele's face, arms, and chest where bruises had formed already.

Talia returned shaking her head. She quietly gathered the comfrey and took it into the kitchen to steep. While she did that, I found a leaf of aloe and cut it, allowing the gel to ooze onto the injuries on Mele's sides that came from Hadar's vicious kicks. Talia returned with a pot of steeped comfrey and a cloth. She dipped the cloth into the comfrey and lay it across the worst of the bruises.

"Hadar did this?" Talia whispered, not wanting to disturb Mele, who finally slept.

I nodded. "She burned his bread this morning, or something stupid like that. The man is out of control. And this is not the first time he has hurt her. The sheets on this bed were covered with blood splatters."

"This has to be the last time," Talia growled in a whisper. "She will not live through another beating."

CHAPTER TWENTY

Gift

After several false alarms, and hours later, Joam and Benjamin led Enoch into the room where Mele still slept. I looked up to him.

"We have Hadar in a safe room." His usual pleasant face was grim.

"What is a safe room?" I whispered.

"I did not know we had one," Talia said, the volume of her voice matched mine. "Where is it?"

We stood and led the men to the kitchen where we could talk without disturbing Mele, sitting in chairs or leaning against the cupboards. I opened the door to the cold storage closet to find something to drink.

"Look here." I brought a jug out. "No wonder Hadar has been so angry."

Enoch took the jug from me and lifted it to his nose.

"Wine," he said in disgust. "He has been making wine. I thought he had been overly industrious in helping with the grapes. He brought some old juice home and made wine of it."

The others drew in their breath, slowly exhaling. Wine could destroy the jugs for any other purpose, as it held the flavor within the pores of its clay if it had not been finished properly.

"How many of these are there?" Enoch asked.

I returned to the closet to examine the contents of the jugs. I brought out three more jugs filled with wine and one filled with milk.

"Three more," Talia said, helping to lift them to the cupboard.

I set the milk and five cups on the table. "I would prefer milk to drink. What would you like?" I nodded at the others.

Benjamin took his cup to the well and filled it with water, the rest chose to drink milk.

"We know part of what Hadar's problem is," Joam said. "Still, his treatment of Mele is inexcusable."

"Not only did he slap her face, leaving the imprint of his hand," Talia said, staring at the jugs of wine, "he kicked her in the ribs. Some are cracked and one may be broken. She is going to hurt for a very long time because of today's beating, all because she burned the morning bread." Her voice was filled with frustration and contempt.

"Because he insisted she go out to the well when it needed to come out of the oven," I growled.

"She has broken ribs?" Enoch's voice rose in surprise. "This adds to the severity of his actions. His penalty will be worse. We must talk with Mele. Is she able?"

"To talk?" A voice came from the hall leading to the bedroom. All eyes turned toward the voice. I jumped up to help Mele join us in the kitchen.

I helped her shuffle into the kitchen, holding her up on the uninjured side. Enoch moved to help, but I waved him away.

When Mele was seated with a cup of cool water in front of her, she looked into Enoch's eyes and said, "What did you need to ask me? Where is Hadar?"

"In a safe room, a nearly empty room in one of the warehouses. There is nothing he can use to hurt himself in there and he cannot leave without permission. James is standing guard by the door, which is locked." Enoch stood with his hands on his hips.

"Locked?" Mele's eyebrows crunched together. "I have found no locked doors in Zion, only the gates to the city walls."

"There is only one," Enoch said, "the door to the safe room. We built the city to be a place of refuge and safety for our people. The locked city gates protect us from those who would do us harm from outside." He waved his hands around. "Because we allow anyone to enter, to investigate our way of life, we built the one safe room, to protect us from those who would attempt to harm us from the inside. Hadar is not the first to be housed there."

Mele spoke in a small voice. "What will happen to him?"

"Is this the first time he has beaten you so severely?" Enoch asked. "I have seen other bruises on you, so do not try to tell me this is the first time."

"No. This is not the first beating, but it is the first time he hurt my ribs so badly." Mele stared into Enoch's eyes.

"He has bloodied you before, too," I said. "I changed the bloody sheets from the bed in your guest room where you have been sleeping today."

Mele turned toward me, then hung her head. "Zehira is right. When he strapped me, I bled. Sometimes, he cut me with his knife."

Joam answered Mele's first question. "He has proved himself to be unworthy to live in Zion. This is a city of peace and love. He is unable to live this way. He will be given a pack with food and water and sent away tomorrow. You may stay, Mele, if you wish. Hadar will not be welcome in Zion." He leaned against a cupboard with his arms folded. "In most cases, we allow people to decide for themselves if the Zion way of life is a good fit for them. If they are not, they usually leave on their own. You did that, yourself, the first time you came to Zion. Sometimes, we are forced to make that decision for them, as we have for Hadar tonight."

"Hadar had false expectations and was not happy here, that first time. He forced me to behave in a way I am not proud of. I am happy here, now." Mele's voice grew stronger. "Zion is a city where everyone can work together, live together. None is better or above the others. Enoch, even you work in the fields and warehouses for your support."

She looked down at her hands. "Hadar seeks for a place where he can be the lord, a place where others will do the work and pay him obeisance. When he found he was required to work, and that sometimes that work was hard, he made wine and began to drink it. I should have told someone ..." Her voice dropped off.

"But, you would have been beaten worse than you were today?" Talia suggested.

Mele's nod was so small it was almost perceptible. She would not look up into our eyes.

In a small voice, she said, "I suppose you will send me away with Hadar, now."

Enoch set the palm of his hand against her chin and gently lifted her face to look into his. "Do you want to leave?"

"I am happier here, even with his beatings, than I have been since before I married Hadar. He is a cruel man and has hurt me many times."

"I saw the scars on your back and arm," I said. "He broke your arm."

Mele nodded. Tears fell from her eyes. "I am his wife. His sins are mine because I married him. Hadar tells me you will send me away if I turn to you for help. He says we cannot be separated. I have tried to leave him before, but he refuses to allow it." Her shoulders heaved with great sobs.

I put my hand on her back, gently rubbing and calming my childhood friend.

When Mele finally managed to gain control of her sobs, putting a hand to her side to support her ribs, she stared at

Enoch. "Is he right? Am I condemned to be abused by Hadar all my life?"

"No, Mele," he said.

The rest of us voiced our support for her.

Enoch continued, "You have a place here with us if you choose. No one will force you to leave. You have shown yourself to be a part of our city. You have been willing to work, willing to help others when Hadar allowed it. Hadar will no longer be a part of your life, if that is what you want. Is it?"

She covered her mouth with a hand, her eyes wide and shining with hope, then licked her lips, swallowed, and nodded. "I do. I want to be away from that man, never again to be joined to him in any way, not even as his former wife."

"We cannot take that from you. You will be his former wife, but never again his wife. Before we send him away tomorrow, I will repeat these words so he will know. 'By the powers given to me by Jehovah to join and separate, I declare you to be permanently separated from Hadar, never again to be considered his wife.'"

I watched Mele's face as the hurt and anger melted away, leaving a woman exuding hope. Then, her face darkened. "How will I be kept safe from Hadar? He will be angry."

"He will be expelled in the morning, never, ever, allowed to return to Zion. You will be safe here with us," Joam said.

"I can never leave Zion, for he will hear of it and hunt me down," she half-whispered to herself. "But, I do not desire to leave. This is not a prison, this is my home." Her face brightened and her calm returned. "Do I have to be there when you tell Hadar?"

"If you are able. The city council will meet with him and share our decision."

Mele nodded. "If you are with me, Zehira and Talia, I can be strong. I will go."

"Thank you, Mele. Benjamin will stay here with you until we are ready. Joam is needed to be there, as part of the council. We will send for you when it is time." Enoch pushed away from the cabinet he had leaned against.

Talia and I escorted Joam and Enoch to the front door, leaving Mele seated at the kitchen table.

"Take care of her. She is very ill," Enoch said. "She would not live if she were sent out of the city with Hadar. I will send for you soon." He kissed me and walked into the afternoon sunlight, followed by Joam.

"Would she change her mind?" Talia whispered. "Would she go with that snake, Hadar?"

"He has a hold on her, and has for much of her life," I said. "I was there when she married him. Even then, I could see he had somehow taken her will. We will need to guard her carefully."

We turned from the door and walked back to the kitchen to find food for us to eat. Grace could feed the boys, if they showed up for a mid-day meal.

CHAPTER TWENTY-ONE

Sentence

While we waited for the message to come that Mele was needed, she returned to her bed and slept, though not well. Her injuries were not all that disturbed her sleep. Her decision to leave Hadar caused her to sleep fitfully, calling out and tossing in the bed. Hadar's control was strong over her mind. I wondered if he used some magic gained from the Destroyer to bind her so deeply to him. Before she confronted him again, she would need a blessing from Jehovah to break the tie and give her peace. I decided to speak of it with Enoch before she faced Hadar.

Mele woke again before messengers arrived to take us to confront Hadar. Talia and I helped her wash and dress in a beautiful blue soft robe. She hobbled to sit on a stool. I stood behind her, brushing the snarls and knots of sleep from her hair. I then braided her hair and looped it into a beautiful style.

"Hadar will be sorry he hurt you so," I said.

Mele frowned. "Hadar filled my dreams. It was not pleasant."

"I could tell. You jumped and hopped in bed. You nearly tore all the sheets from beneath the mattress. He has had control of you for a long time," I murmured. "Will you be able to break away?"

"He tried to force me to leave with him. He entered my dreams, showing me treasures and power if I joined him," Mele whispered, her head bowed, her eyes closed. "And, he showed me horrors, terrible things that will befall me if I do not go." Her body convulsed in a great shiver.

"But the voice of an angel entered my mind, reminding me that Jehovah cares for his daughters and will care for me, if I follow his ways. I know the dreams caused by Hadar are false." She lifted her chin and stared into my eyes. "I will stay in Zion and follow the ways of Jehovah."

I had watched my friend calm and settle into safer dreams before she woke. She spoke the truth.

Talia knocked and entered the room. "Tobiah is here. He brings a message. The council is ready for you, Mele. Are you ready? Can you walk?"

Mele nodded. "If I have help, I can walk."

Talia supported her on one side, I supported the other. We moved to the sitting room where Tobiah and Benjamin waited.

"I can carry her," Benjamin offered. "She is but a tiny little thing."

Mele tittered at that. I had not heard her tinkling laugh for so long, it surprised me. She allowed Benjamin to lift her. I found my crutch, tucked it under my arm, and joined Talia in following the men.

Tobiah carried a torch in front to light our way. He led us farther toward the center of the city. We took several turns before reaching a warehouse I had not yet visited. When we entered, I saw huge piles of wool waiting to be straightened, died, spun, and woven into warm fabric. I sighed, thinking how nice a new cloak of wool would be.

Tobiah led us past the wool into the interior of the building. James stood before a closed door.

"She came?" he asked.

"She is here," Tobiah responded.

Benjamin set Mele on her feet and allowed me to slip my arm around her. Talia did the same on the other side, supporting and balancing our friend. Mele pulled her skirts straight and touched her hair.

"You look beautiful," I whispered as James knocked and opened the door.

Inside, twelve men sat with Enoch facing the door. Each had a sternness about them and a look of sadness. I understood. I, too, felt sadness to know my brother-in-law was in serious trouble. Hadar sat with his back to us. He sat with his head defiantly up, as he stared intently at Enoch. He did not turn or flinch as we entered, accompanied by Benjamin.

Enoch began the proceedings. "Hadar, you have abused this woman, Mele. What have you to say to her?"

He turned to look at her, a sneer filled his face. "This woman is my wife. I have every right to do to her as I choose."

"You have no right to abuse your wife, or any woman. That is not given to men as part of the marriage covenant." Joam spoke with a low, calm voice.

"This woman is mine. I can do as I will."

The anger in Hadar's voice startled me. I had never heard Enoch speak to anyone with such hatred. For his brother to be capable of it forced me to step back a step.

Hadar saw and jeered. "Are you afraid of me, even here, little cripple?" he taunted.

I lifted my chin and stepped forward, dropping my hold on Mele. She wobbled until Talia helped her regain her balance.

"I have no fear of you, Hadar." The calm I felt surprised me. "You are a sorry little man, filled with venom and rage. You cannot hurt me. I pity you."

I stepped back and put my arm around my friend, giving her a quick hug.

"And you, wife? Do you fear me still?" Hadar spat.

Mele lifted her head and stared him in the eyes. "No, Hadar. I do not fear you. You have no more control of me. Jehovah protects me. And, I am no longer your wife."

Rage filled Hadar, his fists tightened, his jaws clenched. "You. Are. My. Wife. And. My. Woman." He shouted, leaving a space between the words. "Nothing can change that."

I looked to Enoch, who stood. Hadar dragged his eyes from Mele's face and stared at Enoch, silently waiting for his words. Enoch allowed the silence to stretch, waiting for Hadar to comment.

At last, Hadar spoke. "What can you do about it, brother?" The word, brother, from his mouth sounded more like a curse than an endearment.

"This." Enoch raised his hands and said, "In the name of Jehovah, and with the power given to me to bind and release, I release you, Mele, from your marriage to this man, Hadar. Henceforth, and forever, you have no connection to him. Amen."

As Enoch dropped his hands, Mele breathed out a deep sigh of relief. Hadar began to rage, trying to move against unseen bonds. I held my breath a moment, until I realized he could not leave the chair, could not lift his arms.

"You cannot take away my wife! She was given to me in Holy Marriage by Papa! You have no right! I was told I would be a great leader, promised wealth and position. Satan promised!"

With that, the counsel stood. Enoch took my arm and we left. Benjamin helped Mele and Joam took Talia by the elbow, escorting them from the room. The rest of the counsel followed. Hadar sat in his bonds, screaming and shouting horrible curses. I covered my ears with my hands until the door shut behind me, closing out the sound. I looked at my childhood friend, who stood with her head down, tears falling to the floor.

"Are you sorry you are parted from him?" I set my hand on her back.

"No." Mele shuddered. "I am sorry I stayed with him as long as I did. I did not know I could be free." She lifted her head and reached for Enoch's hand. "Thank you for freeing me. What will happen to me now?"

"You will return to your home and get a good night's sleep," he said gently.

"I can keep the house? I am welcome?"

"Of course, you are, Mele. You heard the voice of the Lord in your dreams. You are safe here." I brushed the hair back from her face.

She stood staring at each of us, seeking reinforcement of her safety and welcome. At last, she nodded.

"I will take you home, Mele," Benjamin said. "I will sleep by your door to protect you tonight."

He reached out and took her hand and led her through the warehouse and out the door. She leaned on him, her strength waning. Benjamin picked her up and carried her through the warehouse door toward her home.

"James will stand guard here. Hadar will be safe until morning," Enoch said as we walked out of the building. "Tobiah, go with Benjamin and Mele. Watch over your aunt until Benjamin returns with the news that Hadar is safely out of the city."

Tobiah loped off toward Mele and Benjamin. We could depend on him to care for his aunt.

CHAPTER TWENTY-TWO

Patience, Always Patience

The next morning, I walked into my friend's home and found her in the kitchen, reaching into the oven to pull out a warm, crusty, fragrant loaf of bread. The house smelled wonderful. Most of the sense of grief had disappeared.

"Come in, Zehira," Mele called, almost gaily. "Would you like a slice of fresh bread?"

"I would, thank you."

I sat in a chair next to the table as Mele sliced the bread, inhaling the homey fragrance of warm wheat and honey. Tobiah stepped into the room from the back, bringing a jug of water with him.

"Mama, how are you this fine morning?" he asked.

"Well. And you? You seem happy after a long night."

"Benjamin returned an hour ago with the news that Hadar is safely beyond the boundaries of the city. Mele is safe with us in Zion." Tobiah sat next to me at the table.

I reached out to take Mele's hand. We gazed into each other's eyes for a long moment.

"You are free of him. How does that feel?"

"Surprisingly good. I slept without the dreams he often sends me. Only good and loving dreams came to me during the night. For the first time in many long years, I am free of him. I did not know I could be so happy to be free of his presence in my mind."

"He has controlled you for a long time." I sat in a chair and leaned my crutch against the table.

Mele sat next to me. "Since before I married him. Do you remember our mud fight?"

I nodded.

"Even then, I was under his thrall. I thought I loved him, thought he would be a good husband. Your mud in my face nearly broke me away from him, but Hadar reached for my mind and regained control. You were right about him all along. I am sorry."

Mele held my hand tight. I reached out with my other hand and covered Mele's. "You have come to your senses now. You are free of him."

The three of us sat eating bread, enjoying the quiet company of friends.

When the bread was nearly gone, I glanced to Tobiah. "Papa says you may return to your work in the carpenter shop.

Stop by and let Sari know you are well. Aunt Mele will heal. She will be fine, now. Go."

Tobiah reluctantly stood, and then realized what I had said. He leaped into the air and was soon on his way to see Sari.

"Have you removed all of Hadar from your home?" I swallowed the last of the cold water in my cup.

"Not yet. There are still some of his things in what was our room. I have not had the courage to face it."

"Would you like me to help?" I asked as I stood.

"If you would, please."

We walked to the bedroom Mele had shared with Hadar until the night before. She gasped as she opened the door, not remembering the state it had been in the day before.

"A whirlwind must have entered through the window," she said.

"A Hadar whirlwind," I agreed.

Together, we moved through the room, picking up clothing and sorting it. We put Hadar's clothing in one pile, Mele's in another. Some of her clothing had been torn to shreds. These we placed in a separate pile. We removed the dirty bedding from the bed and replaced it with fresh linens and quilts. The piles of Hadar's clothing were carried to the sitting room, to be taken to a central warehouse where people cleaned and stored clothing for new arrivals. We set the pile of torn clothing in another chair in the sitting room, awaiting removal to a storehouse for rags and bandages.

"You are still a best friend," Mele said after we swept and mopped the bedroom floor.

"I am glad you are still my friend." I dropped into a chair to rest. "Do your ribs not hurt anymore? You have been on the go all morning, working hard, after being badly hurt only yesterday."

"My ribs hurt but not as bad as yesterday. I believe my dream helped to heal me."

"What did you dream?" I gazed into her eyes, then dropped mine to gaze at my hands.

Mele glanced at the new rug on the floor and smiled. "I first thought I was visited by an angel who spoke to me. However, now I think it was Jehovah, Himself. It was a blessing I greatly needed. I have felt at ease and safe since He spoke to me."

I sat in shock. *Another friend has spoken to or heard directly from Jehovah. I have not lived in Zion long enough, but Mele came after I did. How did she get to speak to Him? It is not fair. Am I being fair? I am a dumpy, crippled woman. Why would Jehovah speak with me?*

I stared at my hands for a long time, until Grace knocked at the door.

"I thought you two could use some help," she sang out to us.

"Your timing is perfect," I said. "We have these two piles of clothing that need to be taken to two different warehouses. Can you help with one of them?"

Grace found a cart in the back yard of Mele's and filled it with Hadar's old clothing. She pushed it to to the clothing warehouse. Meanwhile, Mele found another cart in the back shed. We filled it with the torn clothing, then shared the effort to pull it down the street to the warehouse where rags and bandages were kept. Soon we were giggling and sharing memories and stories. The empty cart bounced and bumped against our legs, causing us to break into peals of laughter. I thought how those who saw us would never know the serious problems we had survived in the last few days.

I nudged my friend, "Like when we were kids, huh?"

We giggled and chuckled, much like we had as young girls.

As we pulled the cart back to the shed, we met Grace who had just returned her cart. "The people at the clothing warehouse were happy to receive all of Uncle Hadar's clothing. Some of it was much more elegant than any we usually share with our new citizens."

"Hadar had delusions of grandeur," Mele said, sarcasm dripping off each word. "He never knew how low he really is."

"How sad for Uncle Hadar." Grace reached out and took my hand.

"Hadar was deluded and tricked by Satan, who promised him things he could not give. I pity him." I slipped my other arm around Mele.

"Pity is all he deserves," Mele said. "He is gone and I am glad of it."

I wondered at the fierceness of my friend's attitude. I supposed it was because of her having been controlled for so many years. Freedom sometimes allows for submerged bad feelings to surface. I hoped those feelings would soon be tempered.

Later that night, I contemplated the events of the past days as I changed into my night clothes. Enoch pulled me into an embrace and kissed my neck.

"What is wrong?" he asked. "You have been far away all evening."

"Nothing." I kissed him on the chin.

"I know better. You do not get quiet like this for nothing. Hadar is gone. What bothers you?" He pushed me out to better see into my eyes.

"I feel so silly and prideful. Mele heard the voice of Jehovah. Others have heard His voice and seen Him. Will I ever? Am I so unworthy He will not speak with me?"

Enoch pulled me close and brushed my hair back from my face. "Zehira, I cannot say what is in the mind and will of Jehovah. You are a worthy woman. You give of yourself without thinking. Jehovah will speak with you when He chooses, when He has a special message for you. Mele needed to know she was safe."

"I know," I said into his neck. "I try not to be a jealous old woman, desiring things that are not for me, although sometimes I fail."

"No, it is right for you to desire some things. That does not make you a 'jealous old woman'. It is good to desire to speak with Jehovah. It will be your blessing, sometime, though I do not know when. However, I do know it will happen. Lift up your head and be patient."

"Patience, always patience. I will be patient. I do not like to be, but I will. I know you are right."

CHAPTER TWENTY-THREE

Preparations

During the rainy weeks that followed, our family enjoyed the quiet they brought. Great cumulus clouds filled the sky above the city, opened up, and washed the dirt from the air and streets of Zion. When the rains passed, usually each evening, I went for long walks with Mele and Talia, enjoying the freshness and beauty of the rain-washed city.

Other days, when the rains ended, I went with Grace to gather the supplies we needed for our journey to Home Valley. We planned to leave at the end of the rains, so warm clothing would be necessary, as well as sufficient food for the journey there and back. I spent the times when it rained weaving, working to make a few blankets and rugs to trade for goods from other parts of the land. I looked forward to meeting other women from around our world. No one had been invited from Nod, but every other land would send representatives to the great last conference with Adam presiding. The opportunity to meet once more with Eve, Helsa, Rebecca, and Ganet, along with the other matriarchs encouraged my efforts. Their council and support would be welcomed.

Grace spoke of her hope to see Lucas again. "Maybe he will be there to trade horses," she frequently dreamed. Other times, she hoped, "Maybe he will have decided the world is not as exciting as he thought."

I doubted that Grace would be happily surprised by him. I hoped another young man would catch her eye and take her mind from Lucas, for, I feared he was lost to the world.

The rains ended. After we helped with the planting of the fields, we packed up our carts to leave for Home Valley.

"Who will join us in our trip to Home Valley?" I asked as we sat together for dinner shortly before leaving.

"We are all going, are we not?" Noam asked. He had planned his travel for the past month. "I have a new pack, filled with everything I will need."

"Yes, Noam. You are going with us." Enoch tousled his hair. "Everyone who wants to go is invited."

"Will we leave Zion empty?" Grace raised her eyebrows high. "Are you certain that would be smart?"

"No, I do not think everyone is going. Some of our neighbors do not feel close to Grandpapa Adam and Grandmama Eve. They tell me they plan to stay here, caring for the fields, gardens, and trees."

"What about Aunt Mele?" Tobiah asked. "Is she coming with us?"

"She does not feel safe, yet, with Hadar out there somewhere. She feels safer here. Grandpapa Jacob is his papa, too. Perhaps he will want to visit with him and Grandmama Helsa. Because we have so much farther to travel, we will leave earlier than many of the others." Enoch leaned his elbows on the table and set his head in his hands.

We discussed our travel plans for a while, sharing the amount of supplies and other items we planned to take with us.

"Papa, can we not take one of the wagons?" Noam asked. Ben tells me there are big wagons and oxen in his part of the city. He says they are available for citizens to travel long distances. Can we not use a wagon and oxen?"

"It would help Mama if she could ride, rather than walk," Tobiah chimed in. "Noam has a great idea."

"I do not need to be babied," I began, but Enoch interrupted me.

"Not babied, loved and cared for." He turned from the boys to me. "Your sons are right. It will be easier for you if you do not have to walk. We can arrive sooner and you will not be so tired from walking so far. Thank you, Noam, for the great idea."

"Would you like me to check on a wagon and oxen?" Tobiah asked. "I know where to go and who to talk with. Noam can go with me."

"That would be nice son," Enoch agreed. "Tell Joachim we plan to leave in a month."

"Still in a month?" I asked. "Even though we are riding? It will not take as long as it would to walk."

"Yes. We should leave at the same time. I do not know why, but I feel prompted to leave then. We will discover why it is important to leave at that time along the way, or when we reach Home Valley."

Grace and I worked harder to prepare for the journey. Grace completed several clay jugs, some to carry our grains and milk, others to trade when we reached Home Valley. I made seven blankets and two rugs to trade, plus four warm blankets for us to use on the journey. We packed dried fruits, vegetables, and meats into bags. Grains went into two of the jugs Grace made. We checked clothing and packed enough for each member of the family to have enough for traveling and some nice clothes to wear during the conference.

Three days before we were to leave, Tobiah parked a large wagon in front of our home. It was large enough to carry everyone in the family and all the baggage we planned to take with us. Tobiah and Noam carried out everything we planned to take with us, while I directed the packing into it.

The night before we were to leave, Mele visited to say goodbye.

"Did you want to go with us?" I asked.

She thought about it for a long moment. I thought she wanted to go, and may yet choose to join us, but in the end, she decided to stay in Zion where safety was certain for her.

"As long as Hadar is out there, I am safer in here." A frown crossed her face, uncharacteristic since her freedom from Hadar.

She gave me a shawl to wear at the conference and two to trade. Then she kissed me on the cheek and bade us to have a safe journey.

The following morning, Tobiah and Noam left early to retrieve the six promised oxen. All would be needed to pull such a large wagon. Upon their return with the oxen, Grace and I loaded the jug of cool, fresh milk and journey bread we had made for the trip. Enoch carried out the records of Zion he planned to share with Adam. He told me the night before these were copies of the originals. He could not take a chance the originals would be lost.

To my surprise, other wagons lined up on the street, prepared to join us on our excursion. In one, Sari sat with her family. Though I did not expect company, I was not surprised that Sari and her family would join us. Tobiah had quietly courted her during the harvest and raining times, though both were still young. *Perhaps there will be a wedding at the conference.* I smiled at the thought.

Three other families joined us: Joam and Talia; James, with his wife, Tabitha, and their two sons, Jared and Samuel: and Saul, his wife, Pili, and six of their sons and daughters. All were seated in wagons pulled by oxen and ready to leave.

Five families were safer than one while trekking across the wilderness, as bandits now found it easier to rob travelers than to farm to live. These families also probably considered it safer to travel with Enoch, as he was known to protect those who traveled with him in a way that prevented harm or damage to his fellow travelers.

Grace, Tobiah, and Noam clamored into the wagon while Enoch made final arrangements with the other travelers and the city committee who were not leaving Zion. At last, he swung up onto a tall black horse and led the wagons through the city. Tobiah shook the reins leading to our oxen and followed Enoch.

Crowds lined the streets, cheering and waving to us and our small caravan. I nodded and waved at them, perplexed that the crowds cheered louder as we passed. Grace and the boys returned the waves, laughing and shouting at their friends. Our cheerful party finally passed through the west gate and down the road toward Home Valley.

CHAPTER TWENTY-FOUR

Arrival

The trip was uneventful, much of the time, though some mornings we started late as one or another ox had strayed, requiring a search for them before we could leave. Noam became an expert in following the tracks of the missing animals, and even better at hobbling them each evening to prevent the morning search.

Because the animals felt Noam's love for them, they allowed him to milk the ox cows each morning and evening, providing fresh milk for us to drink and use in cooking. Barrels hung on the sides of the wagons carried water, though the water often became stale before we crossed a river and refilled them.

The milk became precious, providing a fresh drink on the days before we reached another river. Many times, the bouncing and shaking of the milk jugs in the wagons churned it into butter, which we appreciated as we spread it on bread. We stopped on the Sabbath, remembering to keep it sacred as we rested ourselves and our animals.

On the twentieth morning from Zion, Enoch told the camp he expected to be in sight of Home Valley by evening. We cheered at the idea and our hearts and eyes lifted at the thought. We were ready for this part of the journey to end. I was glad for the heavy cotton cover over our wagon, though it stifled us in the heat. It kept the sun from our faces. We were happy to not have skin burned red from the sun when we met with Grandmama Eve, Grandpapa Adam, and the other matriarchs and patriarchs.

The news brought me special cheer, for, to be honest, the jouncing and bumping of the wagon tired me and I looked forward to the time I could climb down for a few weeks. I yearned for the quiet and stillness that would allow my body to recuperate from the aches and bruises caused by the ride. That last day seemed to last many more long hand spans of the sun's movement than the past days had.

At last, as the sun set in the western sky, painting it shades of pinks and purples, we crested the rise to Home Valley. We could traverse the final distance that evening. However, we chose to camp on the edge of the valley to enter in the light of day.

That night, we women brushed dirt from our clothing and the clothing of our families, in preparation to meet others from across the land. The men helped Noam brush the dirt from the horses' and oxen's coats. We opened the jar Noam had poured milk into two days before, and found enough butter to trade for other foods from other parts. We sang around the campfire that night. Excitement crackled in the air about us.

I spent much of the time in the journey and that night, wondering if I would be accepted by the other women. Though I had met Grandmama Eve many years ago, when Grandpapa Adam married us, I feared she would not remember me after all these years. Would Grandpapa Adam, although he had visited us once in Aenon many years ago? More than that, I worried about how the other matriarchs would react to my twisted leg.

I remembered, the beautiful Eve and her kindness to me when Adam married us so many years ago. Would she remember this poor little cripple? She was known to be gracious. However, I feared that some of the others would not be as kind. It helped to know that if she had not yet arrived, Helsa would arrive soon, and she loved me.

I woke the next morning with a headache. I splashed col water from the barrel onto my face and vigorously brushed my hair, trying to banish the pain in my head. The morning meal helped. Noam poured the fresh milk from the morning milking into another clean jar, plenty for us to drink and to share. I managed a smile as I climbed into the wagon for the last time for all the days we would be in Home Valley.

We did not travel far down the hill and into the valley before riders raced out to meet us.

"Is Enoch with you?" One young man cried as he neared our wagons.

"I am." Enoch rode forward on his big horse. "Why?"

"Adam sent us to see if you were in this group of wagons. Not many have arrived yet, but he thought you may arrive early. You are needed."

Enoch nodded. "I will join you momentarily."

He rode to the front wagon where I rode. "My dear, I must go with these men. Tobiah, be sure your mama arrives safely. It will not take you long."

He leaned over and kissed me lightly on the cheek. "I will see you soon."

He turned his black stallion and rode away with the young men. Mixed emotions filled me, happiness that my good husband was needed by Adam, fearful he would not be at my side when the time came to be reintroduced to Grandmama Eve, and even anger that he would leave me when we were so close. I knew the emotions came from the headache and fears, maybe even a sense of loss, like when he left me on our way to Zion. However, this was not then. I was safe. I lifted my head and rolled my shoulders back, swallowed my unbidden tears, and smiled at Tobiah, encouraging him to move forward.

More men and women met us as we neared the edges of the community, directing us to a place near an apple orchard for our camp. Few others had arrived yet, giving us choice of a good location to set up our wagons and tents for sleeping. Home Valley residents could not be expected to house all the many expected visitors for this huge conference.

Grace and I found clean robes and ducked inside our tent to change. I hoped to walk through the camp and meet some of the other women. Washed and changed, I took Grace with me in search of a well, each of us carrying one of the new jugs Grace made earlier to trade.

At the well, the design of her jug drew the attention of many women. They stood around the well, and us, sharing stories and laughing. None of the women seemed to notice the crutch I leaned on. They, and I, were almost unaware of its presence.

I remembered the pleasure of meeting women at the well. I still missed it in Zion, though I appreciated the convenience of a well in my garden behind our house.

The women parted as an ancient, bent woman, carrying a small jug, approached. It could only be Grandmama Eve.

"Grandmama Eve," a woman near me said, "this is Zehira and Grace."

I stood still, in shock. I did not expect to meet Grandmama Eve again in this way, by the well, talking and laughing. I drew myself up, standing as straight and tall as I could. Grandmama Eve moved past the other women to stand near me. I expected a close examination, feared she would notice my crutch and twisted foot, and reject me. Instead, she opened her arms wide, welcoming me.

"Welcome to Home Valley, Zehira. I have long waited to see you once more." She stepped closer and enfolded me in her slight arms.

I returned her embrace, trying not to break any bones. Her strength surprised me. At several centuries old, she continued to be strong. Grandmama Eve stepped back, smiling, holding tight to my hand.

"I hoped to find you here, Zehira. And this is your beautiful daughter?" She nodded in Grace's direction, never releasing my hand.

"Yes, my youngest daughter, Grace. Our youngest sons, Tobiah and Noam are settling our things in camp." I waved in the general direction of the apple orchard.

"Wonderful! I look forward to meeting them, as well." She reached to draw water from the well, but Grace stepped forward and pulled the bucket up and filled Grandmama Eve's jug.

"Thank you, dear," Grandmama Eve said. "Would you please carry my jug and the two of you escort me to my home?"

Grace nodded and gathered her jug and Grandmama Eve's in her arms while Grandmama Eve took me by my free arm and turned back in the direction she had come from.

"How was your trip? You arrived sooner than I expected. Zion is far away." Grandmama Eve chattered all the way as we walked toward her home. Her steps were as slow as mine and she seemed to be unaware of the crutch supporting my weight.

"We came in bouncy and jarring wagons, but it was much better than walking would have been. Tobiah requested a wagon from the stores in Zion. It is so large, it required six oxen to pull it." I found myself chattering comfortably with this kind woman, as though it had been only a few days since our first meeting so many years ago. "Four other families joined us, making the journey safer and sharing in the duties of travel. It took us twenty days to arrive on the rim of Home Valley."

"Only twenty days?" Grandmama Eve chirped. "We went that direction, years ago, and it took us more than a month to travel so far. The oxen must have made it easier for you to travel."

We walked together, slowly and cheerfully, until we arrived at Grandmama Eve's door. "Come in, come in," she invited, opening the door wide to allow us to enter

.

CHAPTER TWENTY-FIVE

Eve

I sat on a comfortable chair in Grandmama Eve's sitting room, my jug of water and crutch tucked beside my seat, while Grace went with Grandmama Eve to her kitchen to help her find some apple juice and cookies to share with us. They returned soon. Grace carried the treats on a beautifully carved wooden tray and sat them on a low table in the middle of the room.

"Grace, would you pour the juice?" Grandmama Eve handed me two cookies on a small red plate.

Grace poured each of us juice from a bright, red pitcher into blue and red clay cups. The juice was tart, complementing the sweetness of the cookies.

After some small conversation, I asked, "Do you know why the men came for Enoch?"

Grandmama Eve glanced out the window.

"His brother, Hadar, is here in the guest house. Adam needed his help to solve a problem with him. More than that, I do not know."

"Hadar? He's here?" I stiffened briefly. "I guess it makes sense." I breathed deeply and consciously relaxed.

"He showed up here yesterday, starving and dressed in rags. We fed him and put him to bed in the guest house. This morning, Gavriel came to tell us he heard shouting and banging in the guest house. Adam left with him, but he is not strong enough to handle problems like this anymore. He sent the young men to bring Enoch to help. We will know more when they return here."

"They will come here? Enoch will know to find us here?" My heart beat faster at the thought.

Grandmama Eve nodded. "I thought you would come to the well for water and told the women to send a girl to tell me when you arrived. One of the boys will let Enoch know where you are. Some went to let your sons know not to worry for you."

Grace and I sighed at the same time. Grandmama Eve had thought of everything.

We sat together waiting, sharing stories. Grandmama Eve wanted to hear all about our traveling in the wagon. Grace asked if she knew who was coming, and when the trading would begin. I sometimes lapsed into silence, staring out the window.

"Are Papa Jared and Mama Helsa due to arrive soon?" I asked. "They will want to know Hadar is here."

"We have not heard from them, yet," Grandmama Eve said. "We do not know when they will arrive. Adam was happy to see your campfires on the hill last night. He knew it would be you."

"How ...?" Grace started to say. "Oh. Jehovah speaks to him, too."

Grandmama Eve nodded.

I looked away from the window to gaze at Grandmama Eve. "Enoch felt we should arrive early. He pushed us a bit faster than normal. He did not know why we should come, only that it was important."

Grace raised her eyebrows, while Grandmama Eve just nodded.

My eyes strayed back to the window, where I saw a familiar figure coming our way. "Look. There comes Enoch with some other men. That must be Grandpapa Adam."

"It must be him," Grandmama Eve said. "Now maybe we can find out what is happening."

She stood slowly and straightened her back in time to welcome Adam and Enoch as the entered the house.

"Grandmama!" Enoch embraced the old woman. "How good to see you."

Grandmama Eve returned the embrace and pounded on Enoch's back.

"I have missed you. Where have you been for so long?" she said.

"You know, Grandmama. I have been doing the work of the Lord. Zion keeps me busy."

"I have heard of some things you have been doing. Are they all true?" Grandmama Eve led the men into the room.

Enoch shrugged, then sat next to me, put his arm around my shoulders, and pulled me close for a long kiss.

I brushed my hair back. "How is Hadar? Grandmama Eve says he is not doing well."

"No. Not well at all. He sleeps now." Enoch glanced at Adam. "Will the boys let us know when he wakes again?"

Grandpapa Adam nodded.

"Papa, what is wrong with Uncle Hadar?" Grace asked.

"He is very ill, Grace. The Destroyer no longer supports him, since he left Zion. He wandered in the wilderness in a stupor." Enoch pulled me closer.

"He lost his food in the wilderness and drank only a little water. He was mauled by lions, as well. It is a wonder he still lives." Grandpapa Adam sat next to Grandmama Eve and put a frail, bony arm around her. "His spirit is weak. Last night, he seems to be well enough, now, but he has changed. He rants about people and things not here—wild things."

"What does he say when he rants?" I leaned forward, my hand holding my chin.

"Mele, James, lions, bears, Shuya, other unintelligible things. He is still angry that Mele is no longer under his control. He thinks he loved her, and maybe he did in his own way, maybe more at first. He rambles so much, it is difficult to know what is going on inside his mind," Enoch said. "It is sad to watch."

"What is needed to help him?" Grandmama Eve asked, her once-brown eyes intent on Enoch.

"Grandpapa and I used the Holy Priesthood to cast out the devils who had inhabited his body. They ran, screaming, into the hills. We asked Jehovah to help heal him." Enoch dropped his voice. "He is my brother. It makes me sad to see him in such a terrible condition, but …"

"But," Grandpapa Adam said, "I fear he will not live through the day. He has been held in the Destroyer's will for far too long, and has not the ability to repent. It would be nice if your papa would arrive early. Jared would want to see his son one more time."

"Mama Helsa would, as well," I said. "She is a loving woman and loves all her children, even those who have been a trial for her."

"We all love our lost children," Grandmama Eve murmured. "We have all lost children to the Destroyer. It is the one common sorrow of our lives."

"Is there something I can do for Uncle Hadar?" Grace leaned forward.

"No, dear. He sleeps. And when he is awake, he is dangerous to you." Grandpapa Adam said. "It is good that you care for you uncle, but he is beyond our help, now."

Grace sagged in her chair, bouncing her foot.

Soon, she stood to leave. "I need to check on Noam and Tobiah, make sure everything is in order in the camp." She bent to lift her jar of water and left the house.

I noticed that Grandmama Eve and Grandpapa Adam were tired. Although Ruth came, offering a meal to everyone, I suggested to Enoch that we should return to camp and check on our children and the status of the camp. Grandmama Eve suggested that we could stay, but we could see these beloved grandparents needed an afternoon rest. It had been a tense day for everyone.

"Come back this evening for dinner," Grandmama said as she walked us to the door. "Bring the boys and Grace. There will be enough."

"We will, Grandmama," Enoch assured her and kissed her goodbye.

He took me by the arm, supporting me in his strong arms so I had less need of my crutch. We strolled through the community. Enoch steered me past the guest house to check on Hadar.

"Is he still sleeping?" he asked Gavriel.

"He is," Gavriel said, "but your daughter tried to go in to wake him. It was good that Tobiah passed by just then, for he convinced her that Hadar needed his sleep. They went in the direction of your camp."

"Grace." Enoch sighed. "She does not understand. I will talk with her. Hadar does not need to be wakened by her, and she does not need to be confronted with his attitude and curses."

I raised my eyebrows, not saying anything until Gavriel could no longer hear me. "Hadar's attitude is still bad?"

Enoch shrugged and sighed. "It is. He continues to berate all near him and has nothing good to say about women. He believes Mele is his slave. He raves about returning to Zion to regain his 'property.' Mele was right. She is safer in Zion."

We walked back to our camp, lost in our thoughts. My gratitude for Enoch's protection and goodness swelled within me, glad he was so different from his brother.

CHAPTER TWENTY-SIX

Hadar

We spent a happy evening with Grandpapa Adam and Grandmama Eve, leaving before the sun dipped behind the mountains in the west. Enoch wanted to check on Hadar and I wanted to settle our family quietly into their beds in camp. I managed to get Noam in bed while Tobiah and Grace sat beside the common fire with other young people when Enoch returned.

"Hadar is awake and is more agitated than ever," he said as he sat down next to me. "He believes we have imprisoned him. I suppose we have, for he is not allowed to leave the guest house until he calms down. He is yelling and screaming again that his woman slave was stolen from him. He is in no shape to leave. The lion hurt him badly. I am amazed he still lives."

I took his hand in mine. "Grandmama Eve told me he arrived here in bad shape, starving and injured. It amazes me that he is able to rant as much as he has."

"Grandpapa Adam and I attempted to heal him, not knowing his current state of mind. He slept deeply at the time. We healed some of his injuries, but not all of them. Certainly, we did not heal his mind."

"It is sad for Hadar. How much worse would it be for Mele if she had stayed with him? Has the Destroyer left him to himself?" I squeezed his hand tighter.

"It seems he has. Hadar babbles about taking over Zion and being the leader of our city. He has lost all sense of reality." He returned my squeeze and drew me close.

Hadar's health had not improved the next day. He alternated between sleeping and raging against women and those who stood outside his door, protecting him. Enoch spent some time with Grace, reassuring her that her uncle was much too ill for her assistance and making her promise that she would not attempt to visit him again during his sickness.

Over the next days, more people from other parts of the land arrived for the conference. They set up camp and visited with others who were already there. Grace, Tobiah, and Noam spent their days helping others get settled and meeting other young people. I helped organize the camp and the women. Enoch met with Grandpapa Adam, helping him to plan and organize the upcoming events.

Enoch's grandpapa, and High Priest, Enos, and his wife, Rebecca, arrived the next morning. Papa Jared and Mama

Helsa reached Home Valley in the early afternoon. As their companies settled into the camp, Grandpapa Enos and Papa Jared met with Grandpapa Adam and Enoch to discuss what to do about Hadar.

The new groups were nearly settled with tents up, water found, and space set apart for their animals when a boy came to camp with a message for Grandmama Rebecca, Mama Helsa, and me. Grandmama Eve wanted us to join her, so we walked together into the community to her home. I was grateful the older women now naturally moved at my slower pace.

We were welcomed into the comfort of Grandmama Eve's sitting room, where Ruth helped to serve sweet cakes and pomegranate juice. We exchanged news of our home villages and lives, while we waited for our men to bring us word of their decision.

"Helsa, have you had a chance to visit with Hadar, yet?" Grandmama Eve asked.

"Not yet." Mama Helsa stared into her lap. "Jacob says now is not the time to do such a thing since Hadar's health is so poor. He promised to take me to visit him this evening."

Grandmama Rebecca leaned toward Helsa and set a hand on her arm. "Is Hadar as sick as all that?"

"The men say he is. I have not had a chance to see him. When I passed the guest house where he is staying, the men who stood outside told me he was sleeping." Tears leaked from her eyes and she shuddered as she took a deep breath, trying to regain self-control.

When she did, she wiped her eyes and nose with a square of linen. "The last we heard, Hadar and Mele were moving to Zion. Hadar seemed to think things would be better there for them." She turned to me, staring into my eyes. "Were things better there for him?"

I cleared my throat, wondering how to answer my beloved Mama Helsa without hurting her.

"You can be honest. I know he is argumentative, demanding honors he has not earned. I am not blind to his faults. But," she dropped lifted her gaze from her lap to me once more, "he is my son and I love him."

Mama Helsa's gaze held a hope I could not deny. I thought about softening my answer, making it seem better than it really was, then I remembered Mele's pain. *Mama Helsa did encourage honesty. How could I be truthful and not hurt her?*

I reached across the gap between us and took her hand. "I am sorry, Mama Helsa. Hadar seemed to be better the first few months. He joined with the men working in the fields and helped preserve food for all to use. About three months ago, he stopped showing up to help while Mele joined us alone. She had bruises that prevented her from working as hard as she usually did. One arm was weak. Before the rains, I took her a gift and found her bruised and bloody, her robe torn down the front. Hadar had beaten and kicked her for burning the morning bread."

The older women in the room gasped. Mama Helsa's tears dripped off her chin.

"Hadar cracked or bruised Mele's ribs, badly hurting her. Enoch found Hadar, hoping he would repent of his actions toward Mele. However, Hadar could only rage that she was his property and he had every right to do as he wished with or to her."

I paused to take a breath and squeezed Mama Helsa's hand. "In Mele's dreams that night, Hadar tried to reinstate his control over her. Instead, Jehovah came to her and reminded her that He loves his daughters and will protect them."

I stared into the eyes of each woman who sat near me. "Is that not special to know that Jehovah loves and protects his obedient daughters?"

Each woman nodded, even Mama Helsa as she wiped her eyes with her wet linen square.

"It freed Mele of Hadar's controls. Apparently, he has controlled her much of their time together. When she met again with Hadar, safely protected by Enoch and others, she chose to no longer be bound to Hadar as his wife. Enoch agreed, and through the power of the priesthood, unbound the marriage. Hadar screamed and yelled that Satan had given her to him and it could not be undone. Our men escorted him away from Zion the next morning with food and water."

Grandmama Eve and Grandmama Rebecca sat quietly as Mama Helsa accepted my sorrowful news. I watched her wipe her eyes with her already sopping square of linen, then round her shoulders up to sit straight once more.

"I knew he would not end well," Mama Helsa whispered. "He has been full of pride from his early days. I hoped he would learn … that his life would humble him. He would not listen to me. His words to me were harsh and painful the last time I saw him."

We sat in silence for long moments. Grandmama Eve broke the silence, her voice strong in spite of her great age. "It is the sorrow of women to bear the sins of our children. The pain of birthing them is only the beginning. Watching them turn away from everything you taught them, all you love and know, that is the greater pain."

Rebecca reached up to smooth her hair. "I agree. I once thought the greatest sorrow came when my babies were stolen and sold to Nod, probably into slavery, never to be seen again. I could not be consoled for many weeks until Mama Eve reminded me of our right to be with our children in the next world." She touched Mama Eve's hand gently. "Since then, I have lost other children to war and death, but the greatest sorrow has been to watch them leave the gospel of Jehovah behind."

I breathed deeply and said, "I have thought about myself, my twisted foot and the difficulty I have walking. I became swallowed up in my own pain." I sighed. "Now I know my twisted foot is nothing compared to the sorrow of a child lost to the Destroyer. Watching Hadar and Mele opened my eyes. When we allowed Grace to choose whether she would stay in Zion or marry Lucas, it broke my heart. He left soon after her decision not to go with him to catch wild horses and sell them throughout the land."

I squeezed Mama Helsa's hand and let go. "I am grateful she chose to stay in Zion, safely obedient and happy."

Grandmama Eve took my hand in her gnarly, wrinkled hand. "You have learned a hard lesson. A twisted foot and all the bullying you must have suffered is hard. Your challenges have been difficult."

Her words eased my pain. I relaxed into the back of my chair.

"Have you heard from Methuselah?" Mama Helsa asked. "Is he coming?"

"He met me in Zion last year and stayed for nearly a month. He returned home when the message of this conference arrived. He and his family should arrive soon," I said.

"Adam is expecting all the High Priests to arrive soon," Grandmama Eve said. "Seth and Ganet should arrive tomorrow. Cainan, Mahalaleel, and Lamech are expected to arrive with their families within the week. This will be a great family reunion, a magnificent conference.

CHAPTER TWENTY-SEVEN

Reunion

The other High Priests arrived when Grandpapa Adam expected, along with many others of their families. Even Chayim and his family arrived, camping near us. Half of our little family had arrived.

During the days while others arrived, an atmosphere of a country fair pervaded the camping grounds. Men traded saddles and wagons, horses and oxen. Women traded rugs and blankets, baskets and jars. Women also brought special treats from their homes across the world, many different and new to those of us from other parts of the land. We shared and traded these food items, as well. I traded my rugs and blankets for preserves and dried pineapples, and beautifully decorated baskets. Grace traded her beautifully painted jugs for baskets of taro and breadfruit.

As we enjoyed the trading and sharing, the High Priests met in a special conference. I suppose they discussed the needs of the Jehovah's people. Enoch often returned to our tent late, after I could no longer stay awake waiting for him, and left again early in the morning.

I learned that Hadar spent more time sleeping, less time ranting. Mama Helsa entered the guest house to visit with him during this time. I saw her leave, tears leaking from her eyes. Finally, the day before the Sabbath, two weeks after Enoch and I arrived with our little caravan, he seemed well enough to leave the guest house without ranting at everyone he saw. That day, he left the guest house and walked out, away from Home Valley. When he did not return, Papa Jacob and Enoch searched the community and in the hills. Hadar was gone. No one saw him again during the conference.

I offered a prayer of gratitude. That Mama Helsa had spoken with him without being raged at and that he was gone. His presence dampened our joy at being together as the huge family of our ancient parents.

Our little family joined all the others for the Sabbath worship. Enoch and Methuselah performed the sacred sacrifice, under Grandpapa Adam's direction. The large congregation of several hundred filled the air with songs and prayers.

As planned, the conference began the next morning. While the men sat on a small hill, called Adam-ondi-Ahmen, we women met in the apple orchards. We discussed the needs of women. Many struggled in their villages, trying to keep the fields planted and harvested as they tried to teach their children about Jehovah and the precious skills of reading and writing.

Mama Rebecca stood among them. "Sisters, many years ago, Eve and I were part of our first women's organization. Papa Adam organized us as Ministering Sisters. Do any of you remember it?"

Several voices murmured their agreement, others stared around and shook their heads.

"What is this Ministering Sisters organization you speak of?" one woman stood to ask.

Grandmama Rebecca answered. "Our men are often gone, preaching the gospel or in search of enough food to help us survive. We women stay behind to carry on. When we stand together as sisters, our burdens are lifted. No one should carry the heavy load of family and women's duties alone."

The women in the orchard spoke their agreement.

"Organize yourselves in your communities. Find a sister or two who lives near you." Grandmama Rebecca waved her hands this way and that. "Check on her often, daily if possible, at the well or in her home. Be sure her struggles are known and her needs are met, if at all possible. Watch over each other. Care for each other. This is what we do as Ministering Sisters, minister over each other."

Grandmama Vida, Mahalaleel's wife, added, "Few of us live alone. Someone is always close, there to help you when needed. Spend a few moments now to find your neighborhood groups and organize."

The noise of excited women sounded like the roar of a waterfall. Grace and I joined with other women from Zion, visiting together, though we were already organized.

Ruth called on Mama Eve to share her story. I had not yet heard of her struggles during those early days in this world. I left that evening awed and inspired by her strength and wisdom.

The next two days, while the men continued their discussions, we women were regaled with more stories, from Grandmama Ganet and the next day from Grandmama Rebecca. Each of these women showed us how to manage our lives in love and faith in Jehovah, even during the struggles and challenges brought about by the Destroyer and our own silly mistakes and actions.

At the end of that third day, I sat with the other women, tears rolling down my face as I thought of Grandmama Rebecca's lost children. I heard my name called out by one of the women in the crowd. I looked up.

"What did she say about me?" I asked Grace.

"They want the other wives of our High Priests to write their stories. Can you write yours?"

I stared all around the group. I had never considered my life story to be interesting to others. And now, they wanted me to share.

"We have no time for these women to share in the next days, as we are expected to join the men tomorrow," Ruth said.

"Can they not write their tales and send them throughout the land for all to read?" One bright sister asked.

No, I cannot. I have nothing to tell. Yet, with surprise, I heard other words come from my mouth. "I would be happy to do that."

The women around me quietly cheered. Those closest to me patted me on the back.

Grandmama Elia, Grandpapa Cainan's wife, Grandmama Vida, Grandpapa Mahalaleel's wife, and Grandmama Helsa agreed, saying their stories were short. The crowd of women did not care about length, they only wanted to know more about these matriarchs, these wives of the first High Priests. Why did I agree?

As the women left the orchard, the four of us who had been tasked with writing our stories walked together, discussing the challenges of sharing our stories in writing. I almost wish we had time to share while here. It would be a huge challenge.

The next day, we paraded to the hill, Adam-ondi-Ahmen, for a general meeting with the men of our families. The boys and Enoch spread out one of my rugs on the grass near the top of the hill for us to sit on. There, we waited for Grandpapa Adam and Grandmama Eve to join the crowd. Methuselah's wife, Qutarrah, sat nearby with their children, as did Chayim and his family. Papa Jared and Mama Helsa sat on the other side of us. Though everyone spoke in quiet voices, the roar of voices sounded much like a pride of hungry lions.

Methuselah and three other young men helped Grandmama Eve and Grandpapa Adam to their seats at the top of the hill. Methuselah then found Qutarrah and sat with her. Grandpapa Adam stood and the noise of the crowd calmed. As he spoke, not even the little babes cried out.

Grandpapa Adam spoke of many things with us. He shared his visions of the future, causing me and many others to shed tears of sorrow. I thought the sorrows of disobedient children in our time had been heartbreaking. Grandpapa's visions were worse, much worse.

As he spoke, a light filled the area around Grandpapa Adam. Jehovah stood beside him, honoring our beloved Grandpapa Adam as Michael, a Prince of Heaven. He taught us many sacred things, too sacred to speak or write. I sat in awe, my eyes fastened on Him, listening to the voice I so longed to hear, a smile playing across my face. At last, I could see and hear my God.

The conference ended with an announcement. Grandpapa Adam would provide special blessings to all who desired. Wonder and awe filled the hill as the huge congregation stood and moved to the center of Home Valley. Large kettles of stews, different varieties of breads, fruits, and other foods waited for us there.

I turned to Enoch as we stood, folding our rug. "I am happy. I have heard the voice of Jehovah and feasted my eyes on his face."

Enoch brought the rug to me on its final fold, handed it to Tobiah, then embraced me tightly. He understood.

Over the next days, while families visited with others from all over the world, I watched family groups, large and small, gather in the tabernacle for a blessing at the hand of our great patriarch and Grandpapa, Adam. I patiently waited for our turn, knowing others also waited. At many centuries old, Grandpapa Adam needed to preserve his energy and health.

At last, it was our family's turn. We joined Papa Jared and Mama Helsa, Methuselah and Qutarrah, in the tabernacle. Grandmama Eve tried to have us come to her home, but there were too many of us. Each blessing given was sacred and special. A promise to me filled me with hope, my body would be healed, "in the time of the Lord, as I continued in patience." After this great blessing, and those of all the others in my family, I tucked my crutch under my arm and limped back to our tent that had become our temporary home.

As the families received their blessings, they left Home Valley to return to their homes. Families there waited for their reports and fields awaited harvest. The families who traveled with us from Zion were almost ready to leave, as were we.

Before we left, when only our close family, including Papa Jared and Mama Helsa, remained, Tobiah and Sari stood before Grandpapa Adam while he performed the sacred and simple rite that married them for eternity. We stayed one more night, giving the young couple a night alone in a guest house.

The next morning, Enoch and I trekked to the home of our grandparents to give them our final kisses, and goodbyes. Their warm embraces filled me with joy and love, helping to make the anticipated rough trip easier to bear.

When we returned to the wagons, the boys had our oxen hitched to the wagon. A smaller cart, with one ox hitched to it, stood behind, with Sari and Tobiah patiently waiting. Enoch supported me as I climbed into the tall seat beside Grace and Noam. Noam would direct the oxen on the journey home. He glowed with excitement that we would trust him to direct the team of oxen the long distance home to Zion. When I was settled, Enoch swung up onto the saddle of his tall black stallion and our small caravan departed.

CHAPTER TWENTY-EIGHT

Whirlwind

The journey home to Zion started quiet enough. The oxen plodded down the trail, pulling the heavy wagons. Young people and men and women called back and forth between the wagons. Children laughed and played, often jumping from the slow-moving wagons to run ahead and play.

After the first three days, the calling lessened as exhaustion became more a part of the journey. On the fifth day, Enoch rode back along the caravan, speaking quietly to the people in each of the wagons.

When he arrived at our wagon, he did not kiss me as usual. "We are being followed. Noam, be watchful and ready to draw the wagons into a circle. These men are not seeking knowledge of Jehovah. They plan mischief and are a danger to us."

I nodded, glad he was with us. "Do you know who they are?"

"I do not know who they are specifically. I do know their intent is to cause us harm. Be watchful."

Noam nodded and sat straighter as Enoch turned his black stallion and trotted to each of the next wagons, warning the drivers. Children were called to return to the safety of the wagons. Like the other folk in our small caravan, we traveled quieter and more reserved through the day. At night, we drew the wagons into the usual circle, with the oxen in the middle. It was crowded. Our five wagons and one cart did not make a large circle, but cramped quarters provided safety for us and our animals. The men took turns at watch, watching for an attack.

No attack came that night. The next morning, we prepared to travel, keeping our voices muted. The wagons moved out as fast as possible with slow moving oxen. I noticed Noam's red-rimmed eyes and suspected all the other men stared into the distance with similar looking eyes, red from searching through the bright sunshine for any who would cause us harm.

Near mid-day, Joam raised a cry. Our followers were near and approaching fast. Noam grabbed his sword and leaped to the ground to join in the defense of our small group. I directed our oxen behind the others as we formed our tight circle. Joam, James, Jared, Samuel, Saul and Tobiah joined Noam facing the intruders. I saw Tobiah motion for Noam to return to the wagon and Noam's refusal. My child was becoming a man. Enoch sat on his horse in front of the other men, waiting and watching.

I saw at least thirty men on horses racing toward us, swords drawn, yelling threats and curses. Enoch had told me during the night before not to fear if they attacked. Jehovah would protect us. I sat on the high wagon seat watching and wondering how we would be protected.

The riders came toward our wagons in a rush. I could see Hadar in the lead, shouting curses louder than the rest. *How had Hadar managed this? Too bad he escaped from Enoch and Grandpapa in Home Valley, much as I enjoyed his departure. Now, we would pay.*

Enoch signaled to the men behind him to stand still and quiet. He then stood calmly, arms raised to the heavens. I breathed shallowly as I watched and waited.

As Hadar and his angry men came within almost two arm lengths of Enoch, a whirlwind blew up, swirling dust and bits of rock into the eyes of the invaders. They blinked and brushed at their eyes as they shouted at Enoch and the men who stood between them and the wagons.

The wind blew harder, spinning in place just beyond where the angry men screamed and advancing toward Enoch. The whirlwind increased in speed and size, soon engulfing Hadar and his men. I watched in horror as their shouts and curses became screams of fear when they understood the whirlwind had caught them in its power, lifting and spinning them into the air and away. I watched until the whirlwind spun out of sight, far away.

The noise of the whirlwind's passing stunned everyone in the wagons. Enoch dropped his hands and turned.

"Prepare to move out," he said, not raising his voice.

He turned and walked to our wagon, where Grace and I waited.

"Are you well?" he asked.

I glanced at Grace who nodded.

"Yes. What happened to Hadar and those men? Where will the whirlwind drop them?" The reins to the oxen shook noticeably in my hands.

"It will deposit them somewhere far away." He set his hand on my shoulder.

My hands began to calm. "Will they live?"

"I do not know. They are in the hands of Jehovah. They will live if there is hope for repentance." *That leaves Hadar out. But, it is unfair to think that. Perhaps, this will change him.*

Enoch leaned over and kissed me before riding to the oxen, helping to direct them to turn away and move down the road toward Zion. I grasped the reins tightly in my hands. Noam caught hold of the wagon side and boosted himself inside. He climbed over the seat and nudged Grace aside to sit between us.

"What happened?" Grace looked back the way the whirlwind had taken the men.

"They were taken in the whirlwind, protected by Jehovah as Papa promised." Noam gently took the reins from my hands. "Papa raised his hands and the whirlwind blew up, spinning them into its depths and blowing away, taking them all with it. None came near enough for any to engage in battle." Noam frowned.

I smiled and lay a hand on my young son's arm. "You do not need to be so disappointed. Jehovah protects your papa and those who travel with him whom he loves. I will gladly allow Jehovah to fight our battles and protect my boys and their papa."

Noam bowed his head. "You are right, Mama. It is better to allow Jehovah to fight our battles. None of us were injured."

The remainder of our journey, we plodded uneventfully down the trail at the speed and pace of our oxen. We rested on the next two Sabbaths, worshiping Jehovah in song and prayer.

Nineteen days after leaving Home Valley, we rode once more through the gates of Zion, happy to be home again. Men met Tobiah and Sari, leading them away to their new home. Somehow, they had received word of the need for the young couple to have a home of their own.

While Noam helped Grace unload our possessions and carry them inside our home, I gave Talia, Tabitha, Pili, and Sari's mama, Aleeza, warm embraces as we separated for our own homes.

Though the long journey there and back exhausted me, the conference blessed our lives, especially mine. I unpacked baskets and packs, returning everything to its place. An extra jug of wheat and a bag of dried fruit remained. Grace went with me to return them to the appropriate warehouses for others to use.

As we walked back home, we passed Mele's home. She came out to greet us. "How were the conference and the journey?"

"Wonderful. Grandmama Eve welcomed us, as we heard she would, full of kindness and love. Even Jehovah came to honor Grandpapa Adam. I am grateful to have been there," Grace gushed.

"I would have liked to have joined you."

"Probably a good thing you did not," I said with a frown. "I did not want to say anything so soon, but Hadar was in Home Valley when we arrived."

"Hadar? There?" Mele put her hands to her cheeks. "Is he still there?"

"No. Grandpapa Adam did not know of his behavior here in Zion, and asked Enoch to help heal him from starvation and the injuries he received when mauled by a lion. Though the healing helped his body, his mind and spirit seemed gone. He shouted curses at everyone, especially women, when he was awake. One day the curses ended. The men of Home Valley thought him to be healed, and allowed him to leave the guest house he had stayed in. Hadar walked through the community and away from us."

"And no one saw him?" Mele sat on the front step of her porch.

"No, not then. We saw him once more, on our journey home." I reset my crutch more comfortably under my arm.

"Hadar led a group of at least thirty angry men to attack us. Jehovah interceded, causing a whirlwind that blew them away. We do not know if they live."

"Then it is not safe for me to visit my parents again," Mele whispered. "I hoped to visit them after the harvest to make amends for my behavior over the years. I miss my mama."

"I miss mine, as well," I whispered. I straightened my shoulders. "We can travel to Aenon and visit them sometime soon, when we are certain Hadar is no longer a threat. We can take Enoch with us for safety."

We embraced and Grace walked beside me as I hobbled home, leaning on my crutch.

CHAPTER TWENTY-NINE

Changes

O ver the next year, Enoch continued traveling, teaching, and preaching, calling all who would listen to become followers of Jehovah and residents of Zion. All who obeyed the laws of Jehovah and Zion were welcome. Men enlarged the walls around the city, making it almost twice the size of the city I entered that first day. The new walls enclosed new homes and fields, sufficient to support the increasing numbers of people who chose to live inside.

Many who moved to Zion found peace. Sadly, some could not abide living the full law and were not willing to join in helping with their share of work. None were excluded or asked to leave. We hoped those who were unhappy would repent and find happiness among us.

A few of the discontent were willing to stay and participate in the activities and work of Zion. Other dissenters became uncomfortable with life in Zion, leaving rather than changing their ways and attitudes.

Tobiah and Sari found joy in their marriage. He joined the carpenters, building homes, wagons, furniture for the new residents, and creating new tools to help us with the responsibilities of life in Zion. A son blessed their lives a year after their marriage. They were happy with their life in Zion.

Grace spent another year dreaming Lucas would return and stay with her. At the end of the year, when Zion celebrated the beginning of a new year, Grace ran into the kitchen where I worked, my hands and arms covered with flour, preparing sweet breads for the celebration.

"Mama, Mama," she cried. "He is back! Lucas is here!"

"Lucas is back?" I wiped my face, leaving a dusting of the flour on my cheeks. "Have you spoken with him?"

"Not yet. Ana told me she saw him walking into his parent's home. I rushed home to change into my best robe."

Grace hugged me and raced from the kitchen toward her bedroom. Soon, she stopped by to kiss me on the cheek, then she ran out the door.

I washed my hands and face and cleaned up the kitchen while waiting for the loaves of bread to bake. When they cooled, I set them on a tray and tucked my crutch under my arm. I carried the tray to the tabernacle where many other citizens of Zion celebrated.

I set my tray of breads on the serving table and turned to accept a cup of apple juice from a small boy. I mixed with my women friends, exchanging good wishes and hopes for a happy year. I saw Grace with Lucas, his arm possessively around her. I shivered, remembering the same look on Hadar's face the first time I saw him with his arm surrounding Mele's waist. I hoped Grace would not allow herself to become as hurt as Mele had.

Mele slipped an arm around my waist, murmuring, "Grace's friend has returned, I see."

"Yes. I hope his intents are honorable. Do you see what I see?"

Mele stared a moment at the young couple. Her eyes widened and she inhaled deeply. "His arm around her waist looks loving, but I see a look in his eyes that causes me to cringe. He claims her as his own, as Hadar claimed me."

"As I thought." I glanced at Mele and grimaced. "I hope he does not hurt her."

The look on Lucas's face and fear for my daughter tempered my joy in the New Year celebration. I knew Grace loved Jehovah and usually obeyed without question. She desired to stay in Zion. I feared Lucas would drag her away from Zion and away from the Lord.

Later that night, I heard Grace in her room, quietly sobbing. I knocked and entered.

"Grace, why are you crying?"

"Lucas has changed, for the worse, as I feared. He acts like Uncle Hadar, treating me as his property. He only allowed me to return home because we are not yet wed."

I sat on the bed beside Grace and embraced her. "I saw the look on his face and the possessiveness in the way he held you by the waist. I hoped he had not become like your Uncle Hadar."

"He has, Mama," Grace sobbed. "He has."

I held her close, allowing her tears to soak the front of my robe. After a time, I asked, "What will you do?"

"Talk with Papa. He will know how to tell Lucas I am not his property, nor will I ever become his wife. Until he has talked with Lucas, I must stay here in our home."

"Do you want to speak with him tonight? I can send him to you when he returns." I brushed her tear soaked hair back from her face.

"No, Papa will need his sleep after this long day. I will talk with him in the morning."

I embraced my beautiful daughter, running my hand through her long, dark hair.

"I will tell your papa you need to visit with him before he leaves in the morning. Sleep well."

"Thanks, Mama. I will."

I returned to my bed and found Enoch had returned. We spoke about Grace and Lucas. Enoch had watched the way Lucas treated his daughter earlier and was happy to hear she was home, safely in bed.

"She would like to visit with you in the morning before you leave." I blew out the candle and crawled into bed.

"I will remember." Enoch gave me a passionate kiss.

The next morning, I found Grace sitting in the kitchen preparing our morning meal, humming a quiet tune.

"You are happy today," I said.

"I am, Mama. Papa agreed to talk to Lucas. He is not for me, I know that now. Jehovah came to me in my dreams last night. He promised I would find a good man who will righteously care for me as long as I remain obedient."

"A good reason to be happy." I stooped to take the morning bread from the oven.

Grace and I worked in joyful companionship throughout the day, cleaning the house and preparing food for Enoch and Noam. We sat in the sitting room, reading and resting together, when the door handle rattled. Grace jumped as it opened. Mele entered, come to check on Grace's safety. When Enoch returned, Mele continued to visit with us.

"You are safe to leave home again, Grace." Enoch said.

Grace jumped from her seat to give her Papa a big hug.

"Lucas left Zion today. We reminded him he is welcome to return when his attitude changes. James and Benjamin escorted him away from the city. He cannot return with his current attitude." Enoch sat beside me and put his arm around my shoulders.

Mele raised her eyebrows. "Oh?"

"Yes. Zion is protected. Those who do not have the attitude of seeking truth or obedience are no longer able to find us. Lucas will not return again until he changes."

"How did he find us this time?" I snuggled close to my sweet husband.

"He came to see his parents, allowing us to think he would seek for truth. When he saw you, Grace, his real intentions became apparent to all. We waited to see how you would respond. If he had not allowed you to come home last night, we would have intervened. After our chat this morning, we spoke with him. He is gone now and will not return unless his real intentions change."

"I wondered why Hadar never returned," Mele mused.

"You should have asked," Enoch said. "I would have told you. You have no need to fear in Zion."

Grace brought her hands to her eyes and allowed the tears to fall across them.

I touched her arm. "Sad?"

"No, Mama. Disappointed in Lucas." She wiped the tears from her face. "All will be well if I am obedient." She stood and walked toward the back of the house.

I heard the bucket drawing up from the well in the back garden and splashing water. Eventually, Grace returned to the sitting room, dressed in a clean robe with her dark brown hair neatly braided.

"I am going to help my friends," she said and left the house.

CHAPTER THIRTY

Visit to Aenon

Three years later, Enoch and I decided the time had come to take Noam to visit Aenon once more. I needed to visit my parents and make amends with them. Mele decided to join us on the journey. She, too, desired to visit her parents. Rather than taking heavy wagons pulled by slow oxen, we chose four fast horses from Zion's herd.

Noam, now a young teen and closer to adulthood, chose a tall brown stallion to ride. Over the years, he had continued to work with the animals. He loved them and they felt his love. He chose a roan mare for me and a gray mare for his Aunt Mele to ride. Enoch would ride the tall black stallion he usually rode when he left Zion when not on his own two feet.

Two mules joined the party to pack our food and tents. Behind our saddles were packs for personal items. Even with all our gear, we could travel much faster than in a wagon or a cart.

Most people could walk the distance to Aenon in a week, but it would take longer for me to limp that far, and if I did, I would be sick with exhaustion. Enoch told us we could travel the distance on horseback in about three days, without riding hard. With Enoch with us, none of us feared the enemies who plagued travelers.

We left early the day after the Sabbath, and made good progress. Neither Mele nor I had ridden for a time and Enoch did not push us. He frequently stopped to allow us to climb off the horse and rest our legs. By evening time, Enoch stopped early so our legs could heal and rest.

Noam mocked us, until Enoch reminded him of the misery he felt the first time he went for a long ride. After that, his patience and understanding improved. He brushed and fed all the horses and mules, then set up a tent for Mele and another for himself while Enoch set up one for him and me to sleep in. He reached into his pack and tossed Mele a small jar.

She looked at him with a questioning stare.

"It is for your sore legs. It will help heal them."

"Oh. Oh!" Mele said and slipped into her tent to apply the ointment.

When she returned, she handed me the jar of ointment. "This feels wonderful on sore legs."

I nodded and disappeared into our tent, followed closely by Enoch. He watched as I lifted my robe and struggled to balance.

"Here, give it to me," he said.

"I can do it."

"Yes, you can, if you sit on the bed. Let me help." He held out his hand for the jar.

I stared at him a long moment, then handed it to him. I held up my robe while he gently applied the ointment to my inner thighs.

"Oh," I sighed. "That does feel good."

Enoch grined suggestively.

"Not now. Later. I have to help with dinner." I dropped my robe and bumped his leg with my crutch, giggling.

We left the tent to help with dinner. Enoch helped Noam gather wood and start a small fire while Mele and I gathered the ingredients for a simple meal. We did not want to draw attention to our presence. We wanted this to be a quiet trip.

The next day's ride was painful for Mele and me. Sometimes, we pulled our horses to a stop. I drug my crutch from behind my saddle and slid off the mare. I tucked the crutch beneath my arm and stretched my legs, resting my sore muscles. Walking helped to relieve the pain of sitting in the saddle. It helped when Mele joined me, suppressing her groans. By afternoon, the walking breaks were shorter and the riding lasted longer.

The next day, we rode all the way to Aenon. We escorted Mele to her parent's home, in the darkening evening. Enoch, Noam, and I went to Papa Jared and Mama Helsa's home for the night.

Early the next morning, I tucked my crutch under my arm, while Enoch balanced me on the other side and Noam paced beside me on the other side. I felt loved and special walking between my two men, with very little limp.

We walked to the home of Papa and Mama. We arrived as they were sitting at the table to break their morning fast. I knocked and waited.

Through the door, we heard Lilah grumbling. "Who would come visiting at this hour of the morning?"

The door opened a crack.

"Hello, Mama," I said. "We wanted to visit with you today."

Mama threw the door open and cried out, "Zehira! Enoch! Noam! Gavi, come quickly!"

She hugged me tighter than I could ever remember, then reached out to add Noam and Enoch to the embrace.

Papa hurried to the door at Mama's call. "What is it? Are you hurt?"

He saw the three of us standing at his door. "Oh, Zehira, Enoch, Noam! Come in! Come in!"

We all trooped into the house and toward the kitchen where Mama insisted we join them for the meal. When we were all seated, Mama had dishes set before everyone.

"Before we eat," Papa said with tears in his eyes, "I have to say this. We were just praying to Jehovah. For several weeks now, we have prayed you would come to visit us. We are too old to travel, now, and cannot come to visit you. We prayed this morning, and you knocked on our door."

"Papa." I grasped his hand in mine. "We knew we needed to visit and came as soon as we could. I even rode a horse so the journey would be shorter."

"I needed you to come," Mama said. She stopped to take a deep breath, exhaled and inhaled again. "Zehira, I must apologize for the way I treated you the last time you were here. I treated you like a child, a naughty child. You are a grown woman, a wife, and a mother of grown sons and daughters. I had no right to treat you as I did." She paused again to breathe. "I am sorry."

"Mama," I cried, falling to my knees to hug her. "I love you. I always will. I forgive you."

Noam sat quietly, his face red. Enoch sat watching with a silly grin on his face. I saw them both and knew Noam remembered the way I was treated before. I hoped he could forgive and love them, as I did. I said nothing, too happy to speak.

After eating, Enoch and Noam walked back to Papa Jared and Mama Helsa's for our horses and packs, leaving the mules in their animal pen. We stayed with Mama and Papa for most of the time we stayed in Aenon, remembering, telling stories, and working together.

Mele visited and looked younger than she had for a long time. Much of the fear and sorrow that ravaged her face had been stripped away as her parents gave her the love and attention she had missed for so many years.

One evening, Papa Jared arrived at Mama and Papa's home. His eyes were puffy and red, the skin of his face splotchy. I asked him to sit and called for Enoch.

"Papa, so good to see you," Enoch said. "What news?"

"We just received a message from Home Valley. Grandpapa Adam died two weeks ago. Grandmama Eve followed him home just two days later."

I remembered the ancient women I had grown to love in moments as we visited with them at the family conference. Grandmama Eve lived a good, long time, over nine centuries. No one knew for sure the length of her days, or of Grandpapa Adam's. They only counted after they left Eden. Our world would always be less for their loss.

Papa Jacob and Enoch stayed only a short time, then they left to discuss the responsibilities of High Priests, now Adam was gone. I saw loss in the eyes of both men who had lost their leader.

"I heard Jacob's news," Mama said after Jacob and Enoch left. "Our lives will never be the same, now they are gone."

"No, we lost our first parents." Tears flowed freely down my face.

"They showed their love to all they met." Mama sniffed back tears.

"Did you meet them?" I stared at Mama, surprised at the news.

Mama rolled her eyes up in thought. "Yes, long ago. She graciously accepted all who wanted to meet her. I watched her shake her hand by her side, then lift it up to greet me with a smile."

"She was like that with me when we went to the conference. Our world lost two great people."

The loss cast a pall of sadness over us during the last days of our visit. Our family returned to stay with Papa Jared and Mama Helsa a few days, staying the last night with Mama and Papa. The visit brought me great pleasure, sharing stories and building good memories for Noam, and for me. That last night, we sat late into the night, reminiscing and sharing.

Early the next morning, Noam brought our horses and mules, packed and ready to go, to Mama and Papa's front door. My parents escorted us to our horses. Before mounting, Mama and Papa gave each of us a long embrace. We all hoped this would not be the last time to be together, however, we knew anything was possible.

We stopped by Mele's parent's home for her. She came to the door, clearly not ready to travel.

"Mele," I said, "did you forget today is the day we are to return home?"

"No, I remember." Mele frowned. "Mama and Papa are pressuring me to stay here. They say I have hopes for another marriage if I stay here. Zehira, I am lonely. Hadar was cruel, but I need the company of a man."

"Did not Jehovah promise you the companionship of a good man if you are obedient?" Enoch said.

"He did. I know a good man will be found for me," she threw her hands in the air, "but will it be here in Aenon or in Zion?"

"What do you think, Mele?" he asked. "Remember, Jehovah loves his daughters, but he expects them to obey. Can you obey here in Aenon?"

She stood a long moment, thinking.

"You are right, Enoch. I am drawn away from obedience here. Please wait, I will be ready, soon."

With that, she turned and hurried into the house. We did not wait many finger spans of the sun's movement before Mele returned, dressed, packs prepared, and ready for travel. Her mama and papa followed her out the door, hanging onto her arms and begging her to stay.

"No, Mama, Papa," she said quietly. "I am needed in Zion. There, I have a purpose. There I am obedient. And, there, I will find a new husband who will love and respect me. I cannot take a chance on losing that opportunity. I love you, but I must return to Zion." She gave them each a long hug and mounted her gray mare.

We urged our horses down the streets of Aenon and down the track back to Zion.

CHAPTER THIRTY-ONE

Love

O n our return home, we learned that during our journey Grace found a young man to love her, an honorable man, willing to obey Jehovah and live in Zion. Jonah's tall body had stooped and bent, causing him to appear significantly shorter. Some illness in his youth caused his back to twist, but he had a beautiful spirit. Jonah treated Grace with kindness and respect. All could see his obvious love for her.

Before we had unpacked and returned our horses to the corrals, Grace introduced Jonah to us. Jonah dragged Enoch away to visit with him. Of course, Enoch gave his approval, knowing him from before we traveled to Aenon.

"I am not surprised by this," Enoch told me as we took our packs into the house. "I watched Jonah before we left. He had eyes only for Grace. She finally noticed him."

"She has finally received the blessing promised by Jehovah, a good man to love her." I dropped my pack on the floor in our room.

"We will have another wedding in the family soon. She will not wait long." He dropped his pack by mine.

Our banter about the news brought us closer together in the knowledge Grace would soon be married.

Grace and Jonah looked beautiful at their wedding in the tabernacle two weeks later. Many of the young men and women of her age loved Grace, as did many of the citizens of Zion. They packed into the tabernacle to support her. I watched Grace glow from the love she felt for Jonah. Her smile could not be erased.

Many of Grace's friends helped with the celebration, providing cakes and other sweet treats for those who joined in congratulating the newly married couple. That night, Grace and Jonah made their way to their new home, not many streets from ours.

Only Noam lived as a child in our home after that. He was often gone helping with the animals. He worked to keep them healthy, choosing first born, unblemished rams, he-goats, or bulls to be sacrificed on the days of sacrifice. He helped Enoch in the temple and his training in the temple advanced. I saw that it would not be long before he, too, would find a young woman to marry and leave our home. Then, we would be alone together, as we were at the beginning of our marriage.

It did not surprise me to see Noam helping Penina carry baskets of vegetables or pull carts filled with jars of grains to her home. I remembered him coming home from play as a smaller boy, chattering about this little girl, Penina, who 'throws a ball like a boy,' or 'who loves the animals like I do,' or 'who is so beautiful.'

During the grain harvest that year, I joined the workers threshing wheat on the threshing floor, near the edge of the city. Oxen had already been led through the wheat, breaking away the stalks. I watched Noam, his strong arms bulging as he used the larger winnowing fans to lift the stalks and throw them to the wind.

I watched the wind blow away the chaff, dirt, and all the unusable portions, leaving piles of wheat on the rocky floor. When the men had winnowed away as much as would blow away, I joined the other women, scooping up the piles of wheat and shaking them through large sieves. Penina joined me, scooping the wheat into the big sieve. They shook the wheat through the small opening in the bottom into large baskets, then poured the dirt into other large baskets.

Noam joined us and replaced the basket with an empty one, lifting the full basket of wheat into a cart. Before he pulled it away, he gave Penina a quick kiss on the cheek.

"Do you mind Noam kissing me?" Penina asked in a low voice, peeking at me from beneath her wide-brimmed hat.

"Do you mind that I see?" I smiled at the girl.

She shook her head and giggled.

"No, I have expected this for some time. Noam has come home filled with praises of you since he met you, shortly after we moved here to Zion when you were both very young."

Penina reddened and glanced away.

"If you decide to join our family, it will bring joy to us." I gave the sieve a big shake.

Penina grabbed the sieve tighter. "If Noam asks me, it will be wonderful to be part of your family."

"He has not asked you yet?" I glanced at the girl beside me, who shook her head. "Silly boy. It will come."

"I can wait until it is ready. He is a good man." She glanced up into my eyes. "I love him."

Noam returned many times, that day, to bring us empty baskets, each time kissing Penina on the cheek.

I just smiled.

Over the next days, as we cleaned the wheat and poured it into the jars to await use by the citizens of Zion, Penina and I talked, learning about each other. I learned to love this beautiful girl.

"Penina is a lovely girl," I said one evening at dinner.

"She is, Mama, Papa," Noam said. "I love her. I want to marry her."

"Of course, you do." Enoch leaned forward, resting on his forearms on the table. "I have watched the two of you together. It is obvious to all of us. We have waited for this."

"Have you asked her yet?" I leaned toward him, my head on my hand.

Noam blushed. "I fear she will not accept me."

"Not accept you? The two of you have been close since you came to Zion. Even I, your papa, have seen it." Enoch stared at our son.

"She is waiting for you," I added. "She is ready for you to ask."

"Really, Mama?" Noam dropped his spoon into his plate. "She is waiting for me to ask?"

I nodded. "She told me the other day early as we cleaned the wheat together."

Noam pushed his chair back from the table and stood. "Thank you, Mama. I will be back later. I am going there now." He rushed out of the house.

Enoch turned to me and smiled. "He reminds me of myself when I was a young man in love."

"Did you leave your meal on the table and rush out of the house when you decided to ask me to marry you?" I said with a chuckle.

"No. I was not home. I was in the wilderness. Jehovah had called me and told me to speak with Grandpapa Adam. After our meeting, I traveled toward home, thinking about Grandpapa's direction that I should be married. Who would I marry? It seemed a simple decision. You were always the one for me. I hurried home to Aenon and went looking for you. I had no thoughts that you would not marry me or that your papa would refuse."

"I remember the day you found me. I was on the road. Hadar and his friends were taunting me, as usual. You scattered them, shouting and swinging your staff. I was so grateful to see you then."

"You were stooped in the dust, but showed no fear nor tears. Hadar always wanted to see how many tears he could draw from the 'weak women' he liked to bully." Enoch brushed the hair back from my face. "He never could understand why you did not cry."

I barked a short laugh. "I did cry, but I learned long before him to keep my tears hidden. I keep them from falling out the front of my eyes, I swallow them."

"I have watched you get red, and thought you would cry, and yet, no tears fell. Now, I know your secret!" he teased.

"Now you know. I cannot hide my tears from you anymore," I sighed. "I was so surprised when you asked me to marry you. I never expected any man to want a weak, crippled girl as his wife, especially not you."

"You were never weak. How could I not want you?"

"I have loved you since that day you and Hadar came to get water. Do you remember? You acted like it was no problem for you to bring water to your mama, even though everyone knows carrying water is women's work. I loved you that day."

"And I loved you even earlier than that. I watched you in the rain one day. Your sister wanted you to carry the jug of milk home. It was too heavy for you, especially with your crutch, but you did it anyway. You tucked your crutch under one arm, the jug of milk under the other, and carried it home. I loved your strength of will. I think that is what made me decide to ask you to marry me." Enoch leaned close and kissed me.

"I cried, tears and all, when Papa said he would not allow me to marry you without a bride price. I was grateful when you came and took me away."

"Life has not always been easy for us. I have been required to leave you behind far too often."

I set my knife and spoon across my plate and leaned forward. "But, it has always been to teach and do the will of Jehovah. I survived. And I grew stronger on my own than I ever would have watched and protected by you." I rubbed the back of Enoch's hand.

"See, you have always been strong. That is why I have always loved you."

CHAPTER THIRTY-TWO

Teachers

Penina and her mama and papa agreed to her marriage to Noam. No bride price was demanded. That custom had never become a part of life in Zion. Once again, the tabernacle filled to capacity for the ceremony and the party afterward. I gladly made lemon and poppy seed cakes to share. Penina's friends baked treats to share with the crowds, as well. Everyone enjoyed the singing and dancing that always accompanied wedding parties.

After the party, Noam and Penina moved into a house not far from ours. Enoch and I thought the house would become too quiet, with all the children moved out with families of their own. However, they visited often, bringing our grandchildren with them. Tobiah and Sari had several children who loved to visit their grandmama and grandpapa. I loved to bake them cookies, cakes, and other sweets, and tell them stories.

Sari often teased me. "You give them too much. They will be as spoiled as those tomatoes you forgot to pick.

"And children are made to spoil," I retorted. "I love them and they love me. I want them to remember their grandmama as someone who loves them, not like Tobiah thinks of my mama."

Sari's cheeks reddened. "He has told me of her. He remembers her as a 'mean old woman, who wanted him to work for her.'"

"Exactly. My grand babies will not think of me in this way."

Grace and Jonah soon had nearly as many children as Tobiah and Sari, while Noam and Penina were not far behind in bringing children into the family. I loved to have them all over on days when their parents were busy helping in a warehouse or with the harvest, or just needed a night alone.

I loved teaching children. There were so many children in Zion I accepted a group who came over three mornings a week for lessons in reading and numbers. Each of the grandchildren, and then some of their children were in my classes.

I used flat boards and sticks the children dipped in water and ashes from the fire to write the letters, words, and number problems I taught them. They wrote short stories and read them to me. Sometimes, I asked for a few sheets of velum, a pen, and ink from the storehouse. These, I gave to the older students, for them to copy an especially nice story. I sometimes asked for a second copy for me to keep. I cherished the stories those children wrote. Some of them I used to help the younger ones learn to read.

As the children became better in the skill of reading, I brought out the copies of Grandpa Adam's Book of Remembrance and allow them to read from them. Sometimes, they would be allowed to copy pages for themselves, so they would have pages to read at home and remember the things their first parents had learned and done.

Enoch continued to travel and preach to all who would listen. Sometimes, Noam would join him, other times, another young man traveled with him. Less frequently, he would travel alone. He always called on those he taught to repent and he always taught the word of Jehovah.

"Zehira," he said as I unpacked his bag from his recent journey, "these people seem to desire the truth, but most often, they just want to hear or see something new. It happened again this trip."

"What did?" I poured him a cool cup of apple juice.

"Men of means, owners of flocks and herds, heard of my preaching and left their animals with their servants so they could come to me. They sat at my feet listening to the words of Jehovah, almost believing." He shook his head. "Then, at the end of the day, they returned to their animals. They choose to turn their backs on the truth, preferring their flocks and herds to the ways of the Lord."

"The Destroyer has a tight grip on their hearts. They listen, they almost believe, but he calls them back, determined not to lose any souls." I had seen it when I traveled with him. I saw it with my own Mama and Papa.

"I see it worse every time I leave Zion," Enoch said, bowing his head. "Many years ago, a man named Mahijah came to me, asking who I am, and from where I came."

"What did you tell him?" I sat across from him in our sleeping room.

"I told him and those with him plainly that I came from the Land of Cainan, the land of my fathers, which is a land of righteousness. My father taught me all the ways of God. I told him the Lord commanded me to speak to the people of Earth, and call them to repentance." He leaned forward. "Many more things I told him about the things of God. Zehira, they trembled and could not stand! They feared me, for the Spirit of God was within me."

I moved behind him to massage his shoulders. "And what did you do because of that?"

"I taught them of the fall of Grandpapa Adam and the coming of Satan among the children of men. I called on them to repent and be baptized. Some did. Some of those seekers of truth found us here in Zion." He sighed and shrugged his shoulders.

"But what of this Mahijah? I have not seen nor heard of a man with that name here in Zion?"

Enoch dropped his head, I felt his grief in the shoulders I massaged. "He believed. When it was time to choose to obey or live as he had always lived, he could not give up his wealth and position in his city. I watched him walk away with many of his followers, head bowed. I never saw him again."

"Some men are more willing to accept the cause of Jehovah. You have taught many. Your success is greater than other High Priests who have preached repentance." I moved down to the muscles on his back.

"Ah. That feels nice. I do not boast in my successes. So many I teach choose to follow the will of the Destroyer. The wars and battles between them increase among those who refuse to listen. The Destroyer has too great a hold on their minds and hearts."

I gave him a final tap and sat next to him. "What will you do?"

"Jehovah spoke with me during this journey, calling me to the top of Mount Simeon." Enoch fell silent.

I could almost hear him thinking. I sat quietly, waiting for him to continue.

"Zion is a holy city and the Lord has blessed us, but many of the rest of those on the earth are cursed. There will come a time when all men are wicked and the earth will be washed clean of the wicked. He showed me all the men who will live on the earth. When he showed me the wicked, He wept."

I stared at him. "Why would our God weep?"

"I asked him the same thing. He wept for His creations who would not choose their Father, those who are without affection." Enoch paused, tears falling from his eyes at the memory.

"I saw a grandson of Methuselah who will build an ark and preserve life on earth. There will be but eight people on the ark, protected by the hand of the Lord. Only those on the ark will be preserved. Everyone else, everything else, on the earth will be washed away. The earth will finally be cleansed from their wickedness." He took my hand in his, squeezing it.

I put my hand over his, gently attempting to loosen his grasp. "What of Zion? Will Zion also be washed form the earth?"

"Oh, I am sorry." Enoch loosened his grasp, though he continued to hold it. "Zion is an Holy City and is blessed. In due time, it shall be taken to Him, in the heavens to protect our people from the wickedness of the earth. I suspect this will happen when we have gathered all to Zion who will come."

I sighed. "And Methuselah and our other children? Will they be allowed entrance to Zion?"

"Not Methuselah. He knows of the cleansing, and has been filled with pride that it will be his grandson who preserves humanity. For this sin, he has been denied the privilege of entering Zion permanently. He can visit, but not stay. Besides, his Priesthood will be needed after we leave."

"And our other grandparents? What of Papa Jared and Mama Helsa and all the others? Will they be swept away in the cleansing?"

"The time is not yet set for the cleansing. I only know it will occur. The good people who love Jehovah, our parents and grandparents, will live their lives before the cleansing happens. It will not come the day after we leave. Father and Jehovah will allow the people of this earth to all become fully wicked before then. He will not destroy good people who love him." Enoch pulled me close.

I stared at him. "Do you know when Zion will be taken? Will we have the time to visit our parents again? Visit with Methuselah and our other children? Can we gather Methuselah and the others to Zion?"

"Methuselah can visit, remember? He cannot stay. As to our other children, it is their choice. I do not know if we will have time to visit our parents one more time. We will be given warning to return to the safety of Zion if we leave, but it is safest if we, if you, stay within its walls."

I considered the significance of the news. "Are we to be locked in?"

"Not yet, but it is dangerous out there. The sons of men fight against the sons of God. Word has come that the giants even fight against us, now. Even as we speak, a great army advances toward Zion, intent on our destruction."

My heart dropped. "Would Jehovah allow that? You said we are safe here."

"They will not be able to even attack our walls. Jehovah will protect us."

I leaned close, enjoying Enoch's presence, thinking of all he told me, fearful for my loved ones who lived far away, who would not or could not come to Zion. Among them were our disobedient children and Methuselah, whose mission led him away from life in Zion. Tears leaked past my eyelids.

CHAPTER THIRTY-THREE

Army

It did not take long for the news of the coming army to be known by all of Zion residents. It swept through the city as on a wind of fear. Enoch called us all together to meet in the forty-six tabernacles throughout the city, meeting for a short time with those who met to worship in each tabernacle. He called on us to fast, to give up food and drink during the day, for the next three days. During this time, we were to pray, alone and in our families. We were to pray for protection from the army.

On the third day, we gathered together in the center of the city, filling the square. The numbers of residents had grown so large, many spilled down the streets leading to the square. Enoch led us in prayer, begging Jehovah for protection.

"They come!" James reported as the prayers ended. "We see the dust of many feet along the edge of the hills. They will arrive today."

"Thank you, James." Enoch turned to the crowd. "Thank you for your prayers. I will seek the will of the Lord. Please continue to pray."

He left us. I knew he planned to beseech Jehovah from the privacy within his study in our home. I continued to kneel in silent prayer with the other citizens of Zion.

"I implore a blessing at thy hand," I prayed. "Give Enoch the answer to our need. Bless him to do the right thing to protect our city."

After many long moments, the sun moved almost a hand span across the sky when I saw Enoch leave our home. I followed him. He saw me following and directed me up the wooden stairs along the wall where I could watch. James let him out of a side, walking gate while I negotiated the wooden stairs, wondering why there was no handrail to support me. I clung to the wall, using my crutch on the other side, slowly and painfully lifting myself up the stairs.

"Eighteen, nineteen, twenty," I counted, then looked up. "How many stairs are there? Not so many more. Twenty-one, twenty-two, twenty-three." I counted and climbed the stairs. At thirty, I finally arrived at the top and moved along the walk below the top of the wall.

I peeked over the edge to watch. An enormous army massed outside our gates, many thousands strong of noisy men on foot, and thousands more behind them on horses, screaming obscenities and hatred. Great war machines were pulled behind oxen. I had heard of these, though I had never seen them. They threw boulders to break through walls. Often, they missed the wall and flew over it, injuring and killing those within the walls. In all this, I had no fear of the army.

"These men thirst for our blood," I said.

"They want to destroy our city," Joam answered.

In my desperation to see the army, to see what Enoch would do, and because of the noise of all the men in the army, I did not hear him follow me up the stairs.

"We will be safe. Enoch is the servant of the Lord and He will not allow these men to harm us." Joam shouted over the noise of the army as he faced out toward them.

"Nor will he allow Enoch to be injured." I, too, shouted to be heard above the noise and bounced on my toes to see better.

We stood together, watching in silence as the massive army surged closer and closer. At last, Enoch raised his hands. The marching men at the front slowed. Those behind them stumbled against them. The mass of men faltered and came to a stop. The great noise of the massed men quieted, waiting to see what Enoch would do.

Some of these had seen him stand like this, with his hands raised before an armed camp. I had seen it, too. It had never ended well for the attackers.

The leader of the army pushed himself to the front of the army, past the men who struggled upright after losing their balance from the stumbling men behind them. The leader stood staring at Enoch. At last, he shouted, "You have no hope. Our numbers are greater than yours. We will overwhelm you. Surrender yourself and your city, or you will all be destroyed."

"Repent of your sinful ways," Enoch answered in a voice set to be heard all the way to the back of the mass of men, "or the Lord, your God, will destroy you and all your men. Leave our city, now, and never return. I will give you the span of one hand as the sun moves."

"And I will give you the same span to surrender. At the end of that time, I will unleash my army."

"Do you think he will really wait that long?" I whispered.

"No. Beesus never waits," Joam said.

"You have seen him in battle? How do you know this man who leads this army?" I turned my head to stare at Joam.

Joam spat over the height of the wall. "I know his battle pennant. I stood across from his armies before, beside Enoch. Beesus never honors his word. His honor is as dust."

"Does Enoch know who it is he faces and his lack of honor? Will he still be safe?" I peeked over the wall once more to see what Enoch and this Beesus were doing.

Enoch stood calmly facing the army. I could see him murmuring and knew he conversed with Jehovah. In the distance, I saw the army loading great boulders onto the baskets of the war machines, preparing to hurl them at us.

I nudged Joam. "Do you see? They prepare to send boulders at our walls. Does Enoch see?"

"I am here as his lookout. He will know."

Joam turned and signaled to a young man below us. He turned and ran through the door next to the gate and spoke to

Enoch. Enoch asked a question, nodded, and said something else. The young man ran back through the door and closed and locked it.

"Watch," Joam said, pointing to the army.

Enoch raised his hands again. I heard Beesus scream, "Now!"

All action seemed to slow. I saw the baskets bend toward the earth and slowly rise into the air. The boulders lifted from the baskets. The muffled voices of the men rose to a roar. Joam stared around, then pointed to Mount Jershon, northeast of Zion, forming one side of the pass leading to Home Valley. The mountain seemed to tear itself from its roots, rising in the air.

I glanced back at the army. Boulders arched above the army, floating toward Zion's walls. Turning my eyes back toward the mountain, I stared as it moved toward the army, gaining speed as it tore itself free from the earth beneath.

I tore my eyes from the mountain, turning them back toward the army. The boulders arced above the center of the army, drawing nearer to us. Men in the army heard the roar approaching, louder than the boulders that flew above them. Some glanced in the direction of the greater noise. These, who first saw the mountain flying toward them, jabbed their neighbors and pointed. Almost as one, they turned and froze in fascinated horror.

The mountain hovered for a moment above the army as the boulders reached the front ranks. I wondered momentarily if the boulders would escape the mountain. Then, as though all supports were kicked away, the mountain dropped, gathering the boulders into its face.

Men of the army stood frozen as the mountain fell, crushing them with a deafening rumble. Some of the men near the edges ran toward Zion in an attempt to escape, but an avalanche roared down the sides, crushing and burying any who managed to avoid the bulk of the mountain. I watched as the rock slide nearest the city roared toward the walls and Enoch, who stood still, his arms raised, seemingly unaware of the danger.

I willed for him to move, but knew the sound of the rushing rocks would overwhelm my voice. Rolling and crashing, the rocks, dirt, and dust clouds rushed toward Enoch and Zion. A scream tore itself from my throat. Everything piled up and stopped, as though a wall stood between the rock slide and the city wall, leaving a clear space the distance of a wide road leading away from Zion's walls.

CHAPTER THIRTY-FOUR

Understanding

A cheer rose from all around. I turned to discover hundreds of men on the walls beside me. In my fear, I did not sense the movement of all these men moving along the wall to join me. Their presence and cheering surprised me. I glanced to where Enoch stood and saw him drop his hands and slump his head and shoulders.

Enoch turned toward Zion and raised his arms once more. The cheering ended as abruptly as it began, with only one or two young ones who missed the signal to silence the cheers, and these cheered into the silence, then stuttered to quiet, embarrassed.

"We cannot cheer the loss of so many of Jehovah's children. Hundreds of thousands of men lost their lives here today. It could easily have been the people of Zion whose lives were taken."

Enoch fell to his knees and lifted his arms above his head. "Oh, Jehovah, my Lord and my God," he prayed, "hear our prayer."

All around me on the path of the wall, and on the ground below, citizens of Zion bowed down.

"We offer gratitude unto thee for this great miracle, that thou hast protected our city, our wives, our children, our old men and women, our young men and women, and our own lives. We thank thee that none in Zion were hurt, none lost to the invasion of this man, Beesus, and his army."

The men beside me, kneeling beside the wall listened silently to Enoch's prayer. Everyone in the city listened to his prayer. I realized his voice carried over the wall and into the depth and extent of our huge city. And everyone within understood we had been saved.

Enoch continued, "We ask a blessing upon all the families of the men whose lives were taken today, upon those innocent wives and children, mamas and papas who lost sons and papas today. Many are innocent. Many of these men were drafted into this great army against their will. Some were slaves with no choice but to fight for Beesus."

I heard a stirring as the men around me shifted. I understood their mood. Who would think those in an army, who shouted such awful curses, would be there against their will?

"And Father," Enoch went on. "We know these men were caught up in a society whose aim is the destruction of thy kingdom. Their leaders urged upon them the anger and hatred that led them to find themselves fighting against thee and thy

Holy City of Zion. We sorrow for their loss. We cry for their souls. And we beg that thou wilt, at some time in thy plan, teach them thy laws and enable them to be freed from the prison of sin, that those who would follow thee, under other circumstances, be given the opportunity, at some day in the future and at thy will."

Murmurs and whispers flitted through the great crowd. "Forgiveness? For men who planned to destroy us? "Blessings for those who listen to the Destroyer?"

I understood the murmurs, but I also understood the great love Enoch held for all life, for all men and women on this earth, children of our God.

"Help these, my brothers and sisters, to find the charity within their souls to forgive their enemies. Bless them with an understanding of the pain and sorrows of their enemy's loved ones. Forgive our need to cause such death and destruction upon so many of thy children, I pray."

I understood his grief, heard his sorrow. His responsibility for the deaths of so many men was an awful load to carry. I stood, tucked my crutch tightly under my arm, and made my way carefully down the stairs. I needed to get to Enoch's side. His load was immense. I felt a compelling need to help him carry that load.

As I made my way down the open stair, I slipped once and was caught by arms behind me. Joam followed and managed to catch me before I fell.

"This stair needs a railing to protect us from falling," he said, holding me under my arms and balancing me. "When we built the wall, we never expected to need armed protectors to line the upper wall. We did not think to provide a stair railing, thinking only young men would run up and down them. I will ensure your safe return to the bottom before I locate carpenters to remedy this mistake."

I nodded my thanks and focused on each step, not wanting to fall or cause Joam to fall. It seemed many spans of time before I arrived safely on the ground again, though I knew it had been only moments.

I turned to thank Joam for his assistance, but he had left already. I saw his back as he hurried toward the carpenter shops. I shrugged and limped toward the door beside the gate.

As I reached the door, a young man unlocked and opened the door. I recognized him to be the same young man who carried Joam's message to Enoch. He solemnly nodded to me as he opened the way for me. I returned his nod in thanks to him and hobbled as quickly as possible toward my husband.

Enoch continued to kneel on the earth, tears flowed in rivulets down his cheeks and neck onto his robe. I reached out to him, cradling his head against my breasts. I held him close. In his hour of triumph, so miraculously saving the city of Zion, his reaction was not one of pride or power, but one of sorrow that so many men were lost, that he was responsible for their deaths. He threw his arms about my waist and silently sobbed. I stood quietly and gently rocking him until his sobs stilled.

"You have much pain," I whispered. "You have been required to cause pain to the children of Jehovah. Your love is great, your compassion large. It grieves you that these wicked men would attempt to destroy our beautiful city."

I felt his head nod against my body.

"I understand. I am here to help carry your load. This is my purpose as your wife and companion, to support you, to help carry your load."

Enoch could find no words to speak. I understood. I knelt beside him and brought him close. We embraced until he regained control of his emotions. He then stood and helped me up. I tucked my crutch beneath my arm and he tucked me under his arm. Together, we returned through the gate that now stood open to welcome us.

People lined the streets, silently watching, quietly approving of their leader and me, his wife, as we moved slowly into the city until we reached the door to our home and went inside. I heard the shuffle of the crowd as they returned to their homes, still not speaking or cheering. Only moving in somber silence.

CHAPTER THIRTY-FIVE

Trust

After that day, Enoch and I were closer than we had ever been. Little needed to be said about the experience, but Enoch shared more of his experiences with me, more often. He gave me more of his time, along with other simple, little things that drew us close. Enoch expressed his appreciation that someone understood his heartache and pain when lives were lost, even when those who lost their lives were evil men who tried to take his life.

One day, as we walked in our garden, I asked, "I understand your pain, but did something cause you to be so aware of the lives of all men?"

"Yes, there was an experience." He pulled me onto a bench among the roses. "Do you remember when I returned from Mt. Simeon?"

"Yes. You were told the earth would be washed clean, and Jehovah wept."

"Do you remember why He wept?"

I glanced around me at the beautiful flowers, remembering that conversation. "His children choose to be disobedient."

"Yes. And that disobedience will cause our earth to be washed clean. All our sons and daughters, and those of our first parents, will be washed away leaving only eight to begin the human family anew."

Tears slipped from my eyes as I remembered.

Enoch took my hands in his and gazed into my eyes. "If Jehovah loves all His children and wants them to return to his presence, and I want to be like him, then I love all His children. It hurts me to see His children make choices that destroy their lives, whether they lose their spiritual or physical lives. It hurts me."

I want to live with Him again. Do I love all his children? Even Lucas? Even Hadar? I searched my soul. *Yes, I love, even those men who hurt women I love. I sorrow for the losses of those men, that they listened to the Destroyer. Yes, I love all Jehovah's children.*

We sat together, thinking of all the men and women who had to follow the Destroyer, tears leaking from our eyes. I now understood my sweet husband's great sorrow. "So many lost, so many gone! Do they not realize the Destroyer cannot win against Jehovah?"

Enoch pulled me close to him. "You know the answer to that. Why do they fight against us, against Jehovah?"

I thought a long moment before I answered. "They listen to the Destroyer, who always fights against Jehovah. He wanted the place of importance in the lives of people and lost it in the war in Heaven. Now, he continues the war, using men and women as his weapons."

"Right," Enoch said. "I could not have said it better. Lucifer will fight as long as there are people on earth who listen to him. He has little or no power here in Zion, for we refuse to listen to his lies. Out there, though," he waved his hand broadly in a half circle, "out there, men listen and he believes he will win. He may win this battle, and others, but Lucifer will never win the war."

"I am so grateful for Father's love for me. I never want to listen to the Destroyer."

"You know, do you not, that you listened for a time."

"Me? I never listened to the Destroyer? How? When?"

"You are a good woman, but when you complain that you are worthless or a cripple, your words support Lucifer. Even when you look at Grace and our other daughters, wishing you could be as tall and lithe as they are. He cheers, thinking he has started you along the path to destruction. I have not heard those words for many months, even years, now. I believe you have overcome, have won this battle, without losing any lives."

His arm pulled me tight against him as he allowed me to think about his words. For a time, my face contorted as I considered the truth of his words.

"I have accepted my twisted foot. It is a part of me, as is my crutch. I can accomplish things here in Zion. No one notices when I walk slower, none taunt my crutch. It is as though my twisted foot and crutch are unseen. There is no more reason to wish I could be more like my daughters. I am comfortable with my foot."

"They are, almost, for people here see you for the beautiful, caring, helpful woman you are. The crutch and foot are you. It makes no difference to them, for you do your share to help. You are there in an emergency. You show love to those around you. You do not bring attention to your foot by complaining or trying to avoid work. Why should they notice it when you have so many other wonderful qualities?"

I nodded and gazed into Enoch's eyes. I saw the truth in them and felt the truth in my soul. I smiled and embraced my good husband.

Our lives together became sweeter, as we grew closer in love for each other and for our God.

Shortly after our conversation, Mele came to visit, a smile like I had not seen since we were children stealing time at the stream together, creasing her face. We welcomed her into our back garden, among the fragrant blooms of the roses, lilacs, amaryllis, jasmine, mignonette, and other flowers. We inhaled their beauty and their fragrance as the sun descended toward night.

Mele stopped to inhale the fragrance before she sat on a bench across from where Enoch and I sat.

"I cannot wait another moment to tell you my news." Her eyes sparkled as she struggled to contain her bouncing excitement. She smoothed her robe. "It has finally happened. You can never guess."

I leaned forward, enjoying this friend who I had not seen so joyful in many years. "No, Mele. I cannot guess. What happened?"

"Do you remember Ashram, the tall, blond man who came to Zion a few months back?"

I nodded, searching my memory for a man who fit the description. Many tall blond men had entered Zion in the recent months.

"Ashram, from Shulon?" Enoch asked. "Is that the one you mean?"

"Yes, Enoch, it is."

"With a little scar near his eye?" I asked. The correct tall, blond man clicked into my memory. "What about him?"

Mele leaned forward and giggled, reminding me once more of the young girl who was my friend so many years ago. "He asked me to marry him."

"And you said?" Enoch raised his eyebrows.

"I would think about it and tell him tonight." She crossed and uncrossed her legs and leaned back on the bench. "I have not felt this way in … ever. I thought I loved Hadar, but even he did not make me feel this … giddy! Ashram treats me with such kindness. He never demands from me, it is always a request. He carries wood for my fire with only a nod. He makes my insides melt."

"That sounds good to me," I said, leaning toward Enoch.

"Tell me of his love of Jehovah." Enoch pulled me close. "Will he be one who can stay here in Zion? One who can follow our laws and commandments?"

He sat still, gazing into Mele's eyes as she contemplated his questions.

At last, she answered. "He has joined us in all the harvesting and preservation. He works with the animals, who love him. Horses and oxen come to him when they see him. He always has a carrot or an apple in his deep pockets to give them. He is a kind and gentle man."

"But, his love of Jehovah? Will he be happy with you here in Zion?" Enoch gently prodded.

"I have watched him during our Sabbath worship, wondering the same thing. His expression is one of awe and wonder. He speaks to me of sacred things, shares experiences coming from his obedience. Can that be a lie? I no longer know, for sure, how to tell by myself." She covered her face with her hands. "Enoch, Zehira, I need your help in this. I do not know."

I glanced at Enoch, who shook his head.

He leaned forward and set his hand on Mele's arm. When she dropped her hands from her face, he spoke. "Mele, dear sister. This is yours to decide. I can give you my opinion, but you must learn to trust. You must learn to trust the Spirit of the Lord, and seek for answers from Jehovah. Have you gone to Him? Have you sought your answer in prayer?"

Mele stared at Enoch. "I thought you, as the prophet, could answer my questions, could tell me if this is right."

"And if it is not, would you believe me? And, if I agreed, and told you Ashram was right for you, and later, you argue and fight. Would you blame your arguments on me? No, in this, I cannot offer my opinion. You must place your trust in Jehovah. Pray to him. Seek his will. It will be given to you. Remember the night before Hadar left Zion?"

Mele slowly nodded.

"Jehovah spoke to you in your dreams. Do you remember what he told you?"

A light filled Mele. "He promised me that He loves his daughters and that a good man would come into my life. That is why I am in Zion. I love Jehovah and trust His words. How am I to know if Ashram is that good man?"

"Seek the answer in prayer. Perhaps you and Ashram could pray together. Jehovah will give you the answer."

Mele dropped her hands to her lap. "And how will I know the answer? Will He come to me in another dream?"

"You have been taught this. The answer can come in many ways, a still, small voice or a burning in your bosom, a forgetfulness, or a warm, happiness. All signify answers. You will receive yours as you trust in Him."

Mele stared at Enoch in silence, then turned her gaze toward me. "Is he right? Will I receive my answer?"

"Yes, Mele, you will. I have received answers in this way many times. Trust in Jehovah."

Mele stood, and we stood with her. She threw her arms around me for a long embrace, then gave Enoch a quick hug. "Thank you. I will ask."

As I escorted her to the door, her excitement had subdued, but I felt her joy layered beneath her calm.

"Jehovah will tell me Ashram is the right one."

"He will, but, if he is not? What will you do?"

"Shed many tears of sorrow, and wait for the right man to find me. He will, will he not?"

I pulled her close and hugged her. "Yes, dear friend, the right man will come. Trust in Jehovah."

She pulled away, a small smile on her face. "I hope it is Ashram. I like him."

I watched her walk down my path to the road. I hoped he was the right man for her.

CHAPTER THIRTY-SIX

Sham

Mele shared with me how she had spent long spans discussing her decision with Jehovah. She and Ashram sat together at parties and work. I saw them with their heads close together, as they walked down the street. Perhaps, Ashram was the man for her.

I joined Grace in the preservation of plums, which grew in her block, and we joined Sari in preserving dates. Their children ran back and forth, bringing us supplies or carrying prepared fruits to be placed in jars or the drying shelves. I always enjoyed my time working with the other women as we preserved fruit.

Enoch stayed busy, teaching and helping direct the affairs of Zion, though he left much of the leadership to others. He spent too many days traveling to be responsible for the day to day affairs of our big city.

Some days he returned to me joyfully bringing new families to be a part of our beloved city. Others, he buried his face in my breast as I held him close, and cried about the sins and ugliness of those who lived elsewhere in the world. Their depravity encroached on the few communities that still followed Jehovah. Even Home Valley struggled with sin, now that Grandpapa Adam and Grandmama Eve had returned to their home with Father.

One day, Mele visited me in my workroom, while I wove a new rug to share with one of the new families who was expected soon.

"Zehira, my good friend. Enoch, as always, is right."

I raised my eyebrows. "About?"

"Ashram."

"Ashram? Have you determined to at last marry him?" I pushed my shuttle between the threads on the loom.

Mele dropped into the extra chair in the room. "No. Much as I would love to marry the man, he is not the right man for me." A tear slipped from the corner of her eye.

"Oh? What happened? I thought you two were close." The shuttle passed the other direction, filling in the space and forming a beautiful pattern.

"He plans to leave Zion tomorrow. His piety has been a sham. He came here to entice me away. He planned to take me back to Hadar." Her voice dropped like my shuttle that fell to the floor.

"Hadar? Is he even alive?"

She lifted her gaze to reach my eyes. "He must be. Ashram changed these past few weeks. He no longer shares experiences he had with Jehovah. He insists that I prepare special meals for him. At first, I did it because I loved him. Then, his insistence increased, his desires became harsh. I tried to push away the memories of Hadar, but his actions soon mirrored some of Hadar's."

I bent to pick up my shuttle. "How did Ashram hide his wicked ways? How did he find Zion?"

"He attached himself to a group of honest seekers of truth. When Enoch invited them to visit Zion, he came. For many months, he managed to hide his true face. He found me, as directed by Hadar, and quietly worked to gain my trust."

"You seemed to be happy with him." My shuttle sped through the threads.

"I was, for a time. I prayed, as Enoch suggested, and no answer came. I waited for the answer, as I became closer to Ashram. His kindness soon slipped, and he began to demand little things, pushing me to agree to marry him."

"How have you managed to put him off so long?" I sighed at the thought of another Hadar in our midst.

"Although I agreed to consider marrying him, he would never pray with me. That was the first indication he was not the right man for me. His gentle prodding became pushing, and last night, he threatened me."

I dropped my hands into my lap. "He threatened you? With what?"

"He said if I did not marry him, he would tie me up and drag me out of the gates to Hadar." Tears now flowed freely down her cheeks.

"Drag you out the gates? Does he not understand? Men are at the gates, he could not drag you away without your consent."

"Apparently not. I taunted him and he slapped me, here." She touched her cheek.

I bent close to examine her cheek. A purple bruise, the shape of a hand was taking shape. "Do Enoch and Joam know about this?"

"They do. That is why Ashram will be leaving Zion tomorrow, instead of dragging me away today. He sits in the safe room, waiting for James and Benjamin to lead him out the gates tomorrow. If not, I would not be sitting here, comfortably sharing with you."

I leaned across the space between us, and hugged her. "Would you like to stay in our guest room tonight? It may feel safer."

"No, thank you. I am safe from him in my own home. Benjamin will once again stand guard while I wait for a dangerous man to be sent from the city. I wanted to be the one to tell you. I did not want you to hear from anyone else."

I sat back in my seat. "You will be safe, then?"

"I expect so. Ashram is in the safe room. It held Hadar, so it should hold him."

I sighed. "I suppose you will be safe, then. How are you feeling about all this?"

Mele's elbow rested on the arm of her chair, her hand cradled her chin. "Another bad choice. Oh, Zehira, how is it I always seem to choose men who want to use me. I want a man to love me, like Enoch loves you. What am I doing wrong?"

I shook my head. "I do not know. It looked like Ashram was a good man, one who would love you, and care for you. I could not see through his facade."

"Nor could I. My prayers were never answered, though when he refused to pray with me … It should have been a sign to me. I guess that was the answer, not Ashram. Maybe no man is for me." Her voice dropped.

I leaped from my chair to kneel by her and hug her. "No, that cannot be true. Jehovah told you there is a man for you. It takes trust and faith. You have faith enough to wait, do you not?"

"I do and I shall wait. Jehovah would not have told me there is a man for me if there is not one. No. I shall go home and wait to hear that Ashram is gone. Someday, soon, I hope, I will find the right man. Zehira, do you understand how blessed you are to have a man to love you?"

I bowed my head. "I know I am blessed. As I watch your struggle, I am reminded how blessed I am to have a man like Enoch love me."

Mele stood and helped me stand, then embraced me. "Do not forget that. Hold on to your good man."

She strode out the door toward her own home. I watched her firm step, impressed she could do so without tears.

CHAPTER THIRTY-SEVEN

Lucas Returns

Enoch left to teach two weeks after the men put Ashram out of the city. After the battle with Beesus at our front, east gate, travel to and from Zion through that gate became easier. The mountain across from the gate lifted almost straight up, kept strangers and enemies from sneaking up on the gate. Leaving the city from that gate became less dangerous.

Other gates, however, continued to be dangerous. Enemies lurked behind trees and rocks, waiting to attack those who traveled away from Zion. Occasionally, huge men, called giants, stood outside our walls, hurling insults, curses, and, sometimes, boulders toward us. Some managed to make it over the walls. Once, a boulder grazed a small boy playing near the west wall, trapping his leg beneath it. His injury kept him in bed many weeks. He still limps, but he is able to walk with the aid of a crutch his papa carved, much like mine.

Most often, now, men and women who left to visit others, left from the east gate. A few, however, who needed to travel in other directions, found it necessary to leave by gates on the other walls of the city.

Though Enoch trusted Jehovah's protection, when he left by any but the east gate, he always left early in the morning to avoid the threats waiting for him. For this trip, he slipped out the small door beside the south gate to travel toward the villages located south of Zion. After he left, I heard the giants shouting curses, calling for Enoch to come out to them. I breathed a sigh of relief. Enoch must have made it past them without their seeing him. I fell to my knees, praying for his safety.

Later that afternoon, Grace found me in my sitting room, reading. She gripped the edge of the blanket around Mattan, her youngest boy child as she sat beside me.

"Mama, did Papa leave safely this morning?"

I took the baby from her arms, gently tugging the blanket from her fist. "Yes. He slipped out before the giants began their shouting. Do you fear for him?"

Her chin quivered, her face blanched white. "I am not worried about Papa, not really. I know Jehovah will protect him. I hoped he postponed his journey."

"Why would you want that, Grace?" I cuddled little Mattan to my shoulder and patted his back.

"I hoped he would have a discussion with Lucas for me." She spoke in a soft, flat voice, nothing like my vibrant Grace.

"Lucas? I thought he had been sent permanently from Zion. How did he find his way here?" Little Mattan burped and I wiped his mouth.

Grace dropped her hands to her lap and pleated the front of her robe. "Apparently, he followed the giants to the west gate."

"That would explain how your papa missed him. He left through the south gate. He must have missed Lucas. What does he want?"

"Me. He says he came back for me." She stared at me with vacant eyes.

"Does he know you are happily married?" I bounced the baby against my shoulder.

"I told him that Jonah makes me happy. He mocked me. Asked how a cripple like him could make me happy." A tear slipped down her cheek. "Lucas tried to drag me away until Joam and Benjamin managed to tear us apart. I am amazed you did not hear me scream."

"I did hear something, but it was faint. Where is Lucas now?"

"He wanted to visit his mama. They escorted him there. Benjamin said he would stand guard outside. He has no family waiting for him." Grace shuddered. "Mama, what will I do if he comes looking for me again?"

"Does he know where your home is?"

She slowly shook her head. "I do not know. Mama, I am frightened."

I had not seen Grace frightened like this since, well, ever. She had been angry with her grandmama before we came to Zion, but never frightened. And Enoch was away.

I could leave Grace and Mattan here, but Lucas knows where I live. I cannot send her to Joam for help. He could find her on the streets.

"You say Benjamin is guarding his mama's home?"

She nodded.

"We will need to go together to find Joam and James. They can help us." I tucked the blankets around Mattan and picked my crutch up from beside my chair, using it to push up off the chair, while still holding onto the baby. "Can you manage Mattan? I need to be able to protect us with my crutch."

Grace took the babe from my arms, our hands touched. "Mama, should we say a prayer?"

I nodded and we clutched our hands together while I offered a short, but earnest prayer. Then, we strolled, with all the nonchalance we could manage, down the street toward Talia and Joam's house.

Grace held little Mattan close and looped her free arm through mine, helping to balance me. As we neared Talia's home, Lucas turned the corner.

"Grace!" he shouted.

"Do not respond. Keep walking," I hissed.

We hurried down Talia's walk as quickly as I could hobble. She opened her door and glanced toward the shouting

Lucas, who ran to catch up with us. Talia grabbed me by the arm with the crutch and helped to hurry us inside.

"Is Joam here?" Grace panted. "I need his help."

"Benjamin called him away. Lucas caused a ruckus at his mama's home. And now he is here, pounding on my door." Talia glanced around. "I know. Zehira, can you manage the walk to the orchards?"

I nodded, trying to pull air into my lungs. "I can … I can … do it. Can I get a drink on the way out?"

"Of course." As we passed through the kitchen, Talia grabbed a jug of water and handed it to me. "Take it with you."

We paused long enough for me to sip some cool water, then rushed out the back door, through the garden, and past the gates into the peach orchard.

"Go to the gate to Ana's yard. Her Nathan is home. He can help to protect you." Talia pushed us through the gate.

"But what about you?" I gasped. "How will you stay safe from Lucas?"

"He does not want to hurt me. I will be fine. Now, go, as fast as you can, but go." She pushed us through the gate.

Talia closed the gate behind us. I heard Lucas shout and groaned. "I hope she is safe."

We pushed through the trees, pausing only to sip from the jug of water, then Grace hurried ahead.

"Will Lucas know about this?" I cried.

"Talia told us she would keep him there. We have to trust her. Are you well, Mama? Here it is." Grace pushed open the gate to Ana's back garden.

Usually, no one entered the gardens of others through the orchard, except during harvest time. Ana and Nathan looked startled as Grace and I pushed through their gate, panting. Little Mattan whimpered.

"We are sorry Ana, Nathan, for disturbing the peace of your garden," I gasped. "It is an emergency. Somehow Lucas has returned, and he thinks he can take Grace away with him."

"Lucas?" Ana said. "I thought I saw him."

"I thought he went to his parent's home," Nathan said.

"He left and is now trying to find me. We left him at Talia's and came through the orchard to your garden. Can you help us, please?" Grace took the jug of water from me and guzzled some.

Ana took the babe from Grace's arms and helped us find seats in her garden among their beautiful flowers. Nathan left, telling us he would check the street outside. Ana strode to her back gate and brought the latch down to lock it, then went inside to get us refreshments.

We sat, regaining our breath and sighing in the beauty of her garden, planted in Jacaranda trees and pink crape. The fragrance and colors settled my mind.

Soon, Ana returned with a tray of tart lemon and lime drinks and sweet zucchini bread. She set it on the table in front of us, urging us to eat.

"You need to replenish your energy after your rush to get here. Nathan will look into your problem. No one else knows you are here. You will be safe."

We sat back in our chairs and enjoyed Ana's kindness. Though we sat back, I could see Grace did not relax any more than I did. Until I knew Lucas had been removed, either to a safe room or from the city, I could not relax. My fears for Grace's safety prevented relaxation.

Jonah came through the house to Ana's garden. Walls from the sides of the house to the walls surrounding the neighboring houses prevented entrance into the garden any other way.

Grace leaped from her seat and threw herself into his arms, tears falling onto his robe.

"Nathan told me you are here and why," he stated. "Did you not think to come home?"

"I thought of it, but Lucas would know where to find me, and you and the other children were at your mama's. I ran to Mama's for help."

Jonah nodded.

"We were there, but we came home, and you were gone. I am sorry you have had to face Lucas alone. No more. Finish your refreshment. Then we will go home." He sat beside her.

"But Lucas…" I said.

"Lucas is not a problem. I can handle him. If not, Nathan and Benjamin are outside. Between the three of us, I am certain we can handle one wicked man."

Grace breathed deeply and let it out in a sigh. "You are right. I should have gone home …"

"Not to worry about it. You are safe. I am here."

I remembered times when Enoch said those same words to me and felt a renewed sense of safety.

I ate the last bite of my bread and drank the last of my juice as Grace did. We set our cups on the tray, stood and brushed our robes off.

"Thank you for your hospitality, Ana. We appreciate your willingness to allow us to barge in with our fears." I gave her a hug.

She waved away my gratitude and escorted us to the front door, where she handed back little Mattan, who slept in her arms, to his mama. We walked outside to find Lucas standing between Benjamin and Nathan, cursing and raving that Grace should be his.

Grace walked to him with Jonah by her side. "I am not yours, nor will I ever be. Jonah is my husband. If you cannot find peace with that here in Zion, perhaps you should leave."

The couple walked away, leaving Lucas spluttering in disbelief. I left him to the men, who would resolve his problems, and walked home, as sedately as possible with a crutch supporting my movements.

CHAPTER THIRTY-EIGHT

Mele and Benjamin

The next morning, I woke tired. It had been an energy draining experience, running from Lucas. I went to bed early, though I slept fitfully, often waking from dreams of running. Zion should not require racing through the orchards for safety.

Mele and Benjamin visited early in the day to check on me. Their concern for my safety brought me to silent inner tears. I remembered the years of my early life when it seemed no one cared. And now, here in Zion, love and friendship were as much a part of the fabric of our lives as the yarns I wove into blankets.

"My muscles ache some, from running through the orchard, but I am fine, otherwise," I said.

"Things like this seem to happen when Enoch is gone." Mele plucked at the skirt of her robe. "I worry about you, alone so much."

"You worry about me? When you are alone all the time?" I gazed at her.

Benjamin moved a little closer to Mele and put his arm around her. "Not for much longer. Mele and I will be married when Enoch returns."

My stare danced between Mele and Benjamin. "You ... Benjamin and Mele, you will be married?"

She giggled at my confusion. "I can understand your confusion. But, since Ashram, the friendship between Benjamin and me has developed. He has always been there for me, after Hadar, after Ashram, quietly protecting me, supporting me. I finally opened my eyes to him. Benjamin is a good man." She turned and caressed his face. "I have looked everywhere else, when love waited outside my door."

The smile on my face nearly split it. "I am happy for you, Mele. For both of you." I grabbed their hands. "You both needed someone to love. Congratulations! There is no concern that Benjamin loves Jehovah."

Benjamin shook his head. "I love him more than I love Mele, and I love Mele so much it hurts. I never thought she would see me as someone to love. She is so beautiful."

"Oh, Benjamin. I just had to open my eyes to you. You are a handsome man. Your spirit shines through." Mele's eyes shone.

I left them to their coos and cuddles and found some grape juice and oatmeal cookies. When I returned with them on a tray, they had not moved much, still soaking in the love they shared.

"Mele, Benjamin, I know you will be as happy as Enoch and I are."

Many days later, Enoch returned from his journey, sore and tired from his travels and the efforts of trying not to hurt others. Enemies tracked him, seeking to end his life.

"Father aided me, let me know they were there. I climbed trees and waded through streams to lose them. They are becoming knowledgeable of my tactics. They think if they find me alone, they can kill me."

I hugged him to me, dirty as he was. "I pray Father will always protect you."

"He will, as long as I remember to obey. With him by my side, I am never alone." He dropped into his chair in our bedroom, too tired to remove his clothing.

After giving him time to rest in his chair, I filled the tub with hot water. Then, I helped him undress and into the tub. He lay soaking in the hot water, allowing the dirt and sorrows to wash away.

"Zehira, my dear, if I did not have you to return home to, I could not travel to teach Jehovah's word. You ground me, you are my strength. I love you."

"And I love you, my darling. Let me help you wash."

I soaped a cloth and washed him, then washed his hair. The water cooled and he stood up. Scratches and scrapes covered his body.

"You did have a struggle this time."

He sighed. "There were only three men, but they were persistent. They came close. I slid down a mountain, and still they followed. At last, I was forced to call upon the forces of nature to assist me."

"What did you do this time?" I wrapped him in a big towel.

His face fell. "I called upon Jehovah to send a storm, thinking a heavy rain would cause them to seek shelter. It did not. I crossed a stream, growing wider and faster from the storm. They followed me. A tree crashed down, landing on them, pinning the three men down. A flood raged down the stream. They drowned." Tears leaked from his eyes.

I wrapped my arms around him and led him to bed, where we took refuge in each other.

Only later, did I tell him of our flight from Lucas.

"Is he gone now?" Enoch asked.

"Yes. Joam, Benjamin, and Nathan took care of it. They took him out of Zion and told him never to return unless he truly repents. Jonah has been more watchful and loving with Grace. Their marriage is closer now than it was." I sighed.

He sat in a chair, watching me prepare our mid-day meal. "As is ours. I would have liked to have been here."

"The men of Zion handled it. You have your responsibilities, they have theirs. It gave them all greater self-respect, handling problems without you to take charge. Jonah, too." I turned to see him cradling his head in his hands.

I hugged him from behind.

"I should be here to protect my women."

"Yes, you would like to be, but you cannot always be. Jehovah needs you. And, Mele and Benjamin will need you in a day or two, as soon as they discover you are home."

"Mele and Benjamin? Why would they need me?"

"They waited for you to return to marry them." I returned to my cooking.

"Marry them? Benjamin and Mele?"

I smiled at his confusion. "Yes, silly. They have become friends with all the protecting Benjamin has done for Mele over the years. After Ashram left, they discovered they liked each other. That has matured into a sweet love. You will understand when you see them."

Enoch shook his head. "Mele and Benjamin. I should have known. It was right there, in front of me."

"You can't see everything. That is for Jehovah."

A week later, Enoch married Benjamin and Mele. This one, in Father's way, would last.

CHAPTER THIRTY-NINE

Books of Remembrance

Over the next years, many good people fled to Zion for protection. The wicked were supported by the giants, all had listened to the Destroyer. The giants used their size to reinforce the many armies who fought against each other. Men fought wars in most of the lands outside Zion. Newcomers discussed the many battles between cities and lands.

"They fight for rights to land, for the bounty of crops they believe the land will provide. Yet, after the battles cross and trample the same piece of earth, it becomes barren, refusing to produce new crops for many years," one woman told me.

Another sister, standing nearby, added, "They fight because they desire to control the minds of the others. They desire their neighbors to worship the gods or goddesses of stone and wood they worship, while those in neighboring cities and lands hold tight to their gods and goddesses made of silver and gold created by their own hands. Each believed their god or goddess will protect them against the others. Too many lives are lost in these battles to determine the superiority of idols and false gods."

"That may be," another woman who recently found refuge in Zion related, "they also desire to control our bodies. They search for slaves to work in their mines and fields. Then, they sit idly by and receive the benefit of their slaves' difficult labors. Great battles are fought with the losing people taken into slavery. I have seen tall buildings, obelisks created to honor the victors of battles, huge fields, shops and factories, all built and maintained by slaves."

These stories of sorrow and grief helped me to understand the desires of these righteous people to flee the turmoil of this awful world.

Enoch left the safety of Zion to preach, seeking out those who continued to be true to the faith taught by Adam, Seth, Enos, and the other prophets. Many times when he returned, families and individuals flocked back with him to Zion, seeking the protection of its walls from the battles and wickedness that surrounded them in their home lands. The walls of the city were enlarged on the three sides not bounded by the mountain sitting along the east wall. Men built new homes to accommodate the faithful. None were turned away. We knew they would leave on their own if our rules were too much for them.

Enoch returned home from one journey more sorrowful than usual. After he bathed and sat comfortably in our sitting room, he shared the reason for this increased sorrow.

"Home Valley is no longer filled with righteous people. It is becoming corrupted." He sat back, staring across the room.

"How can they all become wicked? Do not Grandpapa Seth and Grandmama Ganet still live and teach there?" I asked.

He glanced at me, then returned his stare to the wall. "They do, and still, many have left. You remember Ruth and her husband, Dan. They left Home Valley last year, coming to Zion for the protection from evil our walls provide."

I nodded, remembering how Ruth helped Grandmama Eve during the great family reunion. So many fled to the safety of our walls, I did not meet them all, nor remember their names. I did remember Ruth and Dan.

His stare took on a frown. "Some of the residents of Home Valley fled here to Zion, others left for other lands, few remain. After Grandpapa Adam and Grandmama Eve died and returned home to Father, even with Grandpapa Seth and Grandmama Ganet teaching, many have lost their focus on Jehovah, and their determination to be obedient. Too many have gone to other lands and joined other peoples. Many of their homes now stand empty."

"Empty?"

"People loaded up their possessions onto carts and walked away. Grandpapa Adam told me of times when some of their children would do this, choosing to follow the deceptions of the Destroyer, rather than the truths of Jehovah. Only a few families remain there. Without Grandpapa Adam and Grandmama Eve to lead them, they struggle to remember Jehovah's commandments. I never expected to find Home Valley empty of people." Enoch fell into glum silence.

I considered the loss of our first parents, their love for us their grandchildren, and their teachings of Jehovah. "Do they not have the books Grandpapa wrote?"

"No, Grandpapa Adam sent them with me for safekeeping when we left the last family counsel. They are on the shelves of my study. You teach the children from them."

He pulled me up and helped me walk to his study, where he pulled off a book written by Grandpapa Adam many years before.

"I thought these were copies, not originals!" I cried. "Is it right that I use these sacred books to teach the children?"

"Our children, and the children in Zion, need to hear the word and the sacred history of our family. What would be better to learn from than their original Papa? He wanted us to read them, share them with our people." Enoch pulled another book from the shelf and opened the cover. "When Zion is lifted, his Books of Remembrance will be taken with us, protected from the cleansing of the earth by water, and from those who would destroy or change his words. Until then, we can read, copy, and share Grandpapa Adam's words."

He handed me the book and sat in his chair, while I sat in the other one. I leafed through the pages of various thicknesses of vellum Grandpapa Adam used to write his early books on. The pages of the later books were thinner, as he learned more and became more able to create a thinner vellum on which to write his sacred remembrances.

"I believe you have been using copies when teaching the children," Enoch said, "but it does not matter. The books are protected by Jehovah."

"I will be certain to use the copies from now on. I do not want to be responsible for staining, bending, or otherwise destroying these precious books. They are too valuable." I closed the book I held and held it on my lap.

"That is a good plan. The writings of Grandpapa Adam are sacred. Some will call them scripture." Enoch lifted the heavy book from my lap and replaced it lovingly on a top shelf where it would be safe with the others.

Enoch and I spent many hand spans of time examining the Books of Remembrance Grandpapa Adam had been commanded to write shortly after he and Grandmama Eve left the Garden they called Eden. My amazement grew as I read of the struggles our first parents had encountered as they explored and learned to live in this world, new to them.

"I always wondered about their struggles in those early days, like who helped her give birth. She told us some of this when we met with her during the conference, but this is more explicit, giving more details." I turned the page to read more.

"They were the only ones here at the time. It would have had to be Grandpapa Adam."

"Angels could have come to help them," I suggested.

"No, as Grandpapa Adam tells us, they needed to learn to do things on their own. Life was difficult for them. They had to learn to do things for themselves. Angels would not come to help them." Enoch shrugged. "We have the benefit of many things they learned in those early days." He returned his book to the shelf.

I gazed at the many books written by this faithful man and thought of Grandmama Eve, alone with Grandpapa Adam, alone with their struggles. "And the grief of losing their children to the Destroyer had to be painful. I feel some of the same pain with those of our children who have not chosen to join us in Zion, preferring a home in the world. The pain of it still hurts. I suspect Grandmama Eve felt the pain all her life."

Enoch grimaced. "It has been good to see Rachel, Leib, and Miriam return with their families to Zion, but so many continue to live in the world." He took the last book from my lap and replaced it on the shelf.

Together, we walked from his study to the sitting room. We were both surprised to see Methuselah sitting in a chair, resting.

"When did you arrive?" I asked. "I did not hear you come in."

"I arrived some time ago, but I heard you in Papa's study talking and sat down to wait."

"When did you return to Zion?" Enoch asked. "I did not expect you to come here until later."

"I wanted to come visit with you, Papa and Mama. The Lord told me Zion would be taken from the earth in the near future. I wanted one more visit."

"Will you be here with us when we go?" I asked our prophet son.

"I do not know, yet. I have not been given that answer from Jehovah yet. I hoped Papa could tell me it is time to move my family here to Zion. The world becomes more wicked each year."

"I have seen the wickedness increase, son," Enoch said. "I understand your desire to bring your family here to be with us here in Zion. Shall we retire to my study to discuss this or shall we go to the tabernacle?"

"The tabernacle may be best for our needs, Papa."

The two men embraced and kissed me goodbye, Enoch embraced me long and deep, with a kiss promising more later. Then, they left striding purposefully toward the tabernacle. I knew they would be gone for several hours.

I knew the ultimate answer, Enoch told me years earlier, but that was between Methuselah and the Lord. As I waited, I went to the kitchen to prepare dinner. While it cooked, I sat at the table, thinking.

CHAPTER FORTY

Jehovah

I must have fallen asleep, for I opened my eyes to a bright light filling the room. A man stood before me, wearing a white robe, as bright as at the middle of the day. His eyes were a brilliant blue and his curly, brown hair reached just to his shoulder. I recognized this being. The same Jehovah who visited our great conference in Home Valley, honoring Grandpapa Adam as the Father of Nations, stood before me, in my kitchen.

I stared at him.

"Zehira, my daughter," He said. "You have long desired to visit with me. I am here to thank you for the many things you have done for me."

"Wh-wh-what did I do for you?" I stuttered, unable to think of anything good I had done in all the years of my life.

"You have done many things for me. Think back. Do you not remember helping Mele?"

I crunched my eyebrows together in thought. "Mele? She is my friend. No matter what she did to me, I would always help her. She needed someone to stand up for her, defend her against Hadar. He hurt her. He made her do bad things. He tried to control her. I stood up for her. I helped protect her."

Jehovah nodded. "Exactly as I said, Zehira. You helped her when she needed you. You also help Enoch."

"Enoch." I stared at his feet. "When did I help Enoch? He is always here to comfort me."

Jehovah stepped closer to me. "After the army of Beesus attacked Zion, when he was forced to take the lives of that great army, you comforted my son, Enoch. You, Zehira, do many wonderful things each day."

My focus lifted to his hands. I did not consider the things I did each day were a way of helping Jehovah. I stared at my hands, wondering if I should have knelt, fallen to my knees.

I gazed up into His eyes. "I have always tried to do the right thing, but I have had a bad temper, especially with Mama and Papa. I tried to repent. We even visited with them and had a wonderful visit. Can I be forgiven of this?"

"You are already forgiven. You have done your best to listen to your parents and have done your best to obey in difficult circumstances."

"Thank you, Jehovah," I breathed and slipped to my knees.

"You are welcome, daughter." He reached out and took my hand, lifting me to my feet. "I remember your many prayers, begging that your foot be healed and straightened. You have not asked for that for many years."

I glanced at my foot. "I have grown accustomed to my twisted foot, most likely because I am no longer teased and taunted by others because of it."

"I will heal it now if you would like."

My thoughts turned inward, though I spoke aloud. "I have grown used to this foot. It will be strange to walk, using both feet equally, to dance, to feel the earth against the bottom of that foot. Yes, please, Lord Jehovah. I would like you to heal my foot, if it is not too much trouble."

Jehovah expelled a soft laugh. "It is not trouble at all."

He stretched his hand out and touched me on the head. The tingle started there and sizzled throughout my body, increasing as it reached my bad leg and foot. It stretched out, soon touching the floor flat, like my other foot. I watched it straighten, felt it stretch and straighten. A pull, a slight pain accompanied the tingle. When the foot lay smooth and normal beside the other, the tingle escaped out my toes, into the floor of my kitchen.

"Thank you, Lord Jehovah." I fell to my knees and bowed my head in gratitude, tears falling freely on the front of my robe.

"Remember, Zehira, you are loved."

The light withdrew. I gazed upward to discover I was alone in the room once more. I stood and stretched my foot out and took a hesitant step, half expecting to fall without the support of my crutch. The foot held me up, strong and sturdy. The shoe around it no longer fit. I pulled it off and walked across the floor and dropped it into the basket of garbage. I danced around the room, then ran to the sitting room and back to the kitchen. Wearing only one shoe felt weird, so I tugged the other off and set it with my crutch in the corner behind the door, then spun around the room. I checked on my dinner and spun around the room once more. As I danced back to the sitting room, Enoch opened the door and came in, followed by Methuselah.

I giggled as they stood in the open door with their jaws hanging open.

Enoch pushed his chin up and smiled. "Zehira, you are dancing!"

"Mama," Methuselah managed to add, "how is it you can dance? I have never seen you dance."

I laughed again and stopped spinning. "Look at my foot."

Enoch bent to examine my feet. "I know your left foot has been twisted all your life, but I cannot see a difference."

Methuselah bent to examine my foot. "How can this be, Mama?"

"Can you not tell, you who are prophets of Jehovah?" I gazed from Enoch's eyes to Methuselah's.

Enoch smiled into my eyes. "I know how this happened, but tell us."

I tittered and spun once more before sitting in my chair. "I have been healed. Jehovah stood in the kitchen and spoke with me."

Methuselah raised his eyes, glancing upward. Enoch sat in his chair next to me. Both waited for more.

"He told me I am forgiven, even of the hateful words and thoughts I spoke and thought about Mama and Papa. I helped Him in the way I helped others."

"I have seen that," Enoch said. "I am happy He visited you today. You have waited many years for this honor."

"I have waited a long time. And it was better than I expected. He gave me the choice. I could have chosen to not have it healed, but I chose to have it healed. Look! My foot is healed." I jumped up and danced around the room. "Come. Dinner is ready. Let us go eat."

The three of us danced down the hall to the kitchen, singing praises together.

After our cheerful meal, I turned to Methuselah. "In all my joy, I did not ask about your answer. Will you be moving your family to Zion?"

"Not yet. It seems the prophet who will save humanity when Jehovah cleanses the earth with water is to come from my loins. I must remain in the world, teach as many as I can, until the end of my life. I will not be coming to live in Zion." He dropped his head and stared at his hands. "Some of my children are allowed to move here, but I will not be given that honor."

He sat at the table, mixed emotions dancing across his face. "I have known this, felt pride that from my loins the one who will save all life will come," he murmured. "He told me this before, but I hoped my repentance would allow me to go with Zion. I guess I was wrong. I will obey."

I leaned over and touched his arm. "How long will you be here with us in Zion this trip? I love to see you as often as you can come."

He sighed and raised his head. "I will leave tomorrow. There are people who need the message of salvation. Will you not leave Zion again to visit us?"

"No, son," Enoch said. "It is no longer safe in the world for your mama. She is safe here in Zion. Come and bring your children here whenever you can."

Methuselah slept in the guest room that night, leaving early the next morning.

CHAPTER FORTY-ONE

Celebration

The day after my healing, Enoch brought me a new pair of shoes. I slipped them on before I left my crutch in the corner behind our front door and joined my friends to help in picking early fruit. I pushed my cart, loaded with baskets, through the gate from the street into the apricot orchard. Though at home in Aenon the apricots grow so small three or four fit easily in your hand. These were so big, I struggled to hold two in my hands. Plums and peaches were bigger in Zion than at home, as well.

With my basket, I walked to the nearest tree and reached for the golden-orange fruit. I stretched on my feet to tug an apricot from the tree, tucked it in my basket, and stretched for another.

"Zehira! Those apricots are too high for you. Let me help," Chiba cried as she brought her basket to help pick the tree.

"No, Chiba, they are not." I stretched for another, then spun on the foot that had been bad to set the fruit in the basket.

"How are you spinning like that?" She stared all around, her mouth hanging open. "Where is your crutch?"

"Home, behind my front door. I have no more need for it."

"No need?" She gazed at my foot in its new shoe. "What happened? Did Enoch finally heal you?"

I giggled a bit and reached for another apricot. "No."

Talia and Ana entered the orchard, pushing their basket laden carts.

"Talia, Ana," Chiba called. "Come see."

My friends ran to us, panic on their faces.

"What happened, Chiba?" Ana cried.

"Did something happen to you, Zehira?" Talia asked. "Are you hurt?"

I stretched up to pluck another apricot. "No. I am fine. Are you, Talia?"

"But Chib— Your foot! What happened?" Talia squealed.

She began to chortle and I joined in. "I am healed. Look at my foot." I sat down to remove the new shoe and wiggled my toes. "It is straight, now. Jehovah came to visit me yesterday. He gave me a choice, and I said, 'Yes, please. I would like to have my foot healed.' He lay his hands on my head, and healed my twisted food."

My friends grabbed me and jumped up and down in excitement, chortling and shouting. Other women came over to see why we were making such a ruckus. They, too, squealed, joining in my joy.

After many long moments of celebration, we spread out among the trees, gleefully picking the ripe apricots from the tree. Every now and again, a titter could be heard, pealing across the orchard. When all the fruit had been carted to the fruit warehouse for processing, I made my way home, refusing to limp and show that my muscles hurt from their new use.

Enoch massaged my legs for me that night before we went to sleep.

Rather than sitting to peel and slice the apricots the next morning, my friends and I stood over the huge pots, stirring honey into the fruit until it turned to jam. Never before had I been able to do a standing job. My calves cramped to the point I could barely walk home without a limp at the end of the day. With all my pain, I realized they did not hurt as much as they had the day before.

"Why do my legs ache like this?" I cried as Enoch massaged my sore legs until the muscles relaxed. "I thought when Jehovah healed me, all the pain would be gone. I do not complain, I just do not understand."

Enoch brushed my hair back from my face. "Often, when one is healed, that person is completely healed. For some reason, Jehovah left your muscles in need of strengthening. I do not know why. Perhaps he tests your trust."

Over the next days, weeks, and months, my leg muscles strengthened until I no longer watered my pillow with my tears at night. Until that day, Enoch sat beside me squeezing and rubbing my legs until the pain went away. Although my foot was healed, and my muscles enlarged, it took time for them to be strong as I wanted. I did not mind the pain, my foot worked properly, for the first time in my life.

During the grain harvest, I stood beside the others, beating it, after the oxen crushed it until the inedible bits broke away. The next day, we threw the baskets of grains into the air while others waved huge fans and blew away the chaff and bits of dry stalk from the grain. Enoch and I danced late that night along with the others who danced with joy to celebrate the end of the harvest. We had never danced together like that before.

Through the year, I managed to participate in the harvesting and food preservation in ways I never had before. I stood taller, a more complete member of our society.

No one had ever treated me different or unworthy of their friendship in all those days of living in Zion before my healing. I had, in fact, nearly forgotten about my twisted foot. No one teased or taunted me anymore. No one called me a cripple. In all things, I lived as a member of the city of Zion. Now, with my foot straight, with the ability to participate in all the activities, I became complete.

When I expressed this to Enoch, he grinned at me and teased. "What were you before? Missing a body part? Your foot was always there."

"You know what I mean, Enoch." I laughed with him. "In the days when I could not fully participate, there was something missing in me. Not now."

Enoch pulled me close and kissed me. "I understand your pain. I watched you struggle to participate in everything. I cheered when your friends took you in, without concern for your foot, except to help you, stand by you, and assist you when things were tough. Your loving heart won them over. I heard them cheering across the apricot fence as I walked by. The women of Zion, who have known you these many years, did not care if your foot bent and twisted. They love your heart, and love you, as I do."

"You understand, then?" I said, his chest muffling my voice.

"Of course, I do, Zehira. Do you remember that boy who did everything his younger brother ordered? The one who could not speak five words without struggling on three?"

"I remember how you helped your mama and tried to protect me. I always loved you for it."

Enoch sat down, pulling me onto his lap. "I remember the day Jehovah healed me. I no longer stutter over words. I can speak the truths to people across the land. Few remember that boy who stumbled on his words. But I remember. I wake in the night, filled with gratitude that I am now whole. I see that in you. You are now complete." He kissed me deeply.

I found myself skipping down the street, grateful and happy to healthy.

CHAPTER FORTY-TWO

Outside

E noch continued to travel away from Zion, but his treks occurred less often. He stayed with me many weeks longer between his journeys. The wickedness of our brothers and sisters, combined with the strength of the giants, made it difficult to leave.

When Enoch returned from his teaching in the world outside, he brought ugly tales of the depravities of the wicked. He spoke of children given as offerings to their idols one night as we prepared for bed.

"Zehira, they take their precious, little ones, some no more than babes, and do horrible things, things you would not want to hear and I do not want to speak, to them before taking their lives and laying them on the altars to their idols. It sickens me."

I drew him closer to me, cradling him in my arms.

"You cannot imagine the horrors those little ones must suffer. Many of them are dragged from their screaming and crying mama's arms, or their papa's holding them close until the 'soldiers' or 'priests' of their god tear them away."

"How frightening for the little ones. How horrifying for their parents."

I could only murmur words of comfort. The picture he painted with his words caused me to shrink into myself, but I did not want to let him see. Enoch needed to share the horror, the sorrow, and the pain of the things he saw to cleanse himself and prepare to re-enter the wicked world.

Tears dampened my shoulder. "Worse, yet, some of these poor innocents are freely given to their priests, as their parents seek a blessing from the idol god or goddess. The poor children have no knowledge of the terror that is ahead of them."

"The poor babies. Will they be accepted into Father's care?" My tears mixed with Enoch's.

He wiped his eyes with the corner of a nearby blanket and gulped. He breathed in deep and slowly let it out. "How could Father deny these innocents? They have done nothing wrong. Being born into families whose eyes are blinded by the Destroyer is not their fault. Their priests teach lies to their parents. These little children will be welcomed into Father's arms. They are the reason He will cleanse wickedness from the earth. How can He send His beloved children to such wicked homes, with no hope of learning of His love?"

"How long can this continue?" I wailed.

Enoch held me close, saying nothing for a long time. I began to wonder if he heard my plea.

At last, he spoke. "Jehovah says this must continue on yet a while, until all are fully wicked. Only then, will the wickedness be washed away. There are yet pockets of men and women, with their families, who continue to honor Jehovah and choose His path. There are some who will listen, still, who are not yet hardened to the truth. These people are the reason I leave Zion. They are why I continue to preach, and why Zion remains on the earth. We are here to accept any seekers of truth who desire to come to Jehovah."

Not many days later, just one hundred ten years after word of Grandpapa Adam left this earth to the arms of Father, word came that Grandpapa Seth had moved from life on this earth to life with Father and his papa, Adam. His home in Laish lay far to the north, too far for any of us to arrive before his burial.

Enoch led a memorial service for his Grandpapa Seth, honoring his long life and his many years a High Priest who traveled the earth with his wife, Grandmama Ganet for so many years. Only later in their life did they choose to stop wandering and settled Home Valley. Enoch spoke of the cold in Laish, where Grandpapa Seth and Grandmama Ganet had spent so many years, of the rains that froze into snow during the long months when other parts of the land stayed inside while rains fell.

He told of the danger of the long carrots of ice dripping from the edges of the houses. More than one boy had one of the lengths of ice fall on him. Most were injured. Some died. Enoch shared the time when Grandpapa Seth and Mama Ganet first went to Laish. A carrot of ice fell on a boy, taking his life, until Seth prayed, for many long hand spans of time. The child returned to life and lived many long years, dying only a few years before Grandpapa Seth.

In the end, Grandpapa Seth and Grandmama Ganet returned to live in Home Valley, struggling to maintain the teachings of his beloved papa, our Grandpapa Adam. Even with his presence, many in that community failed to obey and left in search of the world. Grandpapa Seth, in his old age, could do little to prevent it.

We honored him and Grandmama Ganet, who left this earth only a few months before Grandpapa Seth did. Our hearts broke from the loss of our parents. And still, we rejoiced in their return home to Father. In all our living on this earth, home to live with Father is always our goal.

After that day, Enoch returned to teach outside our walls, though his journeys occurred less frequently. Less honorable returned with him when he returned than other times. I began to wonder if our time on this earth would soon come to an end.

Methuselah visited us again, with his son, Lamech, who had received the Priesthood of Jehovah since he was a young man. He received his blessing from Grandpapa Seth not many years before he passed into the world beyond. They shared the difficulty he had teaching others of Jehovah.

"Papa, Mama, you cannot believe what they do now." Methuselah paced around the room.

I raised my eyebrows in question.

"The sell their wives and daughters to be used by other men for sexual favors. Even their young daughters are forced into this behavior. They turn to goddesses for the sympathy and love they cannot receive at home from their papas. Sadly, their goddesses are made of stone and clay." Methuselah sighed and dropped into his chair.

Lamech shook his head. "That is not all, Grandpapa, Grandmama. The women sold into this horrible slavery find ways to destroy the babes caused by their forced actions. Women, knowledgeable in the ways of herbs, provide them with a draught to force the unborn child from their wombs long before they can ever survive on their own."

I gasped.

"Stories of men using women have long been told. Some who escaped that slavery have found their way here. However, I never expected to hear of women who would destroy the life of an unborn child. The influence of the Destroyer is strong among those poor women," Enoch said.

"Or they lost all hope of a better life, for themselves or their children. Where could they find hope, when they live among cruel, womanizing men and their blood-thirsty gods? It is no wonder. I cannot believe our loving Father, or Jehovah, who loves all women, can hold them completely responsible for their lost hope," I said.

I glanced around the circle of honorable men, my husband, a son, and a grandson, all who held the High Priesthood of Jehovah. Each shook their head, in agreement with the words I spoke. My heart ached for those women forced into that kind of slavery.

For hundreds of years, those who fell under the influence of the Destroyer took others as slaves, obligating them to work as commanded. Some were worked to their deaths. A few were taken to become a part of the families who purchased them. These unfortunates, sold, stolen, or taken into slavery during war, lost their freedom to act, to behave, and often, to believe. The babies of women slaves, too, were the property of the owner.

Such behavior had long been condemned by Jehovah. His children were given the right of choice. This right, to obey or not to obey His commands, had been given to each person long before the creation of this world. The destroyer poisoned the minds of men, encouraging them to exchange goods for pieces of ore they called money. The lives of many were lost to the slavery of wicked men and women.

Lamech shook his head. "Illness spreads through the land. People become sick and die from them every day."

"And many suffer from accidents," Methuselah added. "Though few suffered broken bones, cuts, or other injuries during the early days of this earth, now mamas and papas are often saddened when a child is burned in a fire, thrown from a horse, attacked by wild animals, or one of the other multiple ways children are injured. Many now die from the effects of these injuries."

"Life in the world is a difficult and dangerous place." I looked around me. "We are safe here in Zion, protected from the evils and dangers of the world outside."

Lamech nodded. "You are blessed to be here, away from the influence of the Destroyer."

Enoch cleared his throat. "The depravities of this people are worse yet. I did not want to share with you, but you need to know why they hate us. Men have lost their love for women, no longer finding a need for children. Many women have also lost their natural desires to be with men. Many no longer choose to create a family. Father's children have few safe and loving homes to come to. How can he send his children as innocents to this wicked place?"

I sucked in a deep breath. "Horrible. How can they make such awful choices?"

"They have fallen under the influence of the Destroyer. They can still choose, but many prefer the dark rather than the light."

The men around me knew this history. The story of these people saddened us all. I sat listening to them, sharing the struggles of the men and women who lived in the world, with tears slipping down my face. We knelt together in a prayer of gratitude for a knowledge of the truths and protection of Jehovah and that we were safely in Zion. Enoch added a prayer of protection for our loved ones, our children who could not, or would not, join us in Zion.

CHAPTER FORTY-THREE

My History

Enoch tells me our time on this earth is short. I must complete this account of my life with my honorable husband, Enoch, to be copied and sent out to the women of our family who participated in the great family gathering and counsel. Perhaps there is something of value to assist those lovely women in their lives on this earth. It may be possible this manuscript will survive the coming washing of the earth, though I do not know how.

These past few years, since Jehovah visited me and healed my foot, have been wonderful. I join the other women in dancing. I am neither the oldest, nor the youngest woman in Zion, at a little more than four centuries, and I enjoy moving in ways I have never been able to before.

More than ever, Jehovah walks through Zion. He tells us he has always done so, though because of our lack of faith, we could not see Him. Now, almost everyone in Zion walks and talks with Him frequently. There is little of the hate and sorrow brought on by Hadar and Ashram. Our sorrows and grief are for those outside of Zion who must continue to face the wickedness, ugliness, and hatred of those who do not believe in Jehovah. I fear for my children and grandchildren who did not, or could not join us.

I know what the future will bring for them, and the rest of Grandmama Eve's and Grandpapa Adam's posterity. It will not always be happy. Many will face much of the same things those outside Zion now face. Someday, many centuries after Jehovah lives as a man on earth, He will come to cleanse it again, this time by fire. In that day, we are promised Zion will return. I look forward to returning.

My crutch still stands, gathering dust beside the cloaks behind our front door. I only touched it once since that sacred day—to set it out of the way, behind the door. I rarely even think of it.

I have taken time, over the years, to write this small history of my life. Though I shared most of the important events of our lives together, as husband and wife, much of what has happened is sacred and I am prevented from writing it. I have read the story Eve told that day in Home Valley, recorded by Ruth, as well as the stories she recorded that both Ganet and Rebecca shared with the women who sat together under the trees that week. My little story is not long, and probably not as interesting as theirs, but it tells the things I am allowed to share from our life together.

Talia, Ana, and some of the other sisters on our block have sat with me for many days copying my poor words to be sent into the world for you to read. We do not have many more days to finish. I go now to assist them with these final words. I will then send the copies out with Lamech, who is here visiting.

Goodbye to all I love until we meet again at the feet of Jehovah.

CHAPTER FORTY-FOUR

After

Lamech took the copied books, the story of his beloved grandmother, and rode through the gates of Zion. He knew he would never return to see either his Grandpapa Enoch or Grandmama Zehira in this life again. The days of Zion on earth were nearly passed. Tears trickled past his cheeks as he waved to his grandparents, who stood along the ramparts of the city, watching him leave.

He rode out onto the plain and slid off his horse to kneel on the earth to pray for the people of the earth. As he prayed, the earth about him shook. Lamech grabbed his horse's reins and searched around him for the cracks in the earth. His eyes were drawn to Zion.

The earth continued to shake. He felt the roots of the city tear away from the earth, much as he had heard Mount Jershon had been torn from its roots before it moved to outside the gates of Zion. In amazement, Lamech stared as the city separated from the soil of the earth, great boulders and small clods of dirt fell from the edges as the city rose, slowly at first, then more rapidly as it broke the bonds tying it to the earth.

Lamech watched until Zion disappeared against the brightness of the sun and was gone. Truly gone. Grandpapa Enoch told him it would depart. He believed and still he stood in amazement for many spans of the rising sun before he stepped into the saddle and rode on.

After that day, men and women flocked to the site where once Zion stood. No walls stood to prevent their entrance. No city of bustling people filled the space. In the space where once Zion stood, a wide, shallow crater covered the ground. There was no doubt it had been the site of Zion.

Some attempted to build in the sacred place, but their homes blew away in whirlwinds, the soil refused to produce. They left the depression as it had been left, a barren, sand-filled crater.

Lamech and Methuselah returned often. One time, Lamech brought his wife and young son, Noah to stare at the place for many long moments.

"I saw it happen, years ago, son. Grandpapa Enoch warned Papa Methuselah when it was no longer safe for Grandmama Zehira to go into the world. She called me to carry her story to the other women obedient to Jehovah, as she promised them at the great family counsel."

"Did you take it to them?" the little boy spoke without turning from the great crater.

"I did, son. Your mama waited many months for my return. She read from the accounts of Grandmama Eve, Grandmama Ganet, Grandmama Rebecca, the book of the other matriarchs, and then the life story of Grandmama Zehira. It is a great gift, to know the lives of our matriarchs."

Angetta, Lamech's wife, nodded. "The books are sacred to me. Without them, we would not know of our early matriarchs.

"What happened to Grandmama Zehira and Grandpapa Enoch?" Noah asked.

"They are gone, Noah. Jehovah took them out of this wicked world, they and all in their city of Zion, to live with Him."

"Gone? Forever, Papa?" The little boy turned his stare toward his papa.

"Until many thousands of years, until Jehovah returns in the end. Only then will Zion return. We will join them at the end of our lives, but they will not return to earth for a long, long time."

Noah's eyes returned to the barren crater. "Why did we not go with them, Papa?"

"I often wonder why we could not join them. Your mama is a good woman and I follow Jehovah. We were denied the privilege, as was your Grandpapa Methuselah and Grandmama Qutarrah. Jehovah needed us, and our High Priesthood, to stay with these wicked people on the earth." Lamech shook his head. "I doubt it will do us much good, but it is our responsibility to teach these people of Jehovah, teach them repentance and love."

The boy lifted his arms and Lamech lifted him into his own. Their tears mixed on his shoulder. Angetta wrapped her arms around her men and felt their sorrow.

The three traced the edge of the crater, returned to their beginning point and stared at the mountain along the edge, a monument to Enoch's Priesthood power. Beneath that mountain lay the bones of the army that tried to attack Zion. Eventually, the family turned from the crater.

A saying crossed the land, "Zion has fled."

The city did flee the wicked earth. Someday, many thousand years in the future, it will return.

Acknowledgments:

The time has come, once again, to thank those who have helped me in the production of this book. Zehira sat by my side, telling me her story as I wrote it for you to read. Like the other early matriarchs, her story was lost to us, perhaps purposefully taken from us. Rebecca would like her story told, as did the other matriarchs.

A big thank you goes to my good husband, Jack, whose patience and continued support enables me to write the stories of the early matriarchs. He listens to my story ideas and helps when I need it. I could not publish my books without his help. I also thank my parents, my children, and my sister, Tina. I can always depend on their love and support.

Thanks to Danica Page, whose careful editing has improved my writing. Thanks, also, to Dar Albert, whose art and design dress my book covers.

Last, but never least, thank you to you, my readers. I look forward to hearing from you. Email me at Angelique@AngeliqueCongerAuthor.com.

Did You Enjoy This Book?

If you did, will you do something for me?

I'm and independent author, publishing my books without the backing of a major publisher. That means no six-figure advances and no advertising budget. This makes it difficult to promote my novels and put them in places new readers can find them. But you can help me.

Honest reviews and genuine "word-of-mouth" advertising makes all the difference. I'm not asking for one of those awful book reports I used to try not to sleep through, that you did in school. What will help me is if you would leave an honest star rating and a couple of sentences on Amazon or Goodreads. Or a short review on your blog. Or tell your friends about it on Facebook or Twitter.

Let people know what you liked about this book and why they might like it, too. And, if there was something you didn't like, you can say that, as well. Constructive criticism helps me write a better book next time.

But, please, No spoilers!

Thanks for reading

Would You Like More?

If you enjoyed this story, you may enjoy a Free Micro Story, written about Eve in her travels with Adam later in their lives. Eve must find a way to rescue Adam after he was taken by servants of the Destroyer. No one else is near and it is up to her.

Avenging Angel is **free** and only available when you subscribe to my Ancient Historical Readers Group.

Go to: http://www.AngeliqueCongerAuthor.com to get your **free copy**.

Other Books by Angelique Conger:

Find these books on your favorite Amazon site, search for Angelique Conger.

Ancient Matriarchs:
Eve, First Matriarch

Eve is a mother to us all. Here is her story of longing, anguish, and hope...

Eve wants nothing more than to fulfill God's two commandments: live in absolute obedience and replenish the earth with her children. But the power of the Destroyer is strong, and when she's told she has a chance to fulfill the second commandment by breaking the first... she takes it.

Into   the   Storms:
Ganet, Wife of Seth

A devastating earthquake. A giant serpent. Can she escape the traps laid to take her life?

Leaving her sheltered community and yearning for adventure, Ganet travels with her new husband, Seth. Imperiled by raging flash floods, land shattering earthquakes, and angry, defiant men who want to sacrifice her to their serpent god, she struggles forward, supported by her profound love for her husband and her God. When Seth contracts a possible life-ending disease that threatens to strand her far from home, can she discover the hidden strength needed to survive?

Finding   **Peace:**
Rebecca, Wife of Enoch

They stole her food, her freedom and her children. Is there peace for Rebecca?

For Rebecca, life in drought stricken Shulon becomes more complicated when ancient feuds explode. Struggling to survive, she is further stricken when raiders take her brother's life and steal her two young children.

Confronting continued brutality and loss, can she overcome hatred and discover the strength to endure continued confrontation and loss?

Coming Soon:

Lost Children of the Prophets, Book 1

Stolen from their parents. Sold into slavery. Torn from each other's arms.

ABOUT THE AUTHOR

Angelique Conger discovered the wonders of writing books later in her life. Books, however, have always been important to her. As a little girl in a small town, she was given her own library card at the tender age of five, highly unusual in those days. She remembers walking to the few blocks to the library on her own to choose the maximum number of books, four, and took them back three or four days later for four more. As she got older and occasionally returned the books a day or two past the limit of two weeks. The librarians allowed her to straighten the shelves to pay off her fines.

Angelique reads a book, or three at once, much of the time. She reads most genres of books and until recently only toyed with writing them. Since beginning, she has spent many hours each day learning the craft of writing and editing.

The stories and mystery of the lives of ancient women enticed Angelique. Little is known about the first patriarchs, beyond their names, and little or nothing is known of their wives. While little is written about our mother Eve, not even the names of the other women who supported their patriarch husbands are known. How then, can she write their stories? They are a work of fiction, though she believes they sat beside her, whispering their stories into her ear. Read their stories in the series Ancient Matriarchs.

Angelique received her BEd (education) from the University of Hawaii and her MS from Utah State University. She taught elementary school for 14 years in Utah after following her husband around the world as he served in the United States Navy. She strives to do her best to obey the command given to Eve to replenish the earth. She has five children and nine grandchildren, so far. Her goal is to be a noble matriarch like Eve.

Angelique lives in southern Nevada with her husband, love bird, and two turtles. She enjoys the visits of her grandchildren—and their parents.

www.ingramcontent.com/pod-product-compliance
Lightning Source LLC
Chambersburg PA
CBHW070049030726
47506CB00002B/412